Death Takes a Gander

Also by Christine Goff
in Large Print:

A Nest in the Ashes

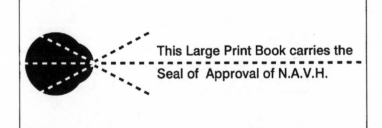

This Large Print Book carries the
Seal of Approval of N.A.V.H.

Death Takes a Gander

Christine Goff

Published in 2005 by arrangement with The Berkley Publishing Group, a division of Penguin Group (USA) Inc.

Wheeler Large Print Cozy Mystery.

The text of this Large Print edition is unabridged.
Other aspects of the book may vary from the original edition.

Set in 16 pt. Plantin by Minnie B. Raven.

Printed in the United States on permanent paper.

Library of Congress Cataloging-in-Publication Data

Goff, Christine.
    Death takes a gander / by Christine Goff.
      p. cm.
    ISBN 1-58724-957-X (lg. print : sc : alk. paper)
    1. Park rangers — Crimes against — Fiction.
2. Women environmentalists — Fiction. 3. Wildlife management — Fiction. 4. Large type books. I. Title.
PS3607.O344D43 2005
    813'.6—dc22   2005000294

To my mother,
Mardee McKinlay Birchfield,
whose spirit lives on in me.
I love you.

National Association for Visually Handicapped
------------------------ *serving the partially seeing*

As the Founder/CEO of NAVH, the only national health agency solely devoted to those who, although not totally blind, have an eye disease which could lead to serious visual impairment, I am pleased to recognize Thorndike Press* as one of the leading publishers in the large print field.

Founded in 1954 in San Francisco to prepare large print textbooks for partially seeing children, NAVH became the pioneer and standard setting agency in the preparation of large type.

Today, those publishers who meet our standards carry the prestigious "Seal of Approval" indicating high quality large print. We are delighted that Thorndike Press is one of the publishers whose titles meet these standards. We are also pleased to recognize the significant contribution Thorndike Press is making in this important and growing field.

Lorraine H. Marchi, L.H.D.
Founder/CEO
NAVH

* Thorndike Press encompasses the following imprints: Thorndike, Wheeler, Walker and Large Print Press

Acknowledgments

Several people helped me by providing technical information for this story. My deepest thanks to: Special Agent Linda Schroeder of the U.S. Fish and Wildlife Service, who lived a real-life version of this story, and shared her insider information; Scott Roederer and Gary Matthews, two birders who put their heads together to dig up obscure facts on the migrating patterns of geese; Yvonne Wallace Blane of Fellow Mortals, a wildlife rehab center in Wisconsin, who provided videotapes of an actual geese rescue operation; National Wildlife Rehabilitators Association and Tri-State Bird Rescue and Research, who filled in the blanks; and John from Johnson's Sporting Goods, Inc., in Rockland, Maine, who gave me a hands-on lesson on the different types of shot.

Additional thanks goes to my fellow writers and friends. To my RMFW buddies, you know who you are; to the members of my critique group, with a special thanks to Suzanne Proulx for the brainstorming and Gwen Schuster-Haynes for the plotting help; to Elisabeth Husseini, for coming up with such a wonderful title; and to my dear friend Laura Ware, who helped me find my way to the end.

Finally, I would like to thank my editor, Cindy Hwang, for her patience and support; Peter Rubie, my favorite agent, for never losing faith; and my family, whose confidence in me kept me going through the toughest of years.

Chapter 1

Wild animals are creatures of habit and environment, with anticipated behaviors. None crave human contact, but when it comes, there are rules of engagement.

People, on the other hand, are unpredictable. They come in all different shapes, sizes, and temperaments, and with multiple agendas. In twenty-four years, Angela had learned to be cautious.

"Will you repeat the message?"

"Your partner is requesting backup at Barr Lake," replied Dispatch. "He was hard to hear. Said something about a sick bird."

Angela wondered if this was Ian's idea of a joke.

"What's your ten-twenty?" asked Dispatch.

"Fort Collins."

"And your E.T.A.?"

Angela glanced at her watch. It was seven-thirty, and Barr Lake was a good forty minutes away.

"Twenty-thirty," she said, tacking on ten

minutes so she could change out of her dress. It was New Year's Eve, and she'd been headed over to her parents' house for dinner. "Is anyone else en route?"

"Negative. He requested we relay the message to you."

"Ten-four."

Angela hung up the phone, called her mother and canceled dinner, then changed into her uniform — a pair of chocolate brown pants and a light-green, long-sleeved shirt. Tugging on her boots, she grabbed a pair of gloves, a wool hat, her insulated coat, and her duty belt. She locked the door, tossed the armload of clothes and her belt on the passenger's seat, and fired up her truck. Backing slowly out of the driveway, she took it easy past the lake, then gunned it on Harmony Road.

Home was a three-room cabin near Boyd Lake. She had moved in her senior year of college, scraping together the rent through odd jobs fitted around her school schedule. Private, tucked in among the cottonwoods, it suited her perfectly. Now that she'd accepted the job with U.S. Fish and Wildlife, she figured she'd have to move. She wasn't required to be in the office that much, but on the days she was, she faced over an hour commute.

Turning onto I-25, Angela pointed the truck toward Denver and wondered what had prompted Ian's call. Ogburn was her field supervisor. Set to retire in a matter of months, he was responsible for training her as a U.S. Fish and Wildlife Special Agent. Her dream job — investigating and apprehending persons suspected of offenses against the criminal laws of the United States, specifically those protecting wildlife.

Unfortunately, Ian was less than a dream to work for. This was the second time in two months he'd called her out unexpectedly, both times centered on reports of a "sick" bird. The first incident had turned out to be a wild goose chase. Someone had reported seeing several dead geese at the edge of Horsetooth Reservoir, but by the time they had arrived on scene, the birds were gone. She and Ian had scoured the shoreline for hours, and turned up nothing.

This had better be for real, Ian.

It was New Year's Eve, and she'd taken the afternoon off. After making a last-minute charitable contribution at Goodwill, she had planned on dinner with her folks, and a late-night date with the VCR.

Even Ian had scheduled the weekend off.

11

According to him, he planned on meeting someone regarding an open case, then heading home for the weekend. She wondered what had prompted the change in plans.

Forty minutes later, and no closer to an answer, she turned off the main highway onto Bromley Lane. Snapping off the radio, she forced herself to focus on the present. Ian had called for backup but hadn't specified what he needed, only that it had something to do with a sick bird. More than likely, she faced a lesson in field evaluation and transportation of a sick animal. But there was always the possibility he had stumbled into trouble.

Gravel crunched under the tires as she parked beside Ian's truck. It stood empty, with a half-inch of powder accumulated on its hood. Directly ahead, the Barr Lake State Park Visitors Center appeared to be all locked up.

So where was Ian?

She checked her watch. He had called in the request for backup over an hour ago. Had he struck out alone?

Law Enforcement 101: If you call for help, you should wait for it to get there.

Angela killed the engine, then cracked open the driver's side window and listened.

Nothing, except the faint whisper of snow striking glass.

Dousing the headlights, she stared into the inky-black night. It stretched in all directions, broken only to the west and southwest, where the city lights from Brighton, Commerce City, and Denver lit the underbelly of the clouds. Corn fields and prairie meandered in black shadows to the east and north. To the south lay the boundaries of Denver International Airport.

Somewhere toward the glow, past the road to the banding station and behind the trees, lay Barr Lake.

She had done some research on the area as part of a college project. Created in the 1880s, the reservoir provided an oasis for wildlife between the edge of the city and farming country. Located in what was shortgrass prairie, Barr Lake State Park now offered a unique combination of grassland, forest, lake, and marsh. Birders and wildlife enthusiasts flocked to the area, and field records dated back to the beginning.

Angela pulled on her hat and tamped down her guilt for not getting there quicker. Once she'd gotten on the road, she had tried setting a land-speed record.

Still, Ian was nowhere in sight. If something had gone wrong . . . like Tonto to the Lone Ranger, or Halle Berry to Pierce Brosnan's 007, she was Ian's backup. The GS-9 to his GS-11. She should have made better time.

Pushing open the driver's-side door, Angela heard the bird as soon as her feet struck ground. Its brassy, trumpetlike voice broke through the trees, past the moan of the pine branches overhead, and drove straight to the core of her bones.

She shivered. There was no mistaking the bird's distress, no mistaking its resonant call. Somewhere on the lake, a trumpeter swan was in trouble.

She'd only seen one once before, in college. She and her college sweetheart, Nathan Sobul, had been assigned to document a pair of trumpeter swans spotted on Long Pond. Nate had bagged out after the first day, but Angela had spent three days observing the birds. She'd determined that on a northern migration the male had been forced down because of ice buildup on his wings. She'd made her report and gotten an A in the class.

Come to think of it, so had Nathan.

Angela leaned forward, and pulled the keys from the ignition. After donning her belt, she checked her gun, then secured it in its holster. It was her duty to check out the bird. She'd lay odds that's where Ian was.

Turning up the collar of her insulated coat, she tugged on her gloves, and grabbed a flashlight from under the passenger's seat. Maybe she could follow Ian's tracks.

The wind struck as she closed the driver's-side door, kicking up the loose snow, and blowing it into her face. She bowed her head. The swan called out again.

The Barr Lake Visitors Center stood between her and the lake. A one-story building comprised of wood, stone, and glass, it hunkered at the edge of the parking lot. Keeping one eye on the structure, she headed for the sidewalk, quickening her pace as she neared the Center. Buildings were people habitat. And dark, empty buildings, stuck out in the middle of nowhere, scared the bejesus out of her. Maybe it was the essence of humanity clinging to the granite. Or maybe it was the mirrored windows reflecting the faint city-glow and masking the building's guts. Either way, she felt uneasy.

Once out of the building's shadow, she

breathed. The cold air flash-froze the moisture in her lungs. She coughed, scaring a small rabbit into the bushes.

A quarter mile past the Visitors Center, the trees and darkness closed in. Underfoot, the snowpack squeaked, adding to the strange symphony composed of wind overhead, snapping branches, and the blueshorn wail of the swan. Angela breathed into her gloves and warmed her nose.

Breaking through to the marshland, she stared out over the basin. Three years of extreme drought had shrunk the lake to a puddle, leaving the surrounding area barren and dry. Fish skeletons littered the ground, creating flattened pockets in waist-high grasses that were originally underwater.

Now covered in a skiff of snow, she spotted a narrow trail recently blazed through the brown, brittle grass. Following the path, she crackled her way through the tall vegetation toward the water's existing edge. The closer she drew, the louder the swan's call, the blare of its trumpeting now joined by a honking of geese.

This was where the action was. So, where was her partner? There was no sign of him anywhere. No flashlight beam cut the night. No one shouted a greeting.

"Ian?" she called out. The wind stripped away her voice, and she cupped her hands around her mouth in an attempt to hold the words together. "Ian?"

She skimmed her light across the surface of the lake. Several yards out, resting on the ice, was a flock of Canada geese. Panning the light back along the shoreline, the beam danced over the swan.

Half-submerged in the water, the large, white bird pounded its wings and bobbed its head up and down. When the animal strained its neck toward the sky, Angela sucked in a breath.

This bird could barely walk. There was no way it could fly.

Exhausted from its effort to be airborne, the swan flopped to the ground, its wings splayed out on either side of its body. Its black bill hammered the earth. After a few moments, it became clear the bird wasn't going to get up.

What now?

From where she stood, the swan looked healthy enough. It carried plenty of fat for migration. So what the heck was wrong with it? Not that it mattered. There was no way she was leaving the bird here to die.

She eased herself closer, and the swan bugled again, its voice pounding in rhythm with the wind. From the lake, the geese honked a warning.

"Stay still, sweetheart," Angela crooned, focusing her attention on the swan. "I'm coming to help."

The words, soothing to her, agitated the bird. It lifted its head and struggled to regain its footing. Flapping its wings, it lurched sideways, beating clouds of snow particles into the air. The swan craned its neck and blared its horn into the wind.

As the swan's voice rose, the honking increased, until the noise became unbearable. Angela pressed her hands to her ears.

Casting about with her light, the flashlight beam hooked on a set of footprints leading toward the banding station in the distance. Had Ian given up trying to help the swan and doubled back to the truck to wait for her?

"Ian?" she yelled.

Still no answer.

The swan collapsed to the ground again, and Angela edged closer. The bird was spent.

Time for a plan.

An adult trumpeter swan weighed anywhere from twenty to thirty pounds, a fifth of her own weight. She could lift the animal, provided it held still. Then, once she got her arms around it, she could follow Ian's footsteps, and carry it back to the truck.

Dropping the flashlight into an empty loop on her belt, Angela knelt beside the bird. "Hey there, baby." Gingerly, she folded the swan's wings into its body. "I'm just going to pick you up, okay?"

The bird writhed as she hefted it off the ground, nearly knocking her onto her butt. "Easy."

Angela gripped the bird more tightly, and struggled to stand. Because of its length, she was forced to cradle the bird in her arms like a toddler, its neck draped over her shoulder. For control, she wrapped her other arm around the bird's body, and gripped both of its legs in one hand.

The wind surged. Sand mixed with snow pummeled her back. Tucking her chin, she headed for the banding station.

Anchored by a platform with benches and a table, the banding station covered a small area of woodland at the edge of the dried-up marsh. Throughout the spring and fall, volunteers came out in the morning and put up mist nets — fine pieces of webbing designed to snag migrating passerines. Part of a catch-and-release program, the volunteers measured, weighed, banded, and otherwise documented each bird captured before sending it on its way.

On a busy day, mist nets filled the lower woods. They were accessed from a maze of paths that wound through the trees then came out onto a flat roadbed, visible from the Visitors Center. That's where she hoped to come out.

Lugging the swan made using her flashlight impossible. Unable to see where to place her feet, she headed toward the woods, keeping her eyes focused on Ian's path. The trampled grass was littered with pitfalls — a fish skeleton here, a piece of driftwood there. Snow slicked the surface of the dead reeds, and she struggled to stay on her feet.

Once out of the marsh, the wind fizzled, and the honking of the geese faded. The swan breathed softly in her arms. Angela slowed her pace. With no moon and no residual light from the cities, blackness engulfed her. She felt like Helen Keller, feeling her way toward the banding station, one step at a time. Cold seeped through her denim jeans. Her knees ached.

"We're almost there, sweetheart," she said, reassuring herself as much as the bird.

Angela paused and rested, allowing her eyes to adjust to this new level of darkness, then scrambled up a small incline to a wide, flat terrace above the old lake bed. *The first mist net site.*

"Two more, and we're home free."

The path forked, and she stayed right, taking the more direct — if not the easiest — route to the road. Her arms burned from exertion. If she didn't know better, she would swear the swan was packing on pounds.

Beyond the clearing, the trees pressed in on both sides, making her claustrophobic. Wind whistled in the tops of the branches, and the swan blasted a low note in her ear.

"It's just a little farther now."

The path jogged left, and up another small embankment to the second mist net area. Cresting the incline, she felt something brush her face.

Angela jerked back. A piece of webbing caught on her zipper, and splayed across her face.

A mist net! What was it doing out?

Unable to wrestle free, she was forced to set down the swan. The bird shook out its wings, and staggered away.

"Don't go too far," she instructed, disentangling herself.

Once freed, she gathered the loose end of the net in her arms. When in use, the net was clipped top and bottom to two ten-foot metal poles, then stretched loosely between them like a volleyball net. When not in use, the webbing was furled around a single pole like a stowed rolling-jib on a sailboat. The wind must have torn this one free.

Reeling in the cloth, she worked her way toward the far pole. Metal struck metal, and she snapped her head up. A dark figure lurked near the pole.

Angela's heart leapt to her throat. Her free hand found her gun. "Ian?"

No answer.

Whoever it was appeared to be standing on a rock beside the mist-net pole. The pole itself leaned at an odd angle and the top appeared wedged in a tree.

"Ian, is that you?" Her voice sounded sharp, and fearful in her ears. Adrenaline pumped through her veins. She fought the urge to turn and run. Instead, Angela raised her arm, and leveled her gun. "Identify yourself."

Again, no answer.

Keeping her eyes and gun trained on the figure, she moved closer. Beneath her feet, the land took on new contours. She stumbled. A gust of wind blasted the trees, filtering through with icy fingers that stroked the back of her neck.

The figure twisted and struck the pole, causing it to bend, and nearly knocking it free of the tree.

Metal struck metal.

Her stomach flipped.

Tangled in the mesh, toes dancing on the ground, Ian's body swung in the wind.

Chapter 2

"It's official." William Kramner, director of the U.S. Fish and Wildlife Mountain-Prairie Division, stood in front of Angela's desk, and rustled a sheaf of papers in his hand. "Come with me."

Angela spotted Ian's name scrawled across the front of the report and rose to her feet.

"Is that the autopsy?"

Without answering, Kramner turned, gesturing for Angela to follow.

"Excuse me, sir, but —"

"Up-p-p-p," the director clucked. He was slight and balding, and thin fingers had worried his remaining fringe of hair into horns at the back of his head. His regulation brown uniform dangled on his frame, his shirt billowing out behind him as he wound his way through the cubicles.

He looked like a greater prairie chicken strutting his stuff, thought Angela, pursing her lips. No doubt her unkind assessment had to do with the fact that Kramner had kept her tethered to her desk for the past two weeks. Maybe, if the investigation on Ian's death was closed, he would assign her back into the field.

"Shut it," he ordered, striding through the doorway of his office, and circling the desk.

Angela swung the door closed.

"Take a seat." He pointed to a chair facing a window that offered a fabulous view. Rooftops and treetops gave way to the mountains, a jagged line of purple peaks crowned by white caps of snow, stretching along the horizon, looking like the negative image of a hot fudge sundae.

Angela pulled her attention back to Kramner and folded herself into the chair. He sat down behind his desk and opened the report. "I'm going to cut to the chase. The investigators ruled Ian's death a suicide."

Angela felt the blood drain from her face.

An accident maybe, but suicide?

"That's crazy, sir."

Kramner folded his hands across the pages of the report. "Maybe, maybe not. There are reasons." He pushed the file folder toward her. "Take a look."

Angela hesitated, then leaned forward and picked up the report. She skimmed the contents.

Two things jumped out. One, Ian's pending retirement wasn't solely voluntary, and, two, the mist net had been tampered with.

According to Ian's doctor, Ian had been recently diagnosed with a heart condition. Instructed to take it easy, there would have been no chance of his passing his periodic physical, and he would have been forced out of the Service. Family members claimed he was despondent.

Then there was the mist net. It had been wrapped three times around his neck, and the pole wedged against the trunk of a tree in order to lend support under the strain of his weight.

Angela closed the report and laid it back on Kramner's desk. "I don't believe he killed himself."

Kramner's head snapped up.

"What makes you so sure?" he asked, standing and circling his desk. He started pacing the floor between the chair she sat in and the window, a trampled strip of carpet signaling the behavior as his standard M.O. "Well?"

"My gut." Not that he would place a lot of stock in her instincts. "Ian had plans for retirement. He'd already lined up another job. He was going to work search and rescue."

Kramner stopped pacing and flicked a finger against the report. "According to his wife, the health issue knocked him out there, as well. He learned about it the day of his death."

Angela swallowed. "Then why did he call me for backup?"

"Who knows? Maybe he wanted to save the swan. Maybe he didn't want some tourist finding his body." Kramner eyed her through thick black glasses that dented the bridge of his nose. "I know it's hard to accept, but —"

"How about his field notebook?" she interrupted.

"Nobody ever found it."

"Doesn't that strike you as odd?"

"Look, Ian was a good man, but we both know he took lousy notes. He kept it all upstairs." Kramner tapped the side of his head, and resumed pacing. "We searched the lake area, searched his vehicle, and had his wife check at home. I doubt he took many notes that night, and, if so, I'll bet you they landed in the lake."

"How do you figure?" She felt the tension building in her body, and considered joining Kramner in his self-imposed march. Instead, she gripped the arms of her chair.

Again Kramner gestured toward the report. "His clothes were wet. The evidence indicates he wrestled with the swan. He must have called for backup when he realized his heart condition wouldn't allow him to carry the bird out."

"So the consensus is, he called for backup, and then hung himself?" Even Kramner had to realize how ludicrous that sounded.

"Do you have a better idea?"

Angela glanced back at the report.

"It could have been an accident."

"Not the way the net was wrapped around his neck, and wedged into the crook of the tree for support. That was staged."

"Then maybe someone murdered him."

Kramner's step faltered.

She took it as a sign to go on. "Ian was meeting with someone that afternoon about a case he'd been working for more than a year. He didn't share the details with me, or a name, but what if that person gave him a lead that led him to Barr Lake? What if his cover was blown?" She gave her words time to sink in. "Do you have any idea what he was investigating?"

"You were his partner," said Kramner. "You tell me."

The words struck home. Angela recoiled against the back of her chair. He was right. She *was* Ian's partner, his brand-new rookie partner. Yet, it was her job to know what he was working on, and to protect his backside. She had failed him, and now Ian was dead.

Kramner pivoted and walked toward her. "It's my policy to let my agents operate with autonomy. If they need help, they can come to me, but I believe in allowing my men to do their jobs without a lot of inter-ference." Reaching the end of his arc, he spun around again. "Besides, we both know what he was doing out at the lake. Dispatch relayed a call about the swan to him shortly after six o'clock."

A little more than an hour before dis-patch had relayed the backup call from Ian to her.

"For now," said Kramner, spreading his fingertips across the folder on his desk, "this report stands."

Angela swallowed. "That means his wife and kids are out the insurance money."

"Unfortunate," agreed Kramner.

"He would never do that to them." Be-sides, Angela had seen him around ani-mals, especially birds. There was no way he would have taken his own life if it had also meant taking the swan's. "Plus, he would have died trying to save that bird."

"Perhaps." Kramner moved back behind his desk. "Sometimes there is no telling what goes through a man's mind. The important thing now is what happens next." Kramner sat down and scooted his chair up to his desk. "With Ian gone, I don't have a supervising agent, and you haven't completed your training yet."

She braced herself for the blow. Was he planning to fire her?

"That means, I am now your acting supervisor, and everything you do must be cleared through me. In your case, autonomy is out of the question."

Angela frowned. "Why is that, sir?"

Kramner pinned her with his googly eyes. "Your own partner didn't trust you, as evidenced by the fact that he withheld information from you on the case he was working on the night he died."

She couldn't refute that.

"For right now, you can tackle clearing out Ian's desk."

"I was hired as a field agent."

"And I'll do my best to get you back out there. But for now, your job is creating order out of chaos. Perhaps in your quest to unearth Ian's desktop you'll find the answers you're seeking regarding his death. Regardless, it should keep you busy for a month."

Much to Kramner's consternation, it had taken Angela five days.

For the first three, she had pored over the rubble, seeking some semblance of order. In the end she had bowed to Kramner. To have called Ian a lousy note-taker was generous. Her partner had scribbled his notes on napkins, bits of paper, tattered legal pads — anywhere one could apply pen to paper. His chicken scratch was worse than any doctor's, lawyer's, or engineer's, and there seemed to be no method of organization — no dates, no case references, few names. In short, she figured it would take a crack decoder months — nay years — to unscramble the mess. How Ian had compiled his cases and earned such respect was beyond her.

Again, the answer seemed to fall in line with Kramner's assessment. Ian kept track of details in his head. According to his wife, he had a photographic memory. He jotted things down, but once written he never looked at the piece of paper again.

Okay, thought Angela, he may have filed everything in memory but he'd amassed a pile of notes. He had to have some system for retrieval. Picking up a piece of paper from his desk, she studied it, then retrieved another. There had to be a common denominator. Her eyes blurred the words. She blinked and focused.

Animals.

Angela reached for another piece of paper. That was it! Every piece of paper referenced an animal. If she sorted the collection by type, taped them onto 8 1/2 x 11-inch sheets of paper, she could bind the collection in spiral notebooks by category.

It took her two days to accomplish the task. If the chicken scratch mentioned an animal, it went in the corresponding notebook — fish with fish, bird with birds. The most recent notes — the pieces at the top of the pile — went into the books toward the front. The pieces farther down went toward the back. Little by little, piece by piece, she applied method to the madness.

"Impressive!" said Kramner, when she'd finished, turning one of the notebooks in his hands. "Did you unearth any information to further your theory?"

"In relation to Ian's death?" She hated admitting defeat. "No, sir."

Kramner's mouth twitched. "I didn't

think so." Setting the notebook down on his desk, he paced toward the window. "I take it you want back out in the field."

"Yes, sir."

"You do understand, without a field supervisor I can't assign you much?"

She nodded, feeling her pulse quicken. A case was a case.

"I do have something I could use your help with."

Never speak ill of the dead.

Or what? she wondered. They'll come back to haunt you? What if you never actually spoke? Could the dearly departed read your mind?

"Don't even think about it," Angela said aloud, chasing back Ian's specter. His death had haunted her for weeks. If she'd gotten out to Barr Lake sooner, he might still be alive. Of course, the same could be said had he trusted her and told her what he was up to.

And *that* was why Kramner had assigned her the duty of checking fish at a local tournament. Not because Ian possessed him to do so. But because Kramner didn't trust her either.

Angela glanced at her watch. Five-thirty a.m. She was on time. So where was John

Frakus, the director of the Elk Park Chamber of Commerce, the man in charge of this show?

Pulling her keys from the ignition, she dropped them into her pocket and reached for her gloves. Except for her truck, the Elk Park Visitors Center parking lot was deserted. Two streetlights bathed the area in a yellow glow, highlighting one set of tracks in the six inches of fresh snow. *Hers.*

Maybe she should check out the building? It was possible he'd come in from the other side.

The center was a large, two-story building with a huge wraparound deck covered with benches and snow. In front, a twice life-size sculpture of a Rocky Mountain bighorn sheep highlighted a circular entrance. In back, the deck jutted out over Black Canyon Creek.

Angela tried the doors on both sides. The building was locked up tight. Above her, wind-pummeled trees shook snow from their branches like dogs shedding water, and she dove for the eaves. Then the wind died, and a high-pitched honking shattered the dawn.

That's odd. To her way of thinking, geese normally honked in oboe tones. These were definitely honking in clarinet.

34

Angela headed down the bike path. Blanketed in snow, it wandered eastward, separated from the golf course to the north by a thicket of willows and alders stripped bare by the winter winds. A playground for warblers in the summer, the thicket now housed a flock of black crows that inhabited the area year-round. In a semicircle to the west, the jagged peaks of Rocky Mountain National Park rimmed the town and lake, like giants at the edge of a frozen pool. And to the south, a copse of ponderosa pines gave way to the lakeshore.

Staring out over the ice, she listened to the honking of geese. The high-pitched sounds interspersed with squeaks indicated something was wrong.

The ice ran deep at this end of the reservoir. In the distance, a dozen small fishing huts, decorated with flag banners, dotted the lake's surface. The huts made Angela think of an R.E.I. winter camping display — no doubt John Frakus's idea in celebration of Elk Park's First Annual Ice Fishing Jamboree.

Her reason for being here, she reminded herself.

She checked her watch again, then turned off the path, heading toward the lake through the Paris Mills Memorial

Bird Sanctuary. Frakus, wherever he was, could wait. The birds were more important. The geese, if they could find some, would be in open water. The only possibilities were where Black Canyon Creek emptied into the reservoir, or near the spillway on the other side. Based on the honking, she opted for Black Canyon Creek.

Circling right, she stayed close to the trees. Arriving at the mouth of the creek, she turned left, skirting the west bank of the promontory. Here, pools of dark water met blue layers of ice, swirling in gentle eddies before giving way to the harder expanse of white.

She tramped along the lake's edge for ten minutes, casting about with a flashlight. She found nothing on the open water, and the honking of the geese had faded. Giving up, she turned back toward the truck.

Wait! Was that movement she'd seen?

She aimed the flashlight across the frozen expanse. Several yards out, away from the open water, a Canada goose pounded its wings, then collapsed on the ice.

Angela flashed on Barr Lake, on the spent swan, on the mist net.

Her heart pounded.

What should she do now?

Call for backup.

She wasn't sure if it was her own internal voice or Ian's that whispered in her head, but she reached for her cell phone and dialed. Unable to locate Kramner, dispatch patched her through to the Raptor House, a bird rehabilitation facility based in Elk Park.

"Linenger."

She recognized his thick accent. He was the park ranger from Norway, a friend of Ian's. She'd met him at the funeral.

"Angela Dimato." She reminded him of who she was, then said, "I've found a bird on the ice. It's not acting right."

"Only one?"

"No, I can hear others." She gave him her location.

"Stay where you are, Angel. I'll be there in five minutes." His use of her nickname endeared him to her, yet angered her at the same time. Only the people closest to her called her Angel — her parents, friends, Ian.

"Better bring help," she replied. "I think we're going to need it."

Putting away the phone, she squatted on her haunches and studied the goose. She'd left a coil of rope behind in the truck.

Maybe she should go get it while she waited for Eric. With a rope, she could tie herself off to a tree and inch her way onto the ice. As things stood, she had no idea how deep the flow was here, and no way to get out to the bird without taking a risk.

A calculated risk, if she took it slow. It was worth trying.

Easing herself onto the lake's crust, she crept toward the bird. It took two inches of ice to hold up a man, six inches to bear a team of horses. Surely there was enough ice here to hold up a short Italian woman, even if she was ten pounds overweight.

With every step, the ice creaked and popped. Normal sounds that now caused Angela's heart to pound. The goose started honking again, its voice rising with the wind.

Where were the others? She raised the beam of her flashlight, and scanned the ice farther out. Between where she stood and the huts, there were hundreds of Canada geese. Some flopped on the ice, others staggered and reeled on their feet like drunken sailors. Most still lay dormant.

"Shit!" Her voice startled the nearest goose. It raised its head, and struggled to its feet, flapping its wings.

Again, she remembered the swan.

"Hey there, baby," she said, drawing near. "I'm just going to pick you up, okay?"

As she hefted it into her arms, the bird writhed, nearly knocking her onto the ice. Gripping the animal more tightly, she struggled to stand.

"We're going to head back now."

The wind picked up, spitting snow in her face, and glazing the ice in front of her. Her feet slipped. The ice snapped.

Fear sliced through her.

Time froze.

She slid until her feet caught on a crust of snow, and she nearly tumbled headlong. Her heart banged in her chest. The goose struggled against her hip.

It took a moment to realize the ice hadn't broken, another to figure out she was back in control of her feet. Puffing out air, she looked down at the bird. "That was close. Shall we try it again?"

Reaching shore, she retraced her footsteps. Dawn gripped the morning, and light now seeped through the cracks in the trees, making it easier to see. The wind died down. The honking of the geese faded. In her arms, the goose breathed softly, and Angela marveled at the beauty of the bird.

"What do you have there, Angel?"

Eric's voice startled her, and she bobbled the animal. The goose's head snapped up. It tried stretching its wings and lashed out with its bill. Angela dodged, struggling to maintain hold. "Don't just stand there. Help me."

Eric tried moving in.

The goose hissed, bobbing its head from side to side like a tall, featherweight boxer.

"From where I stand, this is as close as I get," he said.

"I can't hold it alone."

"Then put it down."

Angela glared up at him. Judging by how much he towered above her, he had to be over six feet, and he looked to be in good shape. "What? Are you afraid of a bird, Eric?"

"Not so much afraid as unwilling to approach. That is not a happy goose."

Spoken in a singsong accent, his words made Angela laugh. "That's an understatement."

With no good way for Eric to get around behind her, Angela realized she was going to have to let the bird go. To her left, through the trees, was Black Canyon Creek. If she could release the goose onto the water, it might have a chance.

She made a beeline for the creek. Clearing the last tree, she lost her grip. The goose spread its wings. Air swirled around her ears. The bird gained its five-foot wingspan, flapped once, then crashed to the ground.

"Great, just great," she muttered, shaking out her arms.

"Are you okay?" Eric moved in closer now that the bird was on the ground. "What were you trying to do with that thing?"

"Save it."

The bird shook out its feathers and glanced side to side. Eric looked skeptical. "It looks fine to me. It's nice and fat."

"Well, it's not fine."

In confirmation, the goose waddled toward the water, then staggered, falling face first into the snow. It flapped about, uttering a series of high-pitched honks and squeaks, and Eric pointed in the direction of the Visitors Center.

"I'll get my net."

Angela squatted down on her heels, studying the bird from eye level. "We'll need more than one. There must be a hundred of them on the ice, most of them near the tournament area." She glanced up. "If I didn't know better, I'd say they'd been drinking the fisherman's beer."

Eric stared down at her. "You're kidding. A hundred?"

"I told you there were others."

"*Ja,* but when you said 'others,' I thought you meant ten or twenty." A lock of brown hair fell across his brow, and he brushed it back with a thick glove. "Are you sure some aren't mallards? Large ducks, gray bodies, green heads?"

Angela bristled. "I know a Canada geese when I see one. Large bird, grayish-brown body, black head, long neck, white chin-strap." She gestured to the bird on the snow.

"*Ja,*" said Eric. "That is a Canada goose. It's just . . . we don't usually see them on Elk Lake in any numbers. Never in the quantity you're talking."

She shrugged. "Then here's your chance. They're down near the fishing huts."

Chapter 3

It had taken Eric twenty minutes to track her down, and ten minutes for the two of them to backtrack to the path. By then, John Frakus, the newly appointed director of the Elk Park Chamber of Commerce, had discovered the geese. Angela heard him barking orders as she and Eric broke free of the trees.

"I don't give a damn how you do it. Just get those frickin' geese off the ice," he yelled into his handheld radio.

Angela glanced at Eric.

He raised his eyebrows, and shook his head.

"I don't think he has the best interests of the birds in mind," she pointed out.

"You'll get no argument from me."

"There you are," hollered Frakus, hailing them from the direction of the boat launch. Lowering his handheld, he stormed up the path. "What the hell is going on?"

"We're not sure, John," replied Eric, tipping his head in Angela's direction. "Angel

43

discovered the geese on the ice. She called me."

Frakus turned on her. "You knew?" he bellowed. "You knew, and you didn't do anything?"

Angela's hand instinctively moved toward her gun. Frakus was a big guy, and she didn't like having him in her face. He was tall, like Eric, though more heavyset, and his neon-green snowsuit made him look like the Incredible Hulk.

"I did something," she replied. "I called him."

Eric leaped to her defense. "She couldn't get out to the birds from where she was."

"Well, I'm damn well going to get to them," hollered Frakus. "We have a fishing tournament kicking off in just under two hours."

Angela wet her lips. "It may take longer than that to —"

Nearby, an engine coughed, then the roar of machinery drowned out her words.

Frakus had already stopped listening. "Alright, boys, let's do it," he said, hollering into the handheld again.

Angela looked at Eric.

"Do what?" she mouthed.

Eric kept his eyes on Frakus, who waved his free arm in the air.

"Start clearing the ice."

On Frakus's order, the roar grew louder. Within seconds, two trucks equipped with plow blades, and a small Bobcat 'dozer with a bucket attachment swerved into view on Highway 34.

Frakus keyed the radio again. "Open the gate."

"Wait!" cried Angela, stepping forward. "You can't just blade those geese off the ice."

Eric cupped his hand on Frakus's shoulder. "You know, John, Angel's right. We need to have a look at the birds. There's no telling what's wrong with them."

Frakus jerked his arm free. "I don't have time for games, Linenger. You, of all people, should understand the stakes. This town has a lot of money tied up in this tournament."

"That may be," said Angela, moving into position to block his path. "But we have a job to do. I'm charged with protecting these animals, and what you're intending to do is against the law."

Frakus glowered. "So arrest me."

"I will, if I have to." She worked at curbing her temper, and waited for his response.

Frakus signaled his men to stand down.

45

The engine noise dropped to an idle.

That's better. "Thank you."

Frakus batted away her words. "Tell me your plan."

"I — we," she said, gesturing to Eric, "need to assess the situation before anyone gets on the ice. Once we know what we're dealing with, I'll make arrangements to have the birds removed."

"How long will it take?"

"Who knows?" she said. "We don't have any idea what's wrong, and —"

"I'll tell you what's wrong," said Frakus, jabbing a finger in her face. "We've got crap on the ice. Loads of crap. Let me tell you something, *Angel . . .*"

She didn't like his gestures, or the way he used her name, and unsnapped the safety strap on her holster.

Frakus leaned in, his warm breath steaming her face. "Geese are not birds. They're pests. I want them off of my ice."

Angela refused to back down. "That may be, Mr. Frakus, but those 'pests' are migratory, and therefore protected by law. You make any attempt to remove them, and I'll charge you with a felony violation under the Migratory Bird Treaty Act."

Frakus's face reddened, making him look like a malfunctioning stoplight. He whirled

46

on Eric. "How about you, Linenger? Do you understand the ramifications of what you're doing?"

Eric nodded. "I'm pretty sure."

"Then perhaps you could explain them to your friend."

Eric scrunched his face, looking doubtful. "I don't know her very well, but I'd have to say, she doesn't seem like much of a listener."

Frakus scowled. "Well I know someone who is. Be prepared to get your marching orders."

Angela wondered who he planned on calling. Kramner? He was the only one with overriding power, and he would back her. He had to. The law was clear.

"Go to it," she said. "Do whatever you've got to do."

Eric moved out of Frakus's line of vision and made a slashing motion across his throat in the universal sign for cut. Did he know something she didn't?

Frakus narrowed his eyes at Angela, as though sensing her anxiety. "Mark my words, Ranger —"

"Special Agent," she corrected. She dug in her pocket and came up with a card. She handed it to him.

He swiped his thumb across the U.S.

Fish and Wildlife emblem, studied the card, then looked up.

"You've got fifteen minutes, Agent Dimato," said Frakus, flashing three fingers on his right hand. "You got that?" He looked at Eric. "Fifteen minutes! After that, my boys are scraping ice."

Angela's hand gripped the butt of her gun, but Eric grabbed her elbow.

"We got it," he said.

"Stupid jackass," she muttered, as Eric hustled her down the path toward the boat ramp. "Who the heck does he think he is?"

"Let it go, Angel. We need to use the time wisely."

She stopped dead in her tracks, and jerked her sleeve free of his grasp. "Excuse me? Are you saying he can make good on his threat?"

"*Ja*, exactly." Eric's mouth formed a hard slash. "In fact, I'm one hundred percent sure he can."

"How?" She pointed toward the lake, the fishing huts with their flapping banners, and the geese. "Those birds are protected."

"So you would think." He took up walking again, setting a pace that forced her to crow-hop to keep up. "But trust me, Frakus is calling Kramner, and Kramner will side with him on this one."

Angela frowned. She and her boss didn't always see eye to eye, but she knew he was ethical. "Is there some loophole in the law I don't know about?"

"*Ja*." Eric glanced down at her. "You're not going to like it."

"Try me."

"Every year, the U.S. Fish and Wildlife Service issues permits to the USDA, the U.S. Department of —"

"Agriculture. I know what it stands for."

"The permits allow for the depredation of geese in areas with overly large populations."

She experienced a sinking feeling. She knew about the special permit policy and disagreed with it. In her mind, it was a political concession to keep the urbanites happy. "It doesn't apply here. You said yourself, Elk Park doesn't have a resident goose population."

"Fort Collins and Denver do."

Angela's mouth went dry, and she licked her lips. "Your point is?"

"Ever hear of a guy named Gurney Crawford?"

"The name's familiar." She tried tapping the vague recollection with no success.

"He was a conservation officer for the

49

Colorado Department of Game and Fish, back in the 1950s," explained Eric.

"That's right." She remembered reading about him in one of her college classes. "Wasn't he the guy who re-established the goose population along the Front Range?"

"*Ja*. He was a man very big on geese. When he came on board, Colorado didn't have many, just a few hundred resident geese in the northwest. Gurney changed all that. He even won a national conservation award for his efforts."

The wind picked up, and Angela repositioned her hat, tucking up a loose curl. "Thanks for the history lesson. I still don't see —"

"Do you have any idea how many geese we have now?"

"Fifteen thousand resident pairs?" It was a guess.

"Close. CDW, the Colorado —"

"Division of Wildlife," she said, huffing out a breath. She was young, not stupid. She knew what the letters stood for.

"CDW put out a release in August of oh-one claiming more than twenty thousand resident pairs," continued Eric. "According to their figures, we may have as many as two hundred fifty thousand geese in Colorado during migration."

Angela whistled. In investigations, you followed the crimes against wildlife, not the studies. "How many are there now?"

"More."

Angela bit back a laugh. "Seriously, do you know how those numbers break down?"

"*Ja.* The original group, the Rocky Mountain group, has around ten thousand birds. The short-grass prairie population —"

"The ones in the San Luis Valley?"

He nodded. "That group comes in at around sixty thousand. The rest belong to the Hi-Line population along the Front Range. You do the math."

She calculated the numbers in her head, twice. "One hundred eighty thousand geese?"

"All along the Front Range, all pooping up a storm."

Angela emitted a half-hearted chuckle. "Still, you're talking city populations. This is different."

"No, I'm talking damage to agricultural crops and city parks." He threw up his hands. "Permission has already been granted for the roundup and removal of four thousand two hundred Hi-Line geese this summer." Eric glanced sideways at her. "Any idea who holds those permits?"

Angela mulled the question. It had to be someone connected to Frakus. Her eyes moved to the First Annual Elk Park Ice Fishing Jamboree banner. One name stood out. "Agriventures?"

"You guessed it. The cosponsor of the Ice Fishing Jamboree."

She didn't know much about the company, except they were a large corporation doing business mostly in the organic foods market. "So, what you're saying is —"

"John Frakus has an ace in the hole."

"Donald Tauer, Agriventures's CEO?"

"None other."

They rounded a bend in the path, and could hear more clearly the high-pitched honking and squeaks that signaled trouble. Another fifty feet and she could see the bodies. According to her watch, they had ten minutes before Frakus sent his men to scrape them off the ice.

"We're going to need reinforcements," said Eric.

On cue, Angela's cell phone rang. The caller ID showed it was Kramner. "Speak of the devil."

She answered, then filled him in on what was happening. "The bottom line is, I told Frakus he can't remove the birds from the ice."

"But he can, Dimato. I told him we'd allow the use of the Agriventures permit, provided — and here's the caveat — the USDA must agree to count the birds in the permit totals. I want their intent to do so in writing."

"That's it? Frakus wins?" Even to her own ears, her voice sounded high-pitched, like the geese's honking.

"It doesn't pay for us to be unreasonable."

"Excuse me, sir, are you suggesting it's reasonable to allow him to plow the birds off the ice?"

"I'm suggesting we choose our political battles. It does not behoove us to antagonize John Frakus over a flock of Canada geese. I told him to have USDA fax their permission, and to be sure you have a copy before he does anything else."

"But —"

"No buts, Dimato. If he gets the documentation, you are to stand down. Do you understand?"

Angela chewed the inside of her cheek, forcing herself to stay calm.

Kramner rephrased the question. "Have I made myself clear?"

"Yes, sir."

After she'd hung up the phone, Eric

crowed. "I was right, wasn't I?"

"Yes." Acid gnawed at her stomach lining. She wished she had a peppermint candy. According to her grandmother, peppermint calmed the stomach and soothed the soul. Angela could use the double remedy. "There has to be something more we can do."

"You could defy Kramner's orders."

Angela reached out, and grabbed Eric's sleeve, forcing him to skid to a stop. "That's it!"

"Defiance?"

"No, an end run." For the second time since graduation, she thought about Nathan Sobul. He was a lousy boyfriend, a lousy lab partner, but he worked for the USDA.

"Kramner hedged," she said. "He made his decision contingent. In order to use the permit, Frakus needs documentation from the USDA to proceed. I may know someone who can intervene." She told him about Nathan.

"What's he do for USDA?"

Angela shrugged. "But he's one of those people who knows everyone. If he can't help, he should know who can."

"Where's he based?"

"Fort Collins."

"That's good." Eric shifted his weight from side to side, and rubbed his hands up and down his arms.

For the first time that morning, Angela felt cold.

But, it was good, she realized. The USDA was headquartered in Fort Collins, and Nate was more apt to know someone with clout working out of the main office.

Peeling off a glove, she punched in Nathan's home number on her cell phone and hoped it was still good. It had been a long time since she'd dialed it. Funny the things you remember. She still knew her junior high school locker combination.

The phone rang, and Angela's heart pummeled her rib cage. What if he wasn't home? What if he was? How long had it actually been since they'd spoken? Three years?

Their breakup had been ugly. She had been thinking about marriage, while he had been sleeping with her college roommate. Time had placed them on civil ground, but the pain lingered.

She let the phone ring, half hoping he wouldn't answer, half praying he would. One thing was certain. At this hour of the morning, if he was at home, he would still be in bed.

The phone clicked.

"Hello?"

Hearing his sleepy voice triggered a tangle of emotions inside Angela, emotions she thought long buried — anger, lust, hatred, fear, betrayal. She struggled to keep her voice even. "Nathan?"

"Yes?" He sounded confused.

The bed covers rustled, and she wondered if he was alone. Not that it was any of her business. "It's Angela."

Eric started walking toward the lake again, and she scurried after him.

"Who?" asked Nathan.

Her chest tightened. Did he really not remember? Or was her call just so unexpected that she was out of context for him.

"Angela Dimato," she said, puffing from exertion and humiliation. "You know, we went to the university together." *Made love in the coed dorms, drank lattes at the "beach," skinny dipped in Bear Creek.* Her memories stretched and stayed with her. His had obviously faded.

"Peeps?"

Angela cringed at the use of the nickname. It stood for "peeping Dimato," from when she'd been caught testing a new scope through the dorm-room window her freshman year. The only available subject had been a couple performing a courting ritual in a dorm room across the way. It figured that's what he'd retain.

"Right. Look, Nate, I need a favor."

She held her breath waiting for his answer. She hadn't asked him for anything, even study notes, since the day they'd parted company. She wouldn't be asking anything of him now if he wasn't her only hope.

"Shoot."

She exhaled, relaxing her shoulders, and explained the situation.

"So," she finished. "If the USDA agrees to count these geese against the Agriventures permit, John Frakus will plow them off the ice."

Her oratory was met with silence. Underfoot, the snow crunched. The geese honked a plea in the background.

"I'm just a commodity grader, Peeps," said Nathan finally, with no trace of sleep left in his voice. "Those permits are handled through the Colorado Division of Wildlife offices."

"But you have to know someone." Angela heard the pleading in her voice, and hated the fact she was begging.

"I'm sorry. I can't help you on this one." He hesitated. "In fact, if you want my advice, Angel, you might want to back off. You're apt to get burned. No sense bucking the brass."

Coming from a brass-kisser . . .

"Thanks," she said. "I'll keep that in mind."

She gained satisfaction in clicking off first, then realized his parting words had sparked an idea she might have to thank him for. "Eric, do you know any birdlovers in town with enough clout to stand up to John Frakus?"

He gave her a confused look.

"What better way to fight fire . . ."

"Than with fire," he said. A slow grin spread across his face. "I know Lark Drummond."

"As in the Drummond Hotel?" Angela's gaze moved to the hotel on the ridge. A designated historical landmark, the five-story Victorian perched on the hillside beneath a pair of rock outcroppings called the Twin Owls. Lights shone from the first-floor windows, and eked out behind curtains in one or two of the windows upstairs. *Talk about brass.*

Angela watched as Eric dialed Lark's number, then explained the situation. Finally, he flipped shut the phone.

"Well?" she asked.

"She's coming. Let's hope she gets here in time."

Angela returned the cell phone to her duty belt. "There's no way. According to my watch, we have under five minutes left."

"Then," said Eric, flashing a smile. "Let's hope she hurries."

The designated fishing area lay due south of the boat ramp. With the water table below normal, the concession stands that typically lined the path now flanked both sides of the exposed launch pad, angling down to the water's edge. Overhead, a large banner stretched between the roofs of two Sanolets proclaimed this the site of the First Annual Ice Fishing Jamboree.

The lake's surface was rough. Snow drifted in miniature mountain ranges and crunched beneath their feet, adding percussion to the wail of the wind and the honking of the geese.

The first pair of geese they came upon were a gander and its mate. Necks intertwined, the birds lay on the ice, the gander still breathing. Angela stooped down, but could see no visible signs of trauma. That ruled out gunshots.

"What do you think, Eric? My guess is some sort of poisoning."

"*Ja,* or they might have some sort of virus."

Angela checked out two more birds, then heard the truck engines roar to life. She whirled around. Frakus stood at the top of the boat launch, one arm raised over his head. He reached up, tapped his watch, then dropped his arm. The trucks careened toward the lake.

"Angel, come on!" Eric grabbed her elbow, pulling her toward the nearest fishing hut.

"No, we have to stop them." She twisted free of his grip, and swung back toward the boat launch. He reached out and clamped an arm around her waist.

"There's nothing we can do," he yelled over the roar of the machines.

"Let me go!" she screamed, arching her body as he dragged her back. His hold tightened, and she kicked her feet. "Frakus, you jerk!"

Eric dropped her beside a yellow-and-white pop-up tent. Grit scattered on the ice bit into her knees, and she wrenched a tear in her pants. Tears stung her eyes. She turned and watched as the first truck lowered its blade, and pushed the gander and its mate along the ice.

The gander struggled to rise. Its wing

caught beneath the blade, and the bird arched, slamming into the plow. Again and again, it struck the metal in a futile attempt to escape. Then, the plow turned, the wing tore, and the gander was pinned to the cold metal blade by the next bird on the ice.

Chapter 4

The human chain had been Lark's idea.

She had set the phone tree in motion after receiving Eric's call, and the Elk Park Ornithological Chapter members had descended upon the lake. Lark was the first of the EPOCH members to arrive. By then, campers awakened by the noise lined the banks, blood smeared the ice, and the pile of geese stood three feet tall. Lark had watched the trucks blade the surface, while several men heaved animal carcasses into the bucket of a small Bobcat 'dozer, then she'd concocted a plan. In minutes, the EPOCH members had Frakus's men outnumbered.

Now, facing down a three-quarter-ton pickup, Lark had doubts. "Hold on, everyone," she directed, clamping her hand more tightly to Dorothy MacBean's. "He won't run us down."

"Are you sure about that?" Dorothy looked skeptical, her gray eyes wide beneath her hand-crocheted hat.

Petey Hinkle revved the plow's engine,

and leaned out the driver's-side window. He was a black man with short cropped hair, and his smile lit up the morning. "Git outta the way, y'all."

"We're not moving, Petey," hollered Lark, white puffs of her breath punctuating the cold morning air.

Petey's smile faded. "Come on, Lark. Play nice."

"Forget it," yelled one of the other EPOCH members. "We're staying right here."

The geese honked.

Dorothy's sister, Cecilia Meyer, chimed in from Lark's left. "Does Gertie know where you are, Petey?"

Lark chuckled. Petey Hinkle's girlfriend, Gertie Tanager, was editor of the EPOCH newsletter, and club president Miriam Tanager's niece. Lark would lay odds Gertie didn't have a clue where her boyfriend was.

"Did we forget to call her?" asked Lark.

Petey flipped her the bird. Ducking his head inside the cab, he ground the truck into granny gear and lurched the plow forward. Lark's heart flipped over.

"You don't scare us, Petey," she shouted, willing her heartbeat to slow down.

"Speak for yourself," muttered Dorothy,

squishing Lark's fingers inside her glove. For a woman in her mid-sixties, she had one heck of a grip.

Petey's head emerged from the window again. "You dang well oughta be scared," he hollered. "Frakus is gonna call the cops, and they're gonna haul y'all's butts to jail." His eyes scanned the row of people stretched across the ice. "Y'all ready for that?" When no one moved, he shook his head. "Where's Miriam, anyways? I reckon she'd listen to reason."

"She's out of town, Petey," shouted Lark. "I'm in charge."

"Wrong," bellowed John Frakus, storming out from behind the pickup. Trussed up in a neon-green snowsuit and matching headband, he planted himself, feet apart, on the ice in front of her. "I'm in charge," he blustered. "And you have no authority here."

Lark straightened her shoulders, and for the first time she could remember willed her five-ten frame to expand. "You are in violation of the Migratory Bird Treaty Act, John."

"We've been granted a dispensation," he crowed, waving a piece of paper in her face. "I have a permit to round up these birds."

Lark glanced behind her. Eric and the small, dark-haired woman who had introduced herself as Special Agent Angela Dimato squatted around the pile of geese. "Is that true?" she called out. "Did John get permission?"

Angela rose off her haunches, and walked toward them. Short and compact, the woman resonated energy. "I'm afraid so."

"Let me see that." Lark yanked the paper from Frakus's fingers, and scanned the document.

The protesters pressed in closer.

"This permit is issued to Agriventures," said Lark, holding it up for the crowd to see.

"Our cosponsor," snapped Frakus. He turned to the U.S. Fish and Wildlife agent. "I want these people off the ice, Dimato. Arrest them if you have to."

"This is public property, Mr. Frakus. They aren't in violation of any laws in my jurisdiction. If you have a problem with their demonstration, I suggest you contact the county sheriff or local police."

Lark noticed that Eric had moved to stand behind Angela, adding some punch to her presentation.

The EPOCH members held the line.

"This is a standard issue permit," Lark noted.

"Have you got a problem with that?" Frakus asked.

"That means standard permit rules apply, unless exceptions are noted. You may have gotten permission to lump numbers, John, but the terms of the permit haven't changed."

Frakus scrunched up his face. "Where are you going with this?" He waited a beat, then threw up his hands. "No, don't tell me, because I don't have time to discuss this with you. The jamboree kicks off in an hour." He leaned toward Lark, and lowered his voice. "You *do* remember who stands to benefit from this three-day event, don't you?"

Yes, she thought. *Me.* The Drummond Hotel was packed with fishermen in for the President's Day weekend. Plus she was hosting the Sunday night banquet — a full course, sit-down dinner for two hundred people. She needed the business.

Heck, between the drought, the fires, and the rash of local homicides, Elk Park needed the business.

All that considered, Lark rustled the paper. "This states, and I quote, 'the birds may only be killed by shooting with a

66

shotgun not larger than number-ten gauge fired from the shoulder, and only on or over the threatened area.' "

"Whatever that means," snapped Frakus. "Most of the birds are already dead, and I'm not going to shoot the ones already down. That stipulation doesn't apply."

Angela stepped forward, and squinted at the fine print.

Lark scanned down the sheet to the next item. " 'Shooting shall be limited to such time as may be fixed . . .' " *Oops.* She glanced at Angela, letting her voice trail off.

"What?" asked Frakus. "You're not going to finish reading that? Do you know why she stopped?" He opened his arms wide, and strutted in front of the EPOCH members "Huh? Huh?" He waited, then continued when no one answered. "Because the hunting season on Canada geese runs from November seventeenth to February seventeenth."

The crowd booed and hissed. Frakus preened like the villain in a melodrama.

Lark ignored him, and kept skimming the pages. The document stated that migratory birds killed under the provisions may be used for food, *yada, yada.* And . . .

"Aha! The birds, and again I quote,

'shall not be sold, offered for sale, bartered, or shipped for purpose of sale or barter, *or* be wantonly wasted or destroyed,' unquote. Any game birds, quote, 'which cannot be so utilized shall be disposed of as prescribed by the Director,' unquote." She pointed to the words, tracing a finger across the page. "There's nothing in here that says they can be scraped off the ice. That's wanton destruction." Lark pinned Frakus with a stare. "Did you get permission to plow the geese, John?"

"Not exactly. William Kramner knew my intentions, but —"

"But what? The Colorado Division of Wildlife policy has always been known to use changes in hunting regulations to manage the numbers of resident geese. Barring that, CDW humanely . . ." She repeated the word slowly, emphasizing the syllables. "*Hu-mane-ly* captures and relocates nuisance birds at specific times of the year. In the case of Canada geese, that's in July, when the birds are molting. That way CDW knows they have members of the resident population." On a roll, Lark moved in, pressing her nose within inches of Frakus's face. "This is far from July, John, and far from humane."

Frakus stepped back.

The crowd cheered.

"I have a right to clear the ice," he blustered. "I obtained permission and have the authority to proceed."

"Not according to the fine print," yelled someone up the line.

"I say get some new glasses," hollered someone else.

"Better yet, get some binoculars."

The crowd erupted with hoots and shouts.

Frakus sputtered a moment, then said, "Fine. Since you're such an expert, Lark, tell me, how do *you* propose we get the birds off the ice within the hour?"

Lark glanced around. There were dead and dying geese sprawled everywhere. Counting those in the pile, she figured there were at least a hundred birds. "How many of us are there?"

Cecilia took a quick head count. "Twenty-three."

"How many have trucks?"

A half dozen hands shot up.

"I have a truck," said Angela.

Eric waggled his fingers. "Me, too."

"Great," said Lark. "Counting mine, that gives us ten trucks. Do we have any pet carriers?" She looked at Eric.

"*Ja,* we have some. Maybe twenty-five or thirty. Not nearly enough."

"I've got a medium-sized one," offered Dorothy.

"The type where the lid comes off?" Eric pantomimed the gesture. "We can't use the type with the wire door. We don't want to stuff the birds through an opening."

Dorothy nodded.

"Okay, look," said Lark. "If we break into groups and divvy up the manpower, we *can* do this. We can put the geese into carriers, haul them up to the Raptor House, unload them, then bring the carriers back down here and repeat the process."

"There's not enough time!" exclaimed Frakus.

"Oh, my," said Cecilia. "Will there be enough room?"

"We'll make room," said Lark. "And we'll beat the clock."

"You'll never make it," said Frakus.

"Give us a chance." Lark paused for effect, then added, "Or if you prefer, John, we can stand here and discuss it some more."

Frakus dropped his arms to his sides, balling his hands into fists. "That's blackmail."

"It's reality."

Angela stepped forward. "She's right, Frakus. I say the fine print gives me grounds to stop you."

He turned to Eric. "What about you? Are you siding with them, too?"

Eric met his gaze. "Lark brought up some valid points."

"Idiots!" Frakus kicked at a clump of snow, wincing as his foot struck solid ice. Hopping on one foot, he waved off his men. "Forty-five minutes. That's all you get."

Before Lark could utter a thanks, Frakus whirled around, and limped back toward Petey's truck. "Climb out of there, Hinkle. Get the rest of the guys, grab some buckets, and start cleaning the ice. We need to get rid of the blood and the crap, before the fishermen show up."

Lark watched for a moment, then gathered the EPOCH members around her. "Okay, everyone, listen up. We need to break into groups — some of us up at the Raptor House, some of us on the ice."

"I'll coordinate the treatment area," said Eric. "We need someone to coordinate treatment housing."

"Cecilia and I can do that," offered Dorothy.

"Good. Then all we need is about ten

volunteers to work with Dorothy and Cecilia. Who doesn't have a truck?" asked
Lark.

A number of EPOCH members raised
their hands.

"Then how about you go with Eric and
Dorothy?" she said, pointing to them.
"Plus we'll need a couple of people with
trucks to fetch the carriers."

"I'll go," volunteered Harry Eckles. "I
even know where they are."

"Me, too." Andrew Henderson lumbered
forward. At nearly four hundred pounds,
Lark would be glad to have him off the ice.

"We don't even know what's wrong with
these birds," pointed out Angela. "We
should be observing them and figuring out
what's making them sick before we move
them. It's possible that it could be something dangerous to humans."

"Good point," agreed Lark. "But we
don't have much time." The lineup of
plows made that obvious.

Angela faltered.

"How about I tell them to wear their
gloves at all times, at least until we figure
out what's wrong?"

"Agreed."

Lark passed on the message, then asked,
"Do you want to coordinate the rescue op-

eration, and I'll float? Or vice versa?"

Angela hesitated. "I guess I'll coordinate from here."

"Great," said Lark. "Then I'll make sure everyone has a job and run outside interference."

"Meaning, you'll keep Frakus off my back?"

"I'll do my best."

Angela smiled, flashing a row of perfect white teeth. "Great!"

Lark smiled back, then turned to the EPOCH members. "Everyone clear on what they're doing?"

The group nodded.

"Okay then, let's go."

The EPOCH members split up. Some raced off to get their vehicles, others focused on the felled geese. Eric and Angela started triage. Dead birds were laid to the side, sick birds designated for transport. The birds waddling around on their feet would be left until last.

Lark moved toward the pile of geese and felt her stomach twist. She didn't handle death well — animals or humans — though she'd racked up a body count in the past year and a half. First there had been the reporter, then Esther Mills, then Owens. It was enough to make her want to barf.

Bernie Crandall, Elk Park's Chief of Police, saved her the embarrassment. He showed up, forcing her to act tough. "So, Drummond, what's the situation?"

Lark swallowed back the bile in her throat and gave him the rundown. "Frakus isn't happy," she concluded, "but he's giving us a chance to save the geese."

"That's big of him." Bernie rubbed his chin. "Look, I'll put out a call for volunteers over the police band. That should bring out a few more hands."

"We'd appreciate it."

The burly cop dipped his head, then jerked a beefy thumb at the geese. "You know, these birds are good eating. What happens to the ones that die?"

"They're disposed of."

"Any chance that means cooked up at the Drummond?"

Her stomach roiled at the thought. "The birds are sick, Bernie! On top of that, it would be a Health Department violation."

He scratched his head Columbo-style. "What's wrong with them anyway?"

"Nobody knows yet." Lark signaled a group of birdwatchers toward a grouping of sick geese, then shrugged. "If you're asking my opinion, I'd guess lead poisoning."

"Why?"

She raised her head, and jutted her chin toward center ice. "Watch the ones on their feet. See how they stagger around like they're drunk? They're disoriented, their honk is abnormal, and they're suffering from diarrhea."

"Aren't they always?"

Lark assumed it was a rhetorical question, and didn't answer. Instead, she flipped her hair over her shoulder and asked, "Don't you have an investigation to conduct?"

Bernie shook his head. "I'm here on the curiosity factor. It's not my jurisdiction. This one belongs to U.S. Fish and Wildlife, though Frakus seems ready to take over."

Bernie jerked his head toward the boat ramp. Frakus simmered on the sidelines, pacing back and forth in front of the concession stands like a caged mountain lion, checking his watch every other lap.

If he boils over, thought Lark, he'll melt the ice. As it was, he had worn a rut in the snowpack. She doubted he'd keep his lid on for long.

The trucks arrived stacked two layers deep with carriers. Birds were stuffed into the carriers, which were then reloaded by single layer into another truck. Several vehicles pulled away, headed to the Raptor House, and several more took their place near the ice. Lark could see the group needed a hand. "I've got work to do, Bernie."

"Go to it."

She stepped around him, and walked toward Eric and the pile of geese. Within a yard of them, she stopped, her stomach churning at the sight of the dead birds. Closing her eyes, she gulped some deep breaths, and struggled for composure.

"Having trouble?" asked Eric. His thick Norwegian accent provided soothing. The tenderness in his voice brought tears to her eyes.

"Yes."

Gripping her elbow, he steered her away, walking her down the ice. "Take my advice. Go for the live ones."

She glanced up. "I'm such a wimp."

"*Ja, vell*, we'll keep it our secret," he said, winking. A brown curl fell across his forehead, and she resisted the impulse to tuck it up into his cap.

"Bernie wants to know why the geese are sick."

"What did you tell him?"

"That my guess was lead poisoning."

"Then *my* guess is, you're right."

His tone caused her to stiffen. "Did you find something?"

"Not me: Angela." He jerked his head in the direction of the U.S. Fish and Wildlife agent.

"Do you know her well?" Lark hoped she didn't sound jealous. In the eight months they'd been dating, she had encountered enough of his old girlfriends to bring out a green streak she worked to deny.

"She was Ian's partner." He released his hold on Lark's elbow, and stepped in front of her. "When Frakus ordered his crew to clean up the ice, she and I were forced to dive behind the fishing huts. She found these." Eric held out his hand.

Lark stared down at the objects in his open palm.

Fishing sinkers! Lead fishing sinkers!

Chapter 5

Hours later, Angela banged on the side of Lark's truck, giving her the go-ahead. Lark waved in return, then crawled the vehicle up the boat launch, hauling the last of the geese off the ice.

"Damn!" Angela exclaimed, watching the truck pull away. Nothing about this was fair.

"Shake the lead out, Dimato," yelled Frakus, taking his post behind the microphone at the registration table.

Was that a Freudian slip, or a pun intended?

Angela fingered the fishing sinkers in her pocket, like worry beads. Who had laced the ice with lead? Or was it an accident there were so many sinkers scattered about near the fishing huts?

Frakus placed his fists on his hips and glared downhill. "We're running late."

"Keep your shorts on," she muttered, sprinting up the incline. "I'm coming."

Not that she wanted to. She wanted to be up at the Raptor House helping. Instead, the others had snared the coveted roles, and Kramner had appointed her Queen of the Jamboree.

Frakus tapped his foot.

Angela slowed to a walk.

The fishermen formed a line to Frakus's left. An eclectic bunch, they ranged in ages from preschoolers to grandmas, and sported every type of fishing gear from high-tech rods to Mickey Mouse poles. Apart from the fishermen who'd been camping near the lake, they'd started arriving half an hour earlier. Some seemed annoyed by the wait, but most were amused at the antics of the rescue operation. Some had even pitched in and offered to help.

By then, "Operation Gander" had degenerated into a goose roundup. Three people would herd a goose down the ice, where a fourth person would net the bird, and wrestle it into a kennel cab. A team of fishermen calling themselves the "Salmon Poachers" had won the illustrious title of "Loose Goose Champions," netting twelve birds in just under fifteen minutes.

"Dimato!" yelled Frakus.

"I'm here," said Angela, stepping up behind him. Muzak blared from the speakers overhead, making her head hurt, and the smell of hotdogs made her stomach rumble.

"Finally." Frakus reached for the microphone. There was a sharp blast of static as he flipped it on, then his voice rasped over the P.A. system. "Welcome, everyone. I am pleased to see such a large turnout for the First Annual Elk Park Ice Fishing Jamboree."

The fishermen cheered.

"Before we get started, we have a couple of pieces of business to take care of. First, I'd like to apologize for the rescue operation you encountered when you arrived. It certainly wasn't in the plans. But, since it seems most of us are rooting for the geese, rest assured . . . I'll keep you up to date on their recovery."

As if you care.

"Next, I'd like to introduce Angela Dimato. She's with the U.S. Fish and Wildlife Service and charged with making sure you know your fish. Angela."

"Thank you, *John*." Angela emphasized the use of his first name, then faced the crowd. "My sole responsibility this weekend is to make sure you all know what a greenback cutthroat trout looks like, and that you release any that you might catch. The greenback is the Colorado state fish and considered a threatened species. It has a green-colored back, large black spots on its body, and a blood-red stripe near its jaw. There are cards at check-in with a picture of the fish. If you have any questions, I'll be around all weekend."

She stepped back from the mike, and Frakus stepped up. "Thank you, Angel. Now I'd like to introduce you to an avid fisherman —"

Another cheer rose from the crowd.

"— and the CEO of our cosponsor, Agriventures, Incorporated, Donald Tauer. Donald, would you like to say a few words?"

Tauer stepped out of the shadows behind them, and Angela stepped aside as he made his way to the mike. She had spotted him earlier on the ice, helping with the geese, but hadn't realized who he was. Forty-ish, tan, with chiseled features and dark wavy hair that bumped the collar of his jet-black snowsuit, he wore no hat, and sequestered his eyes behind a pair of Revos.

"Thank you, John," he said, accepting the microphone and scanning the crowd. "What a day, huh?"

The fishermen stirred impatiently.

Angela squirmed, too.

"How many of you know anything about Agriventures?"

Only a handful of hands shot up.

"Not enough," said Tauer, exaggerating a frown. "Guess I'll have to remedy that." He flashed a bright smile. "Let me give you the highlights. We're an agricultural company that specializes in growing organic crops. We focus on raising food that's safe for you and your families to eat. Food that's free of pesticides and chemicals. Food that's one hundred percent naturally grown." He paused.

The applause was thin.

"Okay, then," he said, wrapping up. "I, too, will be around all weekend. I'm looking forward to awarding the Agriventures's trophy, along with a cash prize, to the individual who catches the biggest fish."

The crowd roared.

Angela shared the sentiment. *Let's get this show on the road.*

Though it was played up as a social event, the Jamboree was strictly a commercial endeavor. While Angela passed out cards on the greenback cutthroat trout, Frakus's staff raked in the dough, checked fishing licenses, and issued tournament numbers and bibs. Grizzly Liquors' concession stand specialized in "beer, hot pretzels, and permits," and anyone without a license, or whose license had expired, only had to purchase one and then get back in line.

By nine a.m., the staff had checked in one hundred fifty-six fishermen, and the hordes had taken to the ice. Enough holes were punched in the lake to make it look like Swiss cheese, and Angela worried the ice might collapse. She seemed to be the only one concerned. Everyone else appeared jubilant.

"I caught one," screamed a little boy holding a young trout up for his grandpa to see. Angela recognized the man as one of the first fishermen to arrive on scene. He had witnessed the carnage from the bank and joined the ranks of the EPOCH members spanning the ice. Later he had helped load the injured and sick birds into crates.

"Way to go, Gabe!" he said.

"The boy needs to throw that fish back," grumbled Frakus. "Go tell him before the thing dies."

Angela studied the boy's face, then eyeballed the fish. Frakus was right. The fish was too small.

"Why don't you tell him, Frakus? You've got being an ogre down to a science."

"Look, girl, you are here to do a job."

"I am doing my job. Kramner assigned me here to ensure the safety of the greenback cutthroat trout. I'm not your personal game warden."

"Maybe not, but I'm going to make sure Kramner hears about your crappy attitude. I'd be careful if I were you."

Angela stood, knocking over her chair. "Fine, you want me to talk to the kid, I'll talk to the kid. But first . . ." she glanced at her watch, "by law, federal employees get fifteen minute breaks in the morning and afternoon, plus half an hour for lunch, and time and a half over eight. I missed my break, and, with four hours clocked, I'd say it's lunchtime."

"By the time you're back, the fish will be dead."

"The fish is already dead, and the boy is only like six years old. Besides, I'll have to measure the fish to be sure, and my tape is in my truck, which is up at the Raptor House."

"You insolent . . . wench."

"Oh, now, now, John. We both know gender-bashing in the workplace is against the law. Trust me, you don't want to go there."

Frakus rolled his eyes, then looked down

at the cash box on the table. "I hope you choke on your hotdog."

Lark Drummond wheeled the truck into the Raptor House parking lot and slowed to a crawl. Trucks and cars were wedged into every available nook and cranny along the perimeter, and parked in a row down the middle.

"Pull up in front of Bird Haven," said Harry, pointing to a narrow slot near the front steps of Miriam Tanager's house.

"I don't know if I can fit the truck in there." Lark cranked the wheel hard, inched forward, and then stopped. "Maybe you should get out first."

"Good thought." Harry jumped out, slamming the door, then leaned over the truck bed railing and grabbed up two carriers from the back. "I'll send out the cavalry," he shouted, his breath a white mist fogging the back window.

Lark lifted her chin and watched him sprint for the barn in the rearview mirror. Still part of the Tanager estate, the tall, green structure anchored the seven-building rehabilitation complex, run in conjunction with the National Park Service. There was a nesting compound for burrowing owls, a place for kestrels and other small raptors, a place for large eagles, a test flight area, and the hospital wing. The barn served as intensive care.

She dropped the truck into low gear, and squeezed forward into the parking spot. Before she could set the parking brake, a flood of volunteers poured out of the barn and emptied the back of her truck. By the time she had wiggled free of the cab, she'd become part of the mop-up crew.

Slamming shut the tailgate, she took her time getting to the barn. The sun was out, the snow sparkled in the light, and the air had warmed to a comfortable breathing temperature. She envied Angela, getting to sit outside by the lake, and eyed the barn with trepidation.

Inside, pandemonium greeted her. Geese and volunteers clogged the open space. Winter clothes had been sloughed off onto the stacks of wire cages that lined the south wall. Dust rose from the earthen floor and mingled with the smell of wet feathers, wool, and fresh hay. Geese honked. People chattered. The noise reverberated off the rafters.

Dorothy and Cecilia perched like a pair of matching bookends on a wooden crate midway to the back. Though two years apart in age, sitting shoulder to shoulder, their ash-blonde perms merging, sweater touching sweater, they looked like gray-eyed twins posing as pinups for a retirement community catalog. Composed against the chaotic background, neither woman looked sixty-something. The only way to tell them apart was by sweater color.

Lark picked her way toward them through a maze of brightly colored tubs, clumps of hay, people, and geese. Many of the birds appeared dead, sprawled on the ground with their necks stretched out. Others writhed in pain or staggered about. One gander with a torn wing seemed frantic to find his mate.

In places, goose dung had turned the dirt floor to mud, and Lark slid to a stop next to the women. A feeling of hopelessness enveloped her. "What do we do now?" she asked.

Dorothy pursed her lips and tipped her head toward the office. "We're still waiting for Eric to give us the word. Meanwhile, we've housed the flock between the barn and the hospital wing, and bought plastic tubs for water. Carmichael's Feed and Tack donated the hay."

"That was nice of them," replied Lark, resting her thigh against the edge of the crate.

"They even sent some of the staff to help." Dorothy gestured toward a group of young cowboys bucking hay bales into the loft.

"So how many geese did we lose in transport?"

"Fifty," answered Cecilia. "We started with one hundred thirty-six."

Lark watched the injured gander lurch drunkenly on his feet. "We're going to lose more if we don't do something."

"Quit preaching to the choir," snapped Dorothy. "Eric's the one who's not ready."

"Why don't I go talk to him?" Lark waved herself off, then wove her way to the back of the barn.

The kitchen area was clear, the noise muted. She ran her hand along a chrome countertop, and stopped at the door of the office. Harry Eckles sat in a visitor's chair across the desk from Eric, who was on the phone. He raised his hand when she entered.

"Then we're in agreement," Eric said to the person on the other end of the line. "*Ja*. What's the procedure?"

Lark saw him grimace.

"You're serious," he said. "Explain it again."

"What?" mouthed Lark.

Eric swiveled his back to her, and she turned to Harry. "How bad could it be?"

He shrugged, peering at her through horn-rimmed glasses, looking every bit the biology professor. Tall and muscular, with sandy hair, he must have broken a few co-eds' hearts, especially when they learned he was gay. "Bad," he ventured. "He's on the phone with the vet."

Eric turned back around. "Okay, thanks." Hanging up the receiver, he planted his elbows on the desk and dropped his face into his hands.

"So?" prompted Lark.

Eric rubbed his eyes. "That was George Covyduck. He says the only way to know for sure that it's lead poisoning is to do a necropsy on one of the geese."

"Who's going to pay for it?" asked Harry. "I doubt we'll get U.S. Fish and Wildlife to pop for it."

"True," said Eric. "Which means, based on what we know, we treat for lead poisoning. The birds show all the clinical signs — weakness, drooping wings, green, watery diarrhea."

"In abundance," said Lark, glancing down at her boots.

"Don't forget the fishing sinkers Angela Dimato found on the ice," added Harry.

Lark's impatience reached an all point high. "Then it's settled. So how do we help them?"

Eric pushed up his sleeves. "According to Covy, the only chance is to remove the lead from the geese's gastrointestinal tracts, then give them chelating agents and pray."

"How do we do that?" asked Lark.

Harry pressed his palms together, up under his chin.

"Not pray," said Lark. "How do we get the lead out?"

Eric's mouth twitched. "It can be surgically removed."

"Do either of you know how to operate?" she asked, glancing between them. "Because I sure don't."

"I've done a few dissections," said Harry.

"We're going for live," said Lark.

Eric nodded. "Which leaves us with lavage. We'll have to flush out their digestive tracts with water."

She froze. There were two ways to do that. Lark raised her hand. "Question?"

"*Ja?*"

"Which end are we washing?"

Eric grinned, crow's feet crinkling at the corners of his eyes, then he burst out laughing. "We go in through the mouth."

Lark's face grew hot.

"You stole my question," said Harry, taking the heat off.

"At the risk of seeming stupid," she said.

"*Ja?*" Both men looked at her expectantly.

"What exactly is a 'chelating agent'?"

Harry spoke up. "It's medication that neutralizes lead in the blood and body tissues. To simplify the explanation, it binds with the lead, and helps cleanse it from the bloodstream." In lieu of an overhead, Harry sketched an illustration on the desk blotter. "I'd guess the treatment would run about ten dollars per goose per day."

"Where are we going to find that kind of money?" asked Eric. "Any chance we could give them something like mineral oil to get the lead to pass?"

Lark grimaced. "They've already got diarrhea. Do we really want to compound that problem?"

"You have a point."

"It doesn't matter anyway," said Harry. "Mineral oil impairs digestion."

Eric rubbed his chin. "How about something that makes them throw up, then?"

Lark brightened. "Like Ipecac syrup? What about trying something like that?"

Harry shook his head.

There was a heartbeat of silence, then the geese honked in the background. Lark met Eric's gaze.

"Fine," she said. "Then we'll pay for it ourselves. Now teach me how to lavage a goose."

Chapter 6

While Eric worked rounding up the medical supplies, Lark broke the news to the EPOCH members. Standing at the back of the barn, using a wooden crate as a podium, she pounded for order.

"Okay, everyone, listen up."

The volunteers gathered around, except for the cowboys, who bucked hay in the hayloft.

"This is what we have to do. We're going to lavage the lead out of the geese's ventricular systems using whatever small tubing we can find. Supplies and resources are limited. Eric's working that problem now. He's on the phone to the pharmacy, and —"

"I've got some aquarium tubing," interrupted Andrew Henderson. The large, bald man stroked his goatee. "I keep fish."

"Perfect. We need some ten millimeters in diameter." Lark made a small circle with her thumb and index finger, and hoped she'd sized it correctly. "Then, once we've removed all of the lead, we'll give the geese

a chelating agent called Calcium EDTA."
She explained what it did for those that
didn't know, then continued. "George
Covyduck, the Raptor House veterinarian,
is calling around trying to obtain the medication, but we'll have to supply syringes."

"What size do we need?" asked Gertie
Tanager. She had shown up at the Raptor
House within an hour of Lark's showdown
with Petey Hinkle. He had apparently
called her himself in hopes of staying clear
of the doghouse. In her purple sweatpants,
speckled with bright-green splotches, she
reminded Lark of a pug-nosed, polka-
dotted Barney doll.

Lark consulted her notepad and the list
of supplies. "Three milliliter syringes, with
twenty-five gauge by five-eighths-inch nee-
dles."

"I can probably get a batch from the
dental office." Gertie's short, dark hair
swung at her shoulders as she glanced
around at the others. "Or from my friend,
who's a physician's assistant at the clinic.
Consider it a perk of my being a dental hy-
gienist."

"Perfect." Lark checked syringes off the
list. "Now here's what we have to do first.
We need to categorize the geese, and tag
them. Move the strong birds to the left side

of the barn, and the critical birds to the right." She made sweeping gestures with her arms, hoping they would get the idea. "Then we'll number each goose using adhesive tape around the leg, and a waterproof pen."

"Why bother tagging them?" shouted someone from the back. "U.S. Fish and Wildlife doesn't care."

Lark stood on tiptoes trying to see who had posed the question. Anger caused her hands to shake, so she steadied them by gripping the crate. "I care. And Eric cares. This is a rehab center. We're going to document treatment."

"What's next?" prompted Cecilia, crushing the spell.

Lark glanced back at her pad. "We'll need to break into teams again. We need several four-man lavage teams, and the rest of you to work hospice. There need to be some changes made in the permanent housing area."

Dorothy's expression hardened. "What's wrong with the way it is now?"

"Nothing," said Lark, trying to placate her friend. "We just need to add a few things."

Dorothy's expression didn't change.

"For one," said Lark, "George Covyduck

wants us to put some powdered electrolyte in the birds' water supply. The geese are stressed, and they haven't been eating."

Dorothy's eyes narrowed. "What else?"

"He wants us to switch their food."

"To what?" The older woman tapped her foot and pointed to the feed sacks. "I'll have you know, we chose the highest quality duck feed Carmichael's had."

"Oh my, Dot," said Cecilia. "I don't think Lark is criticizing the job you've done."

"Of course not," said Lark. "The geese need to be given softer pellets, that's all. Preferably a food that's high in protein and devoid of corn."

"Why?" asked someone in the crowd.

"According to Covy, corn-based pellets can increase the lead toxicity in the birds' bloodstream." She looked at Dorothy. "And hard pellets exacerbate the situation. They force the goose's system to work harder, so any lead inside gets further ground down and absorbed. Covy thinks that by eliminating the corn and mushing up the pellets we can avoid those problems."

Dorothy's stance softened. She dropped her arms to her sides, and whispered something to Cecilia. Lark continued down her list.

"We also need to add a powdered avian lac-to-ba-cil-lus," she sounded out the large word slowly and figured she'd butchered it anyway. "It aids appetite and helps correct diarrhea."

"I'll second that," said Harry.

"You know, I read a paper on lead poisoning in Canada Geese," said Andrew. "Written by a woman in Wisconsin as I recall. In it she mentioned the possible use of aloe-vera gel to provide viscosity and protection to the damaged gastrointestinal tracts of lead poisoned birds."

Leave it to Andrew to add another dimension to the treatment.

To Lark's chagrin, Harry rose to the bait. "There is only anecdotal evidence to support that theory. It's unknown what effect the aloe-vera gel might have on the absorption of protein and calcium from the gut. Therefore —"

Obviously they'd both done their homework.

"Look, gentlemen, can you debate this on your own time?" asked Lark, pointing to Cecilia, who had raised her hand.

"What about the ones who seem too sick to save?" The older woman's gray eyes brimmed with tears.

Lark blinked her own.

"We treat them," she said. "Again, according to Covy, they're not in pain, so we might as well try."

It had taken them hours to tag the geese, dispose of the dead birds, and collect all of the supplies needed to perform the procedure. By the time they were actually ready to start, the crowd of available help had dwindled.

Three volunteers were assigned to work the hospice area, while the rest assembled in the kitchen. Chrome counters gleamed, and the linoleum floor looked freshly polished. A number of pitchers and buckets had been gathered and set by the sinks. Lark noticed the buckets were fitted with screens.

Eric explained the protocol. They would insert a tube down the throat of the goose, and rinse out the stomach, using syringefuls of water.

"Any questions?"

"Are we using anesthetic?" asked Andrew.

"No. The drug we would use is a controlled substance and requires a Drug Enforcement Administration permit. We can't get one."

Andrew elbowed himself toward the front of the crowd. "And what about using a stomach pump?"

"If we had one, we could use it on the larger, stronger birds, but we don't. We're doing this the old-fashioned way."

"What about X rays, then? Shouldn't we at least see how much lead is present before we start this procedure?"

"Again, Andrew, if we had a machine, we'd use it." Eric picked up a length of tubing, and twisted it in his hands. "Covyduck is trying to locate a portable X-ray machine, but we can't delay treatment." He peered over Andrew's head at the others. "Does anyone else have a question?"

No one spoke.

Andrew started to open his mouth again, but Lark cut him off.

"Why don't we break into teams?" she said.

"Good idea," said Eric.

He grouped them, then regrouped them according to size and strength. Finally, he shook his head. "We need two more guys to help hold the birds. There's just no way some of the women will be able to manhandle the geese. Sorry, ladies. No offense."

"I'm stronger than I look," insisted Cecilia, flexing a muscle.

"No, he's right," said Lark. It was one

thing to carry a goose, another to hold it in position for lavage. "Each team needs two strong individuals. We could use some real bruisers."

Dorothy crinkled her forehead in thought, then brightened. "What about the cowboys?"

"Oh my, do you think they'd be willing to help?" asked Cecilia.

"Sure. Why not?"

Dorothy headed for the hayloft. Lark followed, serpentining around the geese. "Ask them nicely."

"What do you take me for?" replied Dorothy, stopping at the foot of the ladder. Cupping a hand beside her mouth, she hollered up, "Hey, you boys in the hayloft!"

Three young men with bright red hair wearing black Stetsons popped their heads up one by one, and peered over the edge. There was no mistaking them for anything but brothers. Lark placed their ages between seventeen and twenty-one.

"Do you need something, Ms. MacBean?" asked the oldest, whipping the hat off his head.

Did Lark detect a quiver in his voice?

"Come down from there," ordered Dorothy.

Spoken like a true schoolmarm. Dorothy had taught middle-school science before retiring, and she sometimes subbed. Had she taught these boys in the past?

"Yes, ma'am," said the boys in unison, scrambling down the ladder. The second-oldest boy straddled the rails, and slid to the floor. Pounding the dust from his jeans with his hat, he stood at attention at the end of the line.

"We need your help," explained Dorothy, pacing before them like a military recruiter.

The boys stared straight ahead, hats in hand, fingers splayed against their blue jeans. All three sported double-pocketed cowboy shirts and wide belts with huge silver buckles.

"You're all strong young men with sharp minds. Have any of you ever tipped a cow?"

They looked at each other, the oldest boy rolling his eyes. "You mean thrown and hogtied, ma'am?"

"Whatever."

All three nodded.

"Then what we're asking should seem tame by comparison."

The two youngest looked to the oldest, then the middle boy raised his hand.

"Teddy?"

Considering how many kids she had taught in the last forty-plus years, it surprised Lark that Dorothy had remembered his name.

"Just what is it you want us to do, ma'am?"

"Didn't I tell you? We need you to wrangle some geese. Follow me." She headed for the back room, the three redheads in tow. Lark took up the rear to prevent escape.

When they reached the kitchen, Dorothy waved her hand toward the boys with a flourish. "Eric, you know the Carmichael boys. They've volunteered to help."

"More like they got roped into it," Lark said softly.

Dorothy jabbed an elbow into her side.

"Terrific," said Eric, ignoring Lark's comment. "We'll put one of you over there." He gestured to the team against the back wall. "And two of you on Lark's team."

The cowboys exchanged glances. Dorothy disappeared, then returned with a large Canada goose.

"Here's number one." Dorothy handed the bird to Eric, then moved toward the back of the room where a magnifying floor lamp hovered over a small wooden table next to a deep washtub sink.

"Dorothy will handle the evidence collection over there." Eric gestured with his head. "Lark and Harry . . ." He handed the goose to Harry, then pointed to the oldest Carmichael boy. "Junior, and . . . you." He jerked his head at Teddy. "Come over here. Let's give everyone a demonstration of how this is done. I need the strongest person to sit on the lab chair." He gestured to Junior. "This tends to be messy."

Cecilia stepped forward and draped a piece of plastic tarp across the boy's lap. "This should help, dear."

The cowboy looked scared.

"You're going to hold the bird's body, like this." He placed the goose in Junior's arms, with the butt held high. "You need to raise the tail and legs to an approximate forty-five degree angle to the head and neck."

The young man looked confused.

"Point the butt between the one and two on a clock face," said Dorothy.

"Gotcha." Junior raised the goose's rear end, then fumbled the bird, trapping it on his lap. The goose hissed, and flapped one wing, knocking Junior's Stetson to the floor. The cowboy's eyes widened. "Is it going to peck me?"

"No, no. It's okay," said Eric, stepping in to reposition the bird. "She's too weak to do much. Hold her tighter. Try raising her butt up and down."

Junior did what he was told.

"Now you're getting the feel of it." Eric stepped away. "Are you comfortable?"

"No!"

Everybody laughed. The boy's ears turned red.

"You're doing great, Junior," said Lark.

He ducked his head and grinned, his whole face pinking.

Eric pointed at the young man. "This is actually the most uncomfortable job. Whoever takes this position has to keep shifting the elevation and position of the goose's body to facilitate the flushing procedure." Eric turned to Teddy. "The other handler keeps the head and neck in an outstretched position."

Eric showed him how to grip the bird under the chin, and stretched out its neck. "The person in this spot is responsible for watching for signs of stress and/or aspiration of lavage fluids and effluent."

"Pardon me, sir," said Junior, hoisting the bird so he could look at Eric. "What's effluent?"

"It's what we want the bird to throw up."

Junior made a sick face, then the goose puckered its anal vent and discharged a blob of bright-green poop. The dung rolled down the tarp, and plopped to the floor, splashing like a raindrop. Junior exaggerated his horror. "Maybe I could switch with Teddy?"

"Sorry, we need you there." Eric patted him on the shoulder. "Look at it this way, it doesn't have much smell."

"Well, it ain't smellin' good."

"Isn't," corrected Dorothy.

Eric turned back to Teddy. "It's your job to monitor the insertion of the tube. You should be able to feel it slide in."

He handed the plastic tube to Harry, who inserted it into the goose's mouth. The bird fought the procedure, but Teddy and Harry held firm.

"Can you feel it sliding past the glottis and down the esophagus?"

Teddy frowned. "I reckon."

"Great, then avoiding the nares —"

For Teddy's benefit, Lark interjected. "The nostrils."

"— clamp the goose's bill over the tubing to keep it from shifting out of place each time another syringeful of water is needed."

Teddy positioned his hand, and Eric

moved around behind Harry. "This person depends on the others to let him know how aggressive to be. We want maximum results, but everything depends on the overall condition of the bird."

The group nodded.

"Once the tubing is in place, Harry flushes water in and out using the syringes Lark hands him."

On Eric's cue, Lark filled a sixty-milliliter syringe with warm water and handed it to Harry.

"How much water is that?" asked Cecilia.

"About a third of a cup."

Harry inserted the end of the syringe into the tubing, and started to squeeze. The goose struggled.

"Real slow!" warned Eric. He watched a moment. "Once he's done, he applies a little suction to bring up the stomach contents."

"Sort of like syphoning gas," said Teddy.

"*Ja*, you've got it," said Eric. "Next it's Lark's job to make sure the effluent drains over the screen into the collection bucket. Meanwhile, Teddy's watching for signs of stress and/or aspiration of fluids. And that's it. The process is repeated."

"How many times?" asked Andrew.

"As many times as possible. The object is to flush clear liquid."

"What happens then?" asked Cecilia.

"We put the bird back and get the next one," Eric jerked his thumb toward the main barn area. "In the meantime, Lark drains the collection bucket and delivers the screen contents to Dorothy, whose job is to sift, sort, and bag any lead found. After that, the bags are tagged with the ID number of the bird, and the process starts over. Any questions?"

Lark was having trouble listening. Harry had begun the lavage, and effluent poured out of the tubing. Hard particles mixed with green vegetation plunked onto the screen, plugging the holes. The fluid backed up, pouring effluent onto her jeans and the floor. "Yuck."

"Clean the screen off," said Eric.

Lark scraped the solids to the edges. More effluent came, and, in between gushes, she filled syringes with water.

The goose choked.

Teddy panicked, and stretched out her neck. "Lift her butt higher, Junior. Lift her up!"

Junior complied, grunting as he repositioned the struggling goose.

Lark glanced at Harry. "Maybe we should stop?"

"Nah," said Teddy, shaking his head. "She's okay. I say we do one more round."

Junior shrugged. Even if his muscles ached, Lark doubted he would have admitted he needed a break.

Harry grabbed another syringe. "You ready, Lark?"

"Go."

The last syringeful of water produced mostly clear liquid. Harry removed the tubing. Junior tipped the goose upright, and slid off the stool.

"Here, I'll take her," said Eric, coming up behind and reached for the bird.

Junior handed her off, then shook out his arms.

"Two things," said Eric. "We need to be sure to mark the collection bucket with the goose's number."

Oops, she had missed that part. Lark reached for a piece of masking tape, marked the bucket, then stood. Her jeans — spattered with the stomach contents of the goose — were hitched up, and she plucked at them with wary fingers. One glance at Junior showed he, too, had suffered. Bright-green dung streaked the lower half of his jeans and covered his right boot.

"Second," Lark said. "Note that the person holding the goose, and the person collecting the effluent, have the messiest jobs."

Everyone but Junior laughed.

"And third," said Eric, giving Lark her due. "If we had the chelating agent on hand, we would administer it now. Unfortunately, we're still waiting for the drugs."

Cecilia flashed her hand in the air. "What if a goose is too weak for lavage? How do we treat it?"

"All we can do is give them the chelating agent and hope it helps."

"What about taking blood lead levels?" asked Andrew.

Lark could see Eric was exasperated.

"It's way too expensive," she said.

Eric nodded. "Once we locate a mobile x-ray unit, we'll start taking radiographs to determine how much lead is in each bird's system. Once the lead is cleared, treatment will be discontinued for ten days, and we'll start doing blood work."

"So, what you're saying is, you'll only run tests once you know a bird will survive?" said Andrew.

Even the birds fell silent, as if awaiting the answer.

"*Ja.*"

109

In the additional silence, Lark picked up the bucket.

"It's the best we can do," she said. "Now let's get to work."

After Eric had left with the goose, Lark dumped the fluid in the sink, and handed the screen to Dorothy. The older woman picked up a pair of tweezers, bent her head over the magnifying lamp, and worried the stomach contents around on the screen.

"Here we go!" she exclaimed triumphantly, plucking several small nodules from the partially digested matter and holding them up. "The geese used it as grit." Then, Dorothy tossed the plant matter into the trash, dropped the lead pieces into a baggy marked with the date and the bird's ID number, and logged in the data.

"Lark, are you about ready?" yelled Harry.

She turned to see him waiting with another bird. Reclaiming the screen, she glanced up at the clock. It was nearly noon.

At last count there were eighty-five geese left to treat — take away the ones that had recently died. At twenty minutes per bird, divided by three, they would be here well into the night. Fatigue settled around her

110

shoulders, and her arms drooped, like the wings of the geese.

When she dropped to her knees beside Harry, the biologist asked, "What did you find?"

"Lead sinkers, like we expected," she answered.

"Did they look corroded?" His intensity surprised her. She tried picturing them in her mind.

"Not really. Why?"

"Something's off." Using a knuckle, Harry pushed his glasses up on his nose. "Lead needs time to be absorbed in the bloodstream."

Obviously.

Her expression must have said she had thought as much, for he pushed on.

"Don't you see? It takes a couple of days for sinkers to erode and leach enough lead into the bird's system to cause poisoning. It wouldn't happen overnight."

Lark slapped a piece of tubing into his hand. "They've been fishing the lake for a month, Harry. Maybe the geese picked some up earlier?"

"Then we should be seeing signs of *chronic* lead poisoning, more weight loss, that sort of thing. These birds were healthy until very recently."

She couldn't disagree with him there.

"Plus, someone would have noticed this number of birds on the ice."

He had a point.

"Maybe someone did," she said. "I'll ask around."

Harry dug in his pocket, then dropped a tiny lead sinker into her hand. "Feel this."

She rolled the small object between her thumb and index finger. "Okay?"

"Notice how smooth and round it is."

"It's similar to what we found on the ice."

"That's my point. A partially digested sinker, one left in a bird's system long enough to leach lead, wouldn't feel like that. It would be distorted . . . just a blob . . . if there was anything left at all."

Lark rested her hands on the edges of the bucket. "What are you saying, Harry?"

"I'm saying, it's not the fishing sinkers that are making the birds sick."

Chapter 7

"Then what is?" asked Angela, walking in on the tail-end of the conversation. She was interested in hearing his theory. On her lunch break, she'd spoken with Kramner and told him about finding the fishing sinkers scattered on the ice. He had told her in no uncertain terms *not* to pursue an investigation. As far as the U.S. Fish and Wildlife Service was concerned, the matter was closed. But if something else was making them sick, maybe he'd reconsider.

Lark glanced up. "How's the fishing?"

"It bites." She thought of Frakus, and his insistence she challenge the little boy's catch.

Harry chuckled.

"I came to pick up my truck and to see how things were going."

She leaned closer to watch the lavage procedure. "Seriously, Harry, I'm interested in hearing your theory. Maybe if . . ."

She broke off, unsure what she was looking for. She needed something with far-reaching consequences. "Maybe if I had a bone to throw him, I could convince

Kramner to let me investigate."

Harry stuck out his hand for another syringe. Lark handed him one, and he jammed the snout into the tubing. "I don't know what's making them sick. I only know it can't be the sinkers. It doesn't make sense."

"Except there was enough lead on the ice to wipe out the entire Hi-Line population." A stream of effluent gushed from the tubing, and Angela pulled back.

Lark guided the flow over the screen. Several fishing sinkers were visible, snagged among the plant matter.

"Angela's right," said Lark. "It wasn't there by accident. There was too much of it. Like I said, maybe the geese picked it up earlier."

Harry shook his head. "If there had been lead on the ice the day before, Frakus would have noticed. They set up the concession area the night before."

"Maybe he's the one who scattered it," said Dorothy.

"Why would he do that?" asked Angela, trying to reconcile her image of Frakus with the image of someone scattering lead on the ice. The merger failed.

"Because he hates geese," answered Cecilia.

"Join the club," said Junior, scooting his chair forward for a better position. "There's lots of people who ain't too fond of 'em."

"Aren't," corrected Dorothy, obviously letting the front of the sentence go.

Junior ignored her. "What about Brett Bemster?"

Where had Angela heard that name?

"Who's he?" she asked.

Junior's look tagged her a moron. "He's the golf pro."

She should have guessed.

"Brett runs the Elk Lake Municipal Golf Course," explained Lark. "Last year, Bernie Crandall ticketed him for bludgeoning a goose on the seventh hole. The bird lived. Brett was fined. After that, he hired Lou Vitti."

That name she recognized. "The guy with the dogs, right?"

"Right on," said Junior.

She had redeemed herself.

"Talk about a sweet deal," said the cowboy. "Elk Park paid the dude five thousand dollars to get rid of them birds, and all he ever did was walk his dogs."

"*Those* birds," corrected Dorothy.

"Heck, I'd've gone out and chased off them dang geese for half that."

"Those."

"Them."

"Those."

"And the town paid for it?" asked Angela.

"It came out of the parks and rec budget," said Lark.

Dorothy sifted a screen of effluent under the light. "Vitti didn't stop with the dogs. He also put out fake owls and Mylar balloons. EPOCH put a stop to that."

"How so?"

"We filed a protest with the town council," said Cecilia.

"The golf course borders the Paris Mills Memorial Bird Sanctuary," explained Lark. "Vitti and his tactics were scaring away all the birds."

Harry passed the end of the tubing to Lark, then swiveled around on his chair. "The point is, neither of those guys would have sabotaged the tournament."

Angela kneaded the muscles at the base of her skull with her fingers. How would Ian have worked the problem?

He would have looked at all possible scenarios. "Unless one of them thought the geese would eat the lead and fly off to die somewhere else."

"Like mice who eat rat poison," blurted

Cecilia. "First they eat the bait, then they look for water, then they die."

"Yuck," said Dorothy.

But it stood to reason. Victims of lead poisoning drank excessive amounts of fluid. Angela could see everyone's mind working.

"I agree with Harry," said Eric, finally logging in his opinion. "Frakus would never take the chance of messing up the fishing."

In truth, Angela agreed with him. From day one, Frakus had been intent on making the ice fishing jamboree a success.

"What else could it be?" asked Lark.

Angela stepped around Lark and the bucket, trying to get a different perspective on the bird. "Maybe the target wasn't the geese. Maybe someone wanted the fishing event to fail."

"Oh my." Cecilia's hands moved from her bucket to her throat, and her fingers fussed with her collar. "That would make us suspects."

Angela assumed she meant EPOCH.

"How so?"

"Things got a wee bit contentious between the bird club and Frakus when the idea for the tournament came up," said Dorothy.

Cecilia nodded. "He wanted to open an access to the ice through the Paris Mills Bird Sanctuary."

"Obviously, he lost the battle," said Lark.

The goose gagged.

"Maybe so," said Angela, "but it's possible he won the war."

"Well, looky here," said Dorothy, holding up a minuscule object with a pair of tweezers.

Angela crossed to her station. "What is it?"

"It looks like a piece of lead shot."

Dorothy moved her head, and let Angela peer through the magnified light. The pellet was tiny. It would have been easy to miss.

"Are there any more?"

Dorothy picked through the vegetation. "Lots." She reached for a Ziploc bag. "One, two, three . . ."

Her voice trailed off. Angela kept count in her head.

Finally, Dorothy dropped the last piece into the bag and announced, "Sixty-four."

Harry whistled. "Is that the first lead shot you've found?"

"Yes, but it's only goose number three."

Pinching closed the seal on the Ziploc,

Angela studied the tiny beads rolling back and forth at the bottom of the bag. "Do you know what this means?"

Nobody answered.

"If the other birds have ingested lead shot, we've widened the search area." She handed the sample back to Dorothy and turned to Junior. "Is there any hunting around the lake?"

"No, ma'am."

"What about places to shoot skeet?" More than likely, with as many birds as were sick, it was a trap-shooting range that was the source of the shot.

"Nope."

The rest of the EPOCH volunteers concurred.

Angela wondered if the shot alone was enough to get Kramner to approve a necropsy of the bird. There was only one way to find out.

Excusing herself, she stepped into the main area of the barn. Standing against the wall, she dug out her cell phone.

"We've got a new development," she said, filling him in on the discovery of the shot. When she finished, the silence hung heavy on his side of the line.

Finally, he spoke. "How long have you been out in the sun, Dimato? We've been over this ground. U.S. Fish and Wildlife considers these resident geese."

"But the presence of shot indicates a possible source of danger to other waterfowl exists." Her mind flashed on the swan at Barr Lake. Whatever had happened to the bird? She didn't remember much after finding Ian.

"Fine. You locate another species who's been harmed by your source, and I'll reconsider."

That's it! If memory served, there were six recognizable subspecies of Canada geese, of which only two wintered in Colorado. They flew in from the north and augmented the year-round populations on the plains. There was bound to be one or two of them in the flock.

"What if I can prove some of the poisoned flock are migrating birds?"

"You do understand, migratory doesn't mean flying back and forth from the Front Range to Elk Park?"

Unable to think of an appropriate comeback, she got right to the point. "I'll grant, some of the geese are members of the Hi-Line population. But if I can prove some of them are migrating, can I have my necropsy?"

He sighed, and she waited for him to

speak. "You don't give up, do you?"

"No." *You might as well cave.* "My folks even considered changing my middle name to Perseverance."

He chuckled. "Okay, Angela *P.* Dimato, you win. You find a migratory subspecies in the bunch, and you can autopsy the bird."

Excitement caused her to dance back and forth on her feet. "Thank you, sir."

"Hey, Dimato."

She didn't like the way he punched out her name. "Sir?"

"For the record, I'm giving you authorization in order to document the lead poisoning, *but* you are not to open an official investigation. I expect you to report back to me with the findings."

"I understand, sir."

"In the meantime, you are to continue to monitor the fishing licenses at the lake. And stay out of John Frakus's way."

Angela wondered if Frakus had complained about her.

"Are you hearing me?" barked Kramner.

"Yes, sir."

Angela slapped the phone shut and raised her arms in the air. Official or not, she'd been granted an investigation. She intended to do a good job.

Now came the hard part, separating the northern migratory subspecies from the flock.

"Good news," she said, returning to the lavage area. "We've got the okay to do a necropsy, provided we can isolate a migratory subspecies to perform the autopsy on."

"Were any of the geese banded?" asked Lark. "That would be an easy way to tell."

They all looked to Dorothy. If one of the geese sported a band from a station up north, the proof was in the record books.

Dorothy flipped through the log she was keeping, then shook her head. "Not unless some of the dead birds are. We didn't check the dead ones in."

"What about measurements?" asked Harry.

"He's right," said Andrew. "Size is the only accurate way to differentiate between the subspecies."

Dorothy snorted. "We didn't have time."

"Then let's make time," said Angela.

Even to herself, she sounded too much like her mother. Lark must have thought so, too.

"Maybe *you* should make time," she said, scowling as a stream of effluent missed the bucket, coating her pant's leg. "In case you haven't noticed, we're all a little busy here."

Angela chalked the sarcasm up to the fact they were all stretched a bit thin. "Do you have a tape measure?"

"Do I look like I have a tape measure?"

"Then does anyone have any idea where I could find one?"

Angela hated to press, but she needed to get back to the lake. It didn't leave her much time.

Eric came to her rescue. "Try the desk in the office. Third drawer down."

She signaled her thanks and slipped out the door. She was glad to get away from the crush of bodies. Too many people jammed in one room made her claustrophobic, not to mention the smell of goose vomit, wet feathers, and sweat.

It was something she and Ian had shared in common. He hated crowds, preferring the solitude of an investigation, the isolation of the hunt. He'd been furious when Kramner had saddled him with her as a partner.

Not that she blamed him. It had to be hard to be forced to train her — a kid straight out of college, albeit one with a master's degree — to take over a job he'd been doing for forty years. Had she been in his shoes, it would have ticked her off, too.

The worse part was, while she knew the latest in theory, in the field she had let him down. Hard.

A cold draft swept the hall, and the hairs on the back of her neck stiffened.

"Sorry," she whispered.

Except for furniture and mounds of paperwork, the office was empty. The clutter didn't faze her. It didn't compare to the mess on Ian's desk.

Kicking shut the door, she sat behind the desk and breathed in the quiet. The room smelled of wood, leather, and aging books. A large oak desk dominated the center space. Leather-bound chairs squared off on both sides. To her right, a built-in bookcase, crammed with notebooks, lined the inside wall. To her left, a bank of windows looked out toward Twin Owls. The only surprise was the small, framed picture of Lark parked next to the phone.

Angela picked up the photograph and studied the woman's face. She was smiling. Laugh lines crinkled the corners of her dark brown eyes. Her blonde hair was pulled back and braided.

How had she missed the connection between Lark and Eric?

Angela set down the frame. Locating the

tape measure, she found a flat package scale on top of the filing cabinets, and pulled *The Sibley Guide to Birds* off the bookshelf. She needed to check the stats on the birds. The common Canada goose — the resident variety — weighed around ten pounds, with a wingspan of sixty inches. The lesser Canada goose was smaller, maxing out at six pounds, and the Richardson's was smaller still.

Using the figures as benchmarks, she headed to the main barn, and started in on the geese. An hour later, she had the results. By her estimations, sixty-three percent of the birds were local, the rest were migrants.

"Guess what?" she said, returning to the lavage room. "We have migrants."

The EPOCH members cheered.

"Can you take a bird down tonight?" asked Eric.

Angela shook her head. "I've been assigned to the Ice Fishing Jamboree for the weekend. I'm bunking at the Drummond through Sunday. Besides, it's a holiday. The Wildlife lab is closed until Tuesday."

"George Covyduck could do it up here," said Lark. She and Eric exchanged glances.

Why not? thought Angela. It would give them some quicker answers. She considered checking with Kramner, then decided against it. She had permission, and he'd never specified which lab to use.

"Can you arrange it?" she asked.

"*Ja.*" Eric bobbed his head. "Consider it done."

The job of selecting a bird fell to Angela. Unable to leave the bodies of the dead geese outside for fear of scavengers, volunteers had piled the dead birds in an unheated storeroom in the back of the Protective Custody House. A small space with ambient heat from the hall, the room's smell — a mixture of rotted flesh, wet feathers, and blood — overwhelmed her. Carcasses stretched along the back wall, stacked like cordwood.

She sucked in a breath, then pulled out the tape measure. Finding a smallish one near the top of a stack, she checked the wingspan.

A lesser.

Gripping its legs, she dragged it from the pile.

She recognized the bird when it hit the floor. Its other wing was bloodied and bent at an odd angle. The goose appeared to have its hand raised. It was the gander she'd seen hit by the plow.

Poor thing.

Gripping its feathers, she straightened the wing, her muscles tensing at the sound of the snap. Maybe she should choose a different bird.

Then again . . .

She gazed down at the gander. His partner had died, and he had paid the ultimate price trying to save her. Now, it was time for the dead to give up their secrets.

Chapter 8

The fishermen were having a party.

The first day of the Elk Park Ice Fishing Jamboree was history. The paperwork was done, dinner was eaten, and drinks were being poured at the bar. More than one young fisherman drank Shirley Temples or Roy Rogers. More than one old fisherman guzzled a beer. But after the day she had endured, the last thing Angela wanted to do was trade fish stories.

Instead, she opted for a hot shower and bed.

Drifting in and out of sleep, she was jarred awake, time and again, by the sound of laughter, glass breaking, and the birds.

The birds.

Her mind sharpened. Somehow, amidst all the noise, rose the high gabbling and cackling of geese. Remnants of the flock?

Angela stirred off the bed. Pulling on the thick hotel robe, she groped her way in the dark to the small balcony facing the water. Yanking open the sliding door, the frigid air assaulted her exposed skin, and goose-flesh pimpled her skin under the terry cloth. Gathering the hotel robe more tightly around her, she stared out at shadows. Stars dotted the sky and a new moon hung low over the mountains like a lopsided grin, taunting her inability to see the geese.

But she could hear them. They were there, lurking somewhere on the hard, flat surface of the lake.

Retreating inside, she reset the alarm. If she went to work early in the morning, she would have time to check on the birds before Frakus showed up.

Crawling back into bed, she was lulled to sleep by the warmth of the blankets, and she dreamed of Ian. In a rewrite of history, she had found him alive near the water, and together they had carried the swan.

The alarm jarred her from the dream at five o'clock, and she grappled with reality. Ian was, in point of fact, dead, and she could no longer hear the geese. With luck, the flock had bedded down safely, in a place outside of the fishing area.

Twenty minutes later, bundled into her winter gear, Angela snatched up the truck keys and headed out to the lake. She had exactly two hours until the Jamboree registration desk opened; exactly two hours to locate the geese.

Parking near the Visitors Center, she grabbed her binoculars from under the seat, looped them around her neck, then dug out a fishing net from the back of the truck. The sky had brightened, chasing away the shadows, and she felt her spirits lift. The honking and gabbling had returned, but it sounded normal.

Other birdsounds seeped in as morning broke over the mountains. Frigid cold temperatures tended to make the birding good, knocking the birds down to take cover.

Crows were abundant in the willow thickets that bordered the path. Perched on the branches like a festoon of large, black ornaments, their *caws* hammered the daybreak like a nagging alarm clock.

Near the seventh green of the golf course, she picked out the hoarse, raspy *tsik-a-zee-zee* of a mountain chickadee. She searched for the small bird, finally discovering it in a small pine tree ten feet ahead. *Fee-bee-bee,* it sang, peering out from its black mask. And, from the ponderosas behind her, came the *shak shak shak* of a Steller's jay.

At the juncture to the Paris Mills Bird Sanctuary, a black-billed magpie — blackheaded with black and white wings, white underparts, and a long black tail — wrestled with a hotdog wrapper on the ground. As she approached, it yanked its prize out of reach. Its black feathers flashed iridescent in the early morning light as it twisted away from her.

Angela turned off the path and followed her footsteps from the day before. She wound through the trees until she reached the tip of the promontory. Ahead of her, on the open waters of the lake at the mouth of Black Canyon Creek, bobbed a large number of waterfowl. Lifting her binoculars, she scanned the groupings, picking out thirty-plus mallards, twelve common goldeneye, and a pair of common mergansers.

The males of all three species were distinctive. The mallards were grayish with shiny green heads, white neck rings, chestnut-colored breasts, and yellow bills. They were one of the first birds she'd learned to identify. The common goldeneyes were just as easy. White with a dark back, greenish-black head, and yellow eyes, they had a prominent white spot behind the bill that was hard to miss.

The first common merganser she'd seen she'd mistaken for a goose. Snowy-white with a black back, greenish-black head, and red-orange bill, they sailed the Colorado waters mostly in the wintertime. She'd been out of college before she added it to her life list.

The females of any species were never as colorful, but of the three ducks, she liked the common merganser the best. Grayish, with a white breast and chin, the female's reddish head had a ragged crest, and there was a wildness about her that appealed to Angela. A goldeneye looked much like her mate, only with a grayish body and reddish head. The mallard females were downright drab.

For ducks, wintertime meant courtship. She chuckled as one of the male goldeneyes tried hard to impress his girl. He would swim near, then throw back his head, point his bill toward the sky, and utter a grunting, nasal quack — *Brrrt!* — kicking his legs back with a splash. The female goldeneye seemed underwhelmed.

After a time, Angela swept the binoculars to the right and studied the far shore near the mouth of the creek.

Her heart sank.

Along the edge of the water, where Black Canyon Creek tumbled into Elk Lake, a small number of Canada geese grazed in the grasses. A few appeared unsteady on their feet, most likely strays from the flock. Beyond them, in the power plant parking lot, someone wearing a dark-colored snow-suit and black cap was loading birds into the bed of a black four-wheel-drive vehicle. An EPOCH member?

It couldn't be. The person wasn't using any carriers. No EPOCH member would transport birds loose in the back of a truck. It was too dangerous for the animals.

Angela zoomed in her binoculars. Whoever it was stopped loading and looked around. Had he, or she, sensed Angela watching?

She tried focusing in on the person's face, but the man — she was pretty sure it was a man from the glimpse she had gotten — looked away, and Angela couldn't make out the license plate number of the truck from this angle. She needed a scope.

She watched for a moment longer, then struck out for the Visitors Center parking lot. If she hurried, maybe she could drive around and catch the person before they took off.

It wasn't to be.

By the time she arrived, whoever had been there was gone. A fresh set of tracks marred the snowpack, but it was not enough to ID the truck.

The remaining geese looked to be in good shape. Camped at the mouth of Black Canyon Creek, they waddled along the shore and floated on the open waters of the river. Not one of them looked sick, which meant the birds could be saved. According to Eric, the best statistical chance of survival came with treating the geese *before* they exhibited symptoms of poisoning.

She called the Raptor House and got the machine. After leaving a message on the voice mail, she dialed the Drummond front desk. Lark answered the phone.

"I've found more geese," Angela said, skipping the preamble. "Do you know where Eric is?"

"No."

"We've got nine birds down here. Someone else picked up the others."

"Who?"

"I have no clue." Angela didn't elaborate. There would be time for that later. "Right now, I need help corralling the rest of the flock."

"Stay there," said Lark. "I'll swing by the Raptor House and pick up some carriers. Give me ten minutes."

Angela waited for her at the truck, sitting inside with the heater blasting. The day

134

was cold and overcast, a rarity for Colorado, where locals expected sunshine three hundred or more days a year. High, white clouds tarped the sky, blurring the edges of the snow-capped peaks. Green trees stretched upwards in jagged lines, creating their own landscape and the illusion of rolling hills along the horizon.

About the time Lark showed up, Angela had started to get antsy. "Finally," she said, climbing out of the truck and stamping her boots on the snow. "What took you so long?"

"I had to wake Miriam Tanager to get keys to the building."

"Eric hadn't checked in?"

Lark's eyes narrowed. "Apparently not."

"What kind of truck does he drive?"

"Why?"

Angela grabbed a carrier from the back of Lark's truck and told her about the person she'd seen in the black four-wheel drive.

"It couldn't have been him, not without carriers. Besides, he doesn't own a black truck."

Nothing more was said, and they walked in silence toward the shore. If it hadn't been for the tension that crackled between them, Angela might have enjoyed the quiet. Instead, the air hummed with the strain of what had gone unsaid.

Unable to take it any longer, Angela said, "You don't like me much, do you?"

Lark's deer-caught-in-the-headlights expression proved it wasn't a question she'd expected.

"We just met," she answered. "I don't even know you."

"But I'm right, aren't I?"

Lark's gaze darted toward Twin Owls and the Raptor House at the base of the giant rock outcroppings.

So that was it.

"You know, you don't have to worry about him."

Lark's eyes narrowed.

"He's obviously sweet on you."

A blush crept into Lark's face. "What makes you say that?"

"For one, he's got your picture on his desk. It's a pretty good one, too." Angela could tell Lark was surprised. "You didn't know?"

Lark shook her head.

"Well, he does. Even if I was interested, I don't think I'd stand a chance."

Lark laughed, looking a little sheepish. "You probably think I'm foolish."

Angela thought of Nate and shook her head. "Not at all. I think you're lucky."

As evidenced by her one true love, relationships were not her forte. She had attended her senior prom with the class geek, now a rocket scientist at Martin Marietta, and accepted the occasional dinner invitation. Unfortunately, most of her dates thought paying for dinner bought them a night in the sack. The only man lucky enough to get reimbursed had ended up falling in love with Angela's college roommate.

"So what's our strategy?" asked Lark, surveying the geese on the lake.

Angela pulled her mind back to the present. "I say the best chance we have is to herd them upstream into the river."

"I agree."

By coin toss, Lark ended up at the bend in the river holding the net, while Angela slogged through the knee-deep snow on the south shore. The top crust shattered with each step, raising a puff of powdered snow.

Several yards downstream of the birds, Angela turned and started moving the birds toward the river. Armed with a fallen branch, she beat at the water and yipped like a cowgirl herding cattle. Startled, the geese flapped their wings.

"Here they come. Go for the big one on the left."

"You mean right," said Lark. Her voice carried, and the geese veered off.

"Shoot!" Angela reached out and slapped the branch on the water. Stepping too close to the bank, her feet slipped, and she ended up ankle deep in the creek. Icy water seeped through the worn seams of her boots and wicked up her socks. *Damn.*

The geese flapped and squawked.

The net swung down.

"Got one." A triumphant Lark loomed into view. Her expression changed when she saw Angela. "Are you okay?"

"I'm fine." *And wet.*

Angela trudged back to the truck through the water at the creek's edge. It was shallow, and she found the rocks easier to navigate than the deep snow. Besides, her feet were already soaked.

Once in sight of the vehicles, she clambered ashore, helping Lark with the bird. The goose didn't want to go into the carrier. It took the both of them to wrestle the bird into the cage, one to hold the goose, one to cram the lid on.

"Ready to do it again?" Lark asked. "If you want, I'll take the river."

"That's okay. I'm already soaked."

They repeated the process eight times, then, with only forty-five minutes left be-

138

fore Angela had to report in to Frakus, the women headed for the Raptor House.

By then, Eric had clocked in, and he helped them unload, lugging the carriers past yesterday's geese and into the lavage area.

"You better get out of those boots," he told Angela on the final trip, hefting the last goose out of the back of her truck.

Snatching up a pair of sneakers from the passenger's side floor, she followed him inside. "Did anyone bring in some birds awhile ago?"

Eric shook his head. "Why?"

She told him about the person with the black truck while she pulled off her socks. Her feet looked bright red and wrinkly. "I figured they headed up here."

"They might have gone to Covy's."

There was a thought. She'd do some checking later. She should have time to make a phone call once the fishermen took to the ice.

Eric disappeared and returned with a pair of dry, wool socks. "Here."

While she pulled on the warm socks, Eric and Lark inspected a goose from one of the carriers.

"This bird looks pretty good," he said. "But we still need to lavage. Dorothy's

139

here. I think the four of us can handle it."

Angela checked her watch for the umpteenth time. It would be tight making the Jamboree, but she hadn't done all this work to have the geese die for lack of care. "Let's do it."

Her feet prickled as she pulled on her shoes, and she rejoiced when they assigned her the easy job of injecting the water. Eric held the goose's body, Lark managed the neck and head, and Dorothy handled the effluent.

The first syringeful produced a gush of half-digested vegetation. Dorothy managed to keep it over the screen and bucket, then after a second and third syringeful announced, "The effluent's clear. There's no more vegetation, nothing."

"Did we pull any lead?" asked Angela, craning her neck trying to see for herself.

"None."

"That's not so unusual," said Eric. "The lead may already be digested. I talked with Covy this morning. He told me that by the time the birds exhibit outward symptoms of lead poisoning, the material is usually broken down and absorbed, or expelled."

"What about the other geese?" asked Angela. "Did you find lead in all of the others?"

"Not all." Dorothy got up and examined the records. "We found sinkers in about a fourth of the geese, lead shot in about half, and there was no lead present in over a third of the birds."

"So where did they come from?" asked Angela.

"Who knows?" said Lark, washing her hands while Eric settled the goose in the main barn with the others. "Nobody saw the flock before Thursday morning, when Opal Henderson spotted them near the spillway."

Angela closed her eyes and dropped her face toward the floor. There had to be a way to track the birds, or backtrack. At this time of year, the geese wintered over, making only local flights.

White flickered on black behind her closed eyelids. *Snow.*

Angela popped open her eyes. "Didn't you get snow here on Wednesday?"

"Yes," answered Dorothy and Lark in unison.

"It was an upslope storm," added Lark.

"Winds heavy, gusts out of the east." Dorothy snapped shut the record book. "Why?"

Excitement pushed Angela to her feet. "How far do wintering flocks move in a day?"

By now, Eric had returned. "Maximum distance?" he said. "About one hundred miles."

"And if the flock had been airborne when the storm came in?"

It took a second, then the room seemed to brighten from the series of light bulbs going off in their heads.

Lark's mouth dropped open. Dorothy chortled.

"*Jumping Jimminy*," said Eric. "The geese would have been blown off course."

Chapter 9

Lark listened in as Angela called Kramner. It was clear the conversation wasn't going the way they wanted.

"He refused to discuss it," Angela said after hanging up. Adjusting make-believe glasses, she mimicked her boss. " 'Do you remember what I told you? No investigation.' "

"He didn't budge at all?" asked Lark.

"He said, and I quote, 'If we learn something definitive from the necropsy, I'll reconsider.' "

It seemed clear to Lark that the director of the U.S. Fish and Wildlife, Mountain-Prairie Division, was not inclined to spend taxpayer dollars pursuing a matter he deemed dead.

"He instructed me to leave the birds to you and get my 'umm' down to the lake. Sorry, guys," said Angela, shrugging on her coat and snatching up her gloves, soggy socks, and wet boots. "I'm outta here. I hope you can handle this without me."

"I guess we'll have to," said Eric, repositioning his hands on the bird while Lark took over Angela's job at the head.

Lark waved, then turned her attention back to the lavage.

Eight geese later, she headed into the main barn. She helped change bedding, then watered and fed the flock. Except for the geese she and Angela had brought in, there were no new intakes. Against all odds, a good number of the treated birds seemed to be getting better.

At mid-morning Lark sought out Eric, finding him hunched over his computer.

"What else did Covyduck have to say?" she asked, plopping down opposite him in a chair. Her eyes drifted to the frame on his desk, and she felt warm inside.

Eric pushed back in his chair. "He confirmed that the necropsy results were consistent with lead poisoning — enlarged gallbladder, impacted proventriculus, and a cracked gizzard lining. Nothing we didn't already know."

"I guess that means we keep on doing what we're doing."

"For now. Angela authorized him to send the shot out for analysis, but it will take a few days to get back the results."

That made sense, thought Lark. It was a

holiday weekend, and not a top priority case.

"She also had him order a toxicology report on the lead levels in the liver and kidneys," said Eric. "Covy put a rush on it, but . . ." Eric let his words trail.

"The birds seem to be doing better."

Eric winced, and his blue eyes clouded. "According to Covy, even if we save them, the secondary losses will be astronomical. The birds are likely to experience reproductive problems, increased susceptibility to disease, infection, predation. He gave them a lousy prognosis."

"Still, they're alive."

Ten hours later, Lark wished *she* were dead. Staring down at the banquet menu, the words "paté de foie gras" pulsed back at her.

"Get me a bag!" she yelled, searching frantically for something to breathe into. Anger had sucked her breath away and now she was hyperventilating.

"Calm down," ordered Stephen Velof, the Drummond's manager. He thrust a brown paper sack into her hands. "John Frakus authorized the menu. In fact, he was quite pleased."

"I don't care if the President of the

United States gave his seal of approval," she replied. "Do you know how they make paté? It's bad enough we serve chicken."

Velof looked blank.

Clamping the bag over her mouth and nose, Lark breathed hard into the sack. Finally, she came up for more air. "They force-feed ducks and geese huge quantities of corn every day, until their livers are oversized, pale, and blotchy. Then they slaughter them. It's barbaric." She found it hard to keep her hands from shaking. "Where's Pierre?"

"In the kitchen." Velof straightened his tie, as if her anger had rumpled him. "I want to go on record as stating, this was his idea."

You weasel. "You hired him!"

The kitchen bustled with activity. The clang of pots, pans, and dishes swirled in the room. Wait staff in black-and-white uniforms congregated in groups near the ballroom doors, while white-hatted cooks grilled chicken, steaks, and salmon over long griddles. Large cauldrons of broccoli bubbled on the stove behind them, belching steam into the air.

"Pierre?" she hollered.

The chef popped his head from behind the freezer door. He was dark and swarthy, and his chef's hat bowed over one eye. "*Oui*, madam?"

"Stephen tells me you made paté."

"*Oui*, and it turned out grand." He kissed his fingers and smacked his lips. "The guests, they are loving it."

"You've served it already?" She felt her blood pressure rise a notch and gripped her bag more tightly.

"*Oui*. I made the Apple Terrine of Foie Gras and Foie Gras with the Blackberry Sauce. Both are scrumptious." He smiled, fat cheeks puffed with pride. "For the Apple Terrine, you take the apple and remove the core. Then you combine the salt, saltpeter, pepper, sugar, and nutmeg, and coat the foie gras."

Lark felt sick. "Please, stop."

"The blackberries you mix with the fat of the foie gras."

"I said, stop!" She clutched her throat with her hand. "How could you?"

"What?" He drew back. "You are not pleased?"

"No, I'm not pleased! You of all people know what they do to the geese to fatten their livers."

"But, of course."

Was his French accent thicker tonight, or was rage affecting her hearing?

"But these birds did not suffer," he said.

"They all suffer."

"Oh, *contraire*. I have found a secret. I took the liver from the game bird."

Fear sparked a stomachache. "From wild geese?"

"Oui." He stuck out his chest. "And I have saved the breast of the bird for dinner tomorrow, and the extra pieces for goose stew. Good, no?"

Paralyzed by the news, Lark wondered whether her heart would ever start pumping again. Ducharme must have been the person Angela had seen down by the lake this morning.

"Do you know what you've done?" she said. "You've served poisoned livers to my guests."

Ducharme blanched. "I do not think so."

"Ducharme, you idiot!" screamed Velof. The noise in the kitchen ended abruptly, and all faces turned in their direction. Lark plucked at Velof's sleeve.

"Keep your voice down," she ordered. Turning to the wait staff and cooks, she said, "Everything's fine, but it's time to clear the hors d'oeuvres. Quickly."

"Vite, vite," said Ducharme, color flowing back into his face. "Pierre Ducharme has a reputation to uphold. I

have created a masterpiece, and now you tell me that the geese I acquired are bad."

"*Oui,*" she replied, wishing she could strangle the man.

"What do we do now?" whined Velof.

She wanted to kill him, too.

"We tell them." She gestured toward the door. She had a reputation, as well. The Drummond was a world-class destination resort known for its location, good food, friendly service, and luxurious rooms — in that order. If word got out that the Drummond had served the guests poisoned birds, and that she knew about it and hadn't told, her business would be ruined.

"But, we don't know that anyone will get sick," said Ducharme, his accent gone.

"What happened to your *Frrrrench?*" she asked, rolling her *r.*

Realizing his mistake, he clamped a hand over his mouth.

"You're fired."

"But you can't just dismiss me like that," he said, accent back in full force. "I am Pierre Ducharme."

"I don't care if you're Julia Child in drag."

Ducharme pulled off his hat and threw it to the floor. "You'll pay for this, bitch."

"Is that a threat?" She pulled to her full

height and stuck her face up close to his.

"*Oui*."

She watched him stomp out, then turned to Velof. "First things first, we need to find out what symptoms the guests who ate the paté might experience. Get on the phone with poison control. In the meantime, I'll collect samples of the food for analysis."

"Good idea."

They reconnoitered in the kitchen a few minutes later. While Lark sorted and marked the gathered specimens in plastic containers, Velof reported the word from poison control.

"They don't think the guests will experience any problems. According to the nurse on duty, it takes an acute dose of lead poisoning for a victim to experience symptoms. Based on body weight, she thinks the geese would have to have been long dead before they would have a buildup large enough to affect anyone."

Lark wasn't convinced. She'd heard of predators getting sick from eating lead-poisoned birds.

"Did she give you the symptoms?"

He consulted his notes. "A metallic taste in the mouth, abdominal pain, nausea, vomiting, bloody or black diarrhea. Enough contamination can trigger neurological symptoms such as headache, confusion, delirium, seizures, coma and . . . death."

"Let's hope the nurse is right about the guests not getting sick, but for the sake of argument, what did she say to do if someone develops symptoms?"

"Have them report to the nearest hospital ASAP."

"We need to call Bernie."

Lark ordered the cooks and wait staff to dispose of the paté and blackberry sauce in a large plastic bag, and she headed to her office. Courtesy of a wait-staff leak, rumblings of trouble rolled through the ballroom. Several people dashed for the bathroom. To top it off, the police chief wasn't in. He was attending the banquet.

"What's going on, Drummond?" Bernie demanded, taking a seat in the hotel office after being hunted down by Velof.

She filled him in, and he clutched his stomach. "Where's Ducharme now?"

Lark shrugged.

"He's very temperamental," explained Velof. "She yelled at him. I think he left."

"He ran?" Bernie looked from Lark to Velof.

Velof looked blank.

"What kind of idiot is this Ducharme?"

asked the police chief.

"A fired idiot," said Lark.

"Are you sure he picked the geese up here?"

Lark exchanged glaces with Velof.

"No. But he admitted he used wild geese." She told Bernie about the person Angela had spotted collecting geese earlier in the day. "Ducharme owns a black pickup."

"Find him," ordered the chief, dispatching Velof to track down Ducharme. "I have a few questions I'd like to ask him."

"What do we do next?" Lark asked once her manager had disappeared.

"First, you tell the banquet guests the truth. Tell them you believe the paté is contaminated, what symptoms to watch for, and what to do if they get sick. Next, the health inspector needs to be notified and the food needs to be analyzed."

"The health inspector will shut down the kitchen."

"You have a problem with that, Drummond?"

"I need to be able to feed my guests."

"Then I suggest you strike a deal with the Elk Park Diner. In the meantime, you need to talk to the guests."

Bernie was right. There were no alternatives. With any luck, no one would get sick, but she couldn't take the risk.

"You realize that the minute we announce this, there will be at least one hypochondriac requiring immediate treatment."

Bernie grinned. "Any bets it's Frakus?"

Lark couldn't help but laugh. Finally, she dropped her head in her hands. "I can't believe this is happening."

"Don't worry, Drummond. With luck, the health department will close you down only until they've cleared all traces of the geese from the kitchen."

"I just pray nobody dies."

He made a clicking noise with his cheek. "You know, Frakus will likely expect a refund of the banquet costs."

"Then, can I amend my prayer, and hope he's the only one who croaks?"

Now it was Bernie's turn to laugh. Lark felt another wave of hysteria building inside.

Velof inched back into the room. He looked as if he thought they were talking about him.

Bernie sobered up. "Did you find Ducharme?"

"He's gone."

The chief reached for the phone. "I'll

153

put out an A.P.B. for the chef, in the meantime . . ."

"We serve dinner?" asked Velof, straightening his tie.

"No!" said Lark and Bernie in unison.

"Gather the staff. Find out how many, if any, ate any of the goose liver paté. I'm going to talk to the banquet guests." She pushed back from her desk.

"You should file a formal complaint against Pierre Ducharme to protect yourself, Lark. Meanwhile, I'll get some of my boys up here to take down the names of everyone who ate the paté." Bernie pushed himself up, and the chair creaked in protest. "I sure hope you're insured, Drummond."

"Why, are you feeling sick?"

Chapter 10

The fishing huts stood like sentinels on the frozen expanse of the lake. Darkness shrouded the ice before dawn, and a stiff breeze whisked across the lake, whipping the flag banners into a frenzy, snapping them like sails in a wind. In an hour, the area would be teeming with kids and adults. It was the last day of the ice fishing tournament. A cause to celebrate.

Not that the work had been all bad. Angela actually enjoyed certain parts of the event — the kids catching fish, the adults acting like kids. The only part she didn't like was kowtowing to the director of the Elk Park Chamber of Commerce.

Cupping her hands around her mouth, she shouted, "Frakus?"

No answer.

A chill crept along her spine. According to Stephen Velof, who had tracked her down having breakfast at McDonald's — not a hard feat considering the kitchen at the Drummond was closed, and fast food was Elk Park's only option at that hour of the morning — the director had called the hotel and wanted her to meet him down at the lake. So where was he?

His car had been in the parking lot, alongside Donald Tauer's SUV and an assortment of RVs, fifth-wheel campers, and Arctic-rated pup tents belonging to some of the fishermen. Camping was not permitted on the ice. A smattering of lights from the makeshift village delineated the early risers, but there had been no lights on at the Visitors Center, and she had passed only one hearty soul on the path between the parking lot and the bathrooms.

"Frakus?"

This time the echo of her own voice slithered into the early morning hours and came back accompanied by the hoot of a great-horned owl. Taking heart, she pressed on toward the ice, past the registration table, past the concession stands and Sanolets, until she stood at the edge of the lake staring out.

Why did she have a bad feeling about this?

The cold air pinched the skin on her face, drawing it tight across her cheek bones. She scanned the contours of the shoreline. Her gaze drifted over the miniature houses dotting the ice until it halted abruptly. A faint glow eked out from inside one of the fishing huts.

That's odd.

Could it be Frakus? What would he be doing out there at this time of the morning? From what she knew, the huts belonged to individual fishermen, most of whom were competing in the tournament. Had Frakus caught someone camping on the ice? Or worse, cheating?

Why call her? Her authority extended to Fish and Game violations — fishing without a license, keeping a green-backed trout. Tournament rules fell into his baili-wick, and camping violations fell under Bernie Crandall's jurisdiction.

Unless . . . Had he found more dead geese on the ice?

There was only one way to find out. Easing herself onto the lake's surface, Angela inched her way toward the hut, keeping her eyes open for unmarked holes. The last thing she wanted to do was go swimming.

The hut in question sat farthest out. Made of corrugated metal and painted army green, it measured the size of a small living room. The pipe from its wood-burning stove towered above a small antenna affixed to the peak of the roof. The wind howled, skittering snow across the ice, and a snake of air slithered up the leg of her snow suit.

"Frakus?"

Again, no answer.

"Is someone there?"

Metal clanged.

A vision of Ian sprang unbidden to mind. Spinning around, she drew her gun and peered into the darkness.

If this was Frakus's idea of a joke, it wasn't funny.

The door of a Sanolet banged on its hinges. Angela jumped.

Keeping one eye on the outhouse, she moved sideways toward the hut. Light seeped from underneath its edges in the places where metal didn't meet ice and through the cracks in the structure where the sides didn't quite fit together.

Standing off to one side, she rapped on the door of the hut. "Hello?"

No answer.

Nearby, the Sanolet door banged again, and a shot of adrenaline raced through her veins. Listening, she thought she heard a faint squeak, like the sound of a buoy scraping a dock.

She drew a deep breath, exhaled, then

knocked again. "Who's in there?" This time she pounded on the door, determined to raise the occupant. "This is Special Agent Angela Dimato. Please, open the door!"

Still no answer. Maybe the owner had come down earlier, and left a light on.

She tried the handle. The door was locked.

That's weird. No one locked their fishing huts. It was part of the code of honor. Others were free to take shelter, provided they replenished used supplies.

She heard another noise from inside and circled the hut, trying to peek through the cracks in the seams. She caught glimpses of color but was unable to make out anything more. The light seemed to be coming from near the ice.

The bottom of the hut was raised half an inch off the ground in back. Angela stretched out on her stomach and peered under the edge. From this vantage point, she could make out a chair, a cooler, a small table, and stove. In the middle of the hut the hole in the ice was uncapped.

Scooting around for a better angle, she pressed her face to the ice. A strange glow spread through the layers beneath her. The light seemed to be shining up from below the surface. And it looked like something was stuck to the edge of the hole.

A black glove.

A hand.

Her breath left, and she sat upright, huffing for air. Digging out her cell phone, she hit 9-1-1.

"This is nine-one-one, please state your emergency," said a cheery voice.

"This is Special Agent Angela Dimato."

"Who?"

"Special Agent Dimato. I'm calling from Elk Lake. There is someone in the water down near the fishing huts. I'm requesting backup and emergency personnel."

"Yes, ma'am. Please stay on the line. Tell me, how do you spell your last name?"

"Just get an ambulance, and Bernie Crandall, down here, stat! Elk Lake, by the fishing huts."

The town siren blared as she kicked in the door. It took two tries to knock it off its hinges. The first sent a jarring shock wave through the pad of her foot, up her calf, and into her knee. The second slammed the door inward, buckling the metal jamb.

She darted inside. The room glowed eerily, illuminated from under the ice. In addition to what she had seen through the cracks, a couch lay tipped on its back, knocked aside in a scuffle. A nice stereo system stood in the corner and four Bose speakers were mounted on the walls.

Lark moved toward the body in the water. Gouges in the ice indicated that the person in the hole had tried climbing out. Or, that someone kept pushing him back in. The hand belonged to a big man.

Frakus?

There was no way she could pull him out by herself. His glove was frozen to the ice at his wrist. He must have fallen through, then reached back out, the wetness of his clothes securing him to the lake's surface like a tongue on frozen metal. A flashlight bobbed in the water, half-encased in new formed ice.

Afraid to grab him for fear of losing him into the hole, she searched for something — anything — to safeguard his position. A rope?

All she could find was a roll of fifty pound–test line. *It's not heavy enough.*

Suddenly, the hut filled with firemen. No-Mex–clad men hauled the body out of the water. A National Park Service insignia flashed from the victim's shoulder.

Angela sank to a chair. Her ears rang. Her head spun. The man in the water wasn't Frakus. It was Eric Linenger.

161

★ ★ ★

What was Eric doing in the fishing hut? And why was the door locked?

The second question nagged at her.

Staying out of the firemen's way, she walked over and examined the lock. Her kick had knocked off the catch plate on the inside of the door frame, but the door-handle mechanism was still in place. Made of stainless steel, it was keyed on only one side. The outside. Which meant someone had locked Eric in.

Who?

Who would have had a key? The owner of the hut, anyone he had given a key to, and possibly Frakus. It ran in her mind that the owners of the ice fishing huts were required by permit to provide one for entry in the case of an emergency. Keys were normally kept in the marina office — in this case, the office was in the Visitors Center.

"Chief." She tried catching Bernie Crandall's gaze, without drawing the attention of the reporters and film crews who had arrived on site, but several heads turned at the sound of her voice.

"What?" The beefy police chief left his post beside the ambulance and swaggered toward her.

162

She noticed one reporter edging over with him and dropped her voice. "Who locked the ice hut?"

Crandall gave the reporter a mean glance, took Angela by the elbow, and led her farther away. "Let's go over your story again."

She had told it a number of times — about Velof passing the message to meet Frakus, the vehicles in the parking lot, the eerie light, and the Sanolet door — but she told it again.

"And Velof told you it was Frakus who called?"

"That's what he said."

Crandall jotted something in a notebook. Slapping it shut, he eyeballed her. "Now, what was your question?"

"Do you know who this hut belongs to?"

"Yep," he answered, but his attention seemed drawn by some commotion near the ambulance.

"Whose is it?" she prompted, flashing her fingers in front of his eyes.

He broke his stare. "Donald Tauer's."

The CEO of Agriventures? What had Eric been doing inside Tauer's fishing hut?

Just then a cheer rose from the firemen. Crandall made a dash for the ambulance. Angela scrambled behind.

"What's going on?" she asked, standing on tiptoes trying to see over the heads of the firemen. Their broad, No-Mex–clad shoulders blotted out the view.

"He's alive!" someone shouted. "We have a pulse."

"What?" Eric was alive. A giddiness washed through her, followed by a chill of fear. How long had he been under water?

"This is good," said Crandall, elbowing his way back through the crowd. "When he can talk, maybe he can tell us what happened."

"If he can talk," she muttered. She hated to be pessimistic, but she was afraid of getting her hopes up. "It's my guess he was under there quite a while."

"It's a cold-water drowning." Crandall ducked under the crime scene tape and moved back onto the ice.

Angela followed. If he was trying to make her feel better, she wasn't convinced. She knew they could warm him up slowly, but as often as not victims like Eric didn't remember anything once they woke up — not even how to tie their own shoes.

"What this?" Frakus's voice cut through the crowd behind them, and Angela groaned.

Now he shows up.

"I'll second that," mumbled Crandall.

"Will someone tell me what the hell is going on around here?" Frakus bullied his way through the firemen packing up gear and tugged down the yellow ribbon cordoning off the fishing area. Behind him, Donald Tauer and another man picked their way past the concession stands.

Nathan Sobul. The sight of her former boyfriend caused Angela's breathing to shallow and her legs to tremble. What was he doing here? She wondered if it was too late to throw up.

"Someone get that tape back up," hollered Crandall. "Dammit, John, you're messing up my crime scene."

Like three more people mattered, thought Angela. Between the firemen, policemen, and Angela, any evidence on the ice had been trampled by now, or contaminated. Inside the hut was a different story. Besides herself, four firemen, Crandall, and the crime scene investigators, only Tauer and anyone else with a key could have been inside.

By the time the men reached the hut, Angela had pulled herself together. She'd also figured out the connection between Nate Sobul and Tauer. Nate worked for the USDA. Tauer was in organic foods. No doubt they'd met on the job. No wonder Nate wouldn't help block the use of Agriventures's geese-depredation permit. He and Donald Tauer were friends.

Nate looked up.

Their eyes met.

Angela knew, in this business, sooner or later she would see him again. Why did it have to be now?

"I am talking to you, Dimato," barked Frakus.

"Sorry." Angela glanced at Crandall, hoping to deflect Frakus's negative vibes. "Eric Linenger fell through the ice. They're transporting him to the hospital."

To his credit, Frakus blanched. "Is he okay?"

"It's too soon to say," answered the chief. Crandall eyed the three men. "What brings you gentlemen down here so early?"

"It's the last day of the fishing tournament," said Frakus. The "duh" was implied.

Tauer moved forward and pointed to the lit-up fishing hut. "Is everything still intact? Was anything damaged?"

Angela scowled. A man was in critical condition, and Tauer was worried about his things?

Crandall ignored him. "According to

Special Agent Dimato, you called her about an hour ago, John, and asked her to meet you down here?"

"I what?" Frakus looked surprised. "I didn't call anyone."

Now Angela frowned. "Velof tracked me down at McDonald's. He said you wanted to meet me here early."

Frakus stared at her like she'd lost her mind.

"No?" Crandall jotted another note in his book.

Why would Stephen have lied? wondered Angela. Her mind drew a blank. More likely Frakus was lying, except he seemed truly surprised. Had someone else called pretending to be Frakus? But who? Eric? No way. Velof would have recognized his accent. Someone else who wanted her down on the ice to find Eric? Or had Eric come down to the ice and stumbled into an ambush meant for her? The thought sent chills up her spine.

One thing was certain; someone had locked Eric inside the fishing hut after pushing him into the water. Someone had wanted him silenced. But why?

"What time did you get here this morning, John?" asked Crandall.

"Why?" Frakus glanced around, absorbing the scene. "Are you suggesting this wasn't an accident?"

"The thought crossed my mind."

"Well, I didn't do anything. I've been with Donald and Nate here, all morning."

"He's telling the truth," said Nate. "We met in the parking lot at about five-thirty and took my car into town to the Elk Park Diner for breakfast."

Tauer suddenly pushed past them and stepped through the door of the fishing hut.

"Hey," Crandall blustered, going in after the man. "This area is off limits."

"I want to know what that guy was doing inside my fishing hut."

"So do I," said Crandall, jostling Tauer out of the hut. "Now, move back, or I'll bust your heinie for hindering an investigation. All of you. You too, Angela."

Crandall started to shoo them up the hill, when Angela thought of the one-sided lock on the door. "Hold on a second! Mr. Tauer, do you have a key for the hut?"

"Sure."

"May I see it?"

He pulled off a glove, and produced a key on a blue coil.

Crandall showed a sudden interest in Angela's line of questioning. "Were you in

168

the hut this morning?"

Tauer shook his head. "I never ventured past the parking lot."

"Do you keep the hut locked?" asked the chief.

"Most of the time. I keep some expensive equipment in there. I don't want anything stolen."

"Right. Except Angela here kicked the door down."

"Well, you know what they say about locks," ventured Nate. All eyes turned toward where he stood shivering in the dawn, hands tucked into his armpits.

"No," said Crandall. "What?"

"Their only purpose is to keep honest people honest."

Crandall's eyes narrowed. "And you are?"

"Oh, I'm sorry," said Tauer. "This is Nate Sobul, U.S. Department of Agriculture." Tauer gestured towards the chief. "Bernie Crandall, Elk Park Chief of Police, and this is Angela Dimato, U.S. Fish and Wildlife."

Nate shook hands with Crandall, then stuck out his hand to Angela. She refused it, tucking a stray curl into her cap instead.

"Who else has a key?" she asked.

"Any number of my associates, and the town has a copy."

"Do you keep a spare key inside?" asked Crandall.

"Yes. Why?"

"Someone had to unlock the door to get inside."

Tauer gestured toward the hut. "I keep an extra key on a screw to the left of the door."

Crandall stepped back to the door of the hut, and poked his head inside. Angela heard him tap on the metal, then he emerged empty-handed. "It's not there now."

"Are you positive?" asked Tauer. "It should be on a red string."

"It's gone. Any idea when it went missing?"

Tauer shook his head. "I was in and out of the hut all day yesterday. I didn't bother to lock it, there were so many people around I figured nobody would try and take anything in broad daylight."

Wrong, thought Angela.

Crandall rubbed his chin. "It looks like somebody took the key planning to come back here and burglarize the hut. Eric must have caught them in the act."

"That doesn't explain the phone call,"

said Angela, unable to shake the feeling it should have been her floating under the ice.

Silence shrouded the ice, until Crandall broke the veneer. "Maybe Velof can shed some light on the subject, but first I need to tell Lark about Eric."

Telling Lark about Eric wasn't going to be easy. No doubt she would take it hard. She was going to need a lot of support. Thank heavens she had some close friends like Dorothy, Cecilia, and Harry to help her get through it.

Angela smiled sympathetically, then said, "Unless there's something I can do. . . ."

"There is," said Crandall. "I need you to make sure the Raptor House volunteers put someone else in charge up there."

"Sure, I can do that." In fact, she would relish the chance to get away from the crime scene.

"Great. I'll notify the National Park Service."

Angela figured NPS already knew. Elk Park was a small town, and the fire department and ambulance service were primarily volunteer. She would be surprised if half of the town — and maybe even Lark — didn't know by now.

Frakus pushed forward. "Hold on a cotton-picking minute, Bernie. Dimato's been assigned to oversee the fishing."

"She's a sworn peace officer. Do you have a problem with that?"

Getting no support from the others, Frakus backed down. "When are you going to take down this yellow ribbon?"

The combination of Eric's situation, Nate Sobul's presence, and Frakus's attitude had proved too much to bear. Anger flashed inside of Angela and burned hot.

"Is that all you care about?" she asked, unleashing her temper. "Opening the ice?"

Frakus looked startled and took a step backward.

Angela advanced. "What's the problem? We're not being hush-hush enough for you? Are you afraid that someone's near-fatal accident might ruin your little party?"

Crandall pressed a hand to his mouth, and Nathan laughed out loud. "Oooh boy, watch out!"

Frakus looked dumbstruck. At first he stared at her, his mouth agape, then he started sputtering. "You better . . . how dare you . . . I don't think you . . ."

"Yoo hoo!" called out a female voice.

Angela's back was to the woman, but she noticed a shift in Frakus's attitude. He dropped his shoulders and plastered a smile on his face.

Turning to see what had caused the transformation, Angela spotted a reporter with bleached hair and makeup visible from a distance making her way toward them. She had a cameraman in tow, and a television station logo was embroidered on the right-hand shoulder of her parka. Balanced on high-heeled boots, she spread her arms to the side like a tightrope walker and picked her way down the slippery path.

"May I have a word with you?" she asked, with a pointed look at Angela.

"Smile, Dimato," Frakus ordered. "This may be the only thing that saves you."

"Are you threatening me?"

"William Kramner is a friend of mine."

Fraternization, the buzz word of the day.

"How could I forget?" asked Angela. She figured she'd pay for the outburst, but didn't care.

"Watch what you say to this woman," he warned. "That is, if you value your job."

The flames of anger fizzled. Frakus was right. She was already skating on thin ice with Kramner. One more incident, and she might easily find herself out of a job.

"Linda Verbiscar, KEPC-TV," announced the reporter, once she'd slid her way onto the ice. "This is Charlie." She flicked her finger in the air, and the cameraman began rolling tape. "I understand you're the one who found the body," she said, jamming a microphone in Angela's face.

Angela nodded, turning away from the lights.

Verbiscar signaled for Charlie to change angles. "We're live in ten."

Crandall stepped forward, looking official in his uniform. "Give the kid a break, Linda. I'll give you an interview. Or better yet, talk to John. After all, this is his Jamboree."

Frakus plastered a PR grin across his pudgy face.

"I'm going for the human interest angle," said Verbiscar, dismissing the men. "We're live in three . . ." Reaching around Crandall, she grabbed Angela's arm and drew her forward. "Two . . . one . . . Hello, Dan. We're at the site of Elk Park's First Annual Ice Fishing Jamboree where a body has just been pulled out from under the ice."

Verbiscar mugged for the camera, while Angela tried wiggling free.

"The victim is a thirty-five-year-old National Park Service employee whose name is being withheld pending notification of his family. All we know at the moment is the man fell through the ice sometime early this morning and now clings tenuously to life at a local hospital. We are joined this morning by U.S. Fish and Wildlife Special Agent Angela Dimato, the woman who found him."

Linda shoved the microphone in Angela's face. "Special Agent Dimato, in your own words, tell us what happened."

Angela stared at the woman. Dressed in a tight, white, Bogner ski suit, she appeared to Angela to be the anti-Christ. "I'm not at liberty to discuss this case. Suffice it to say, Eric fell through the ice."

Verbiscar's face drained of color behind her makeup. "Folks, we have just learned that the victim's first name is Eric."

Angela kicked herself for letting his name slip. Kramner would have a field day.

"Special Agent Dimato, is it true that you are investigating the alleged poisoning of a flock of migratory geese?"

"Yes."

"Is it also true that the National Park Service rehabilitation center has been helping with the geese?"

"Yes." Where was Verbiscar headed with this line of questioning?

"I'm just trying to help our viewers understand the situation," said Verbiscar, as though answering Angela's question. "Isn't the poisoning of migratory geese against the law?"

"Yes it is."

Verbiscar made a mean face, indicating Angela should expound.

"Migratory birds are protected under the Migratory Bird Treaty Act," added Angela. "Harming them is a federal offense."

Verbiscar cracked a smile, then gazed at Angela intently. "Then you're saying it's possible this wasn't an accident?" She gestured toward the fishing huts behind them. "That the ranger might have been the victim of foul play?"

Angela swallowed. "I never said that."

Verbiscar switched tacks. "According to my sources, a man left word for you to meet him here early this morning. Was that person 'Eric'?" Her voice caught on his name.

Where had Verbiscar gotten her information? wondered Angela. Velof? "No comment."

Verbiscar pressed. "Perhaps he wanted to meet you to disclose the identity of the person, or persons, responsible for poisoning the geese?"

Angela's mouth went dry. Was Verbiscar trying to create a story, or did she know something Angela didn't? "I said, no comment."

The reporter looked grim. "My source also informs me that those poor individuals sick from eating the paté served last night at the Drummond banquet may, in fact, have been eating paté made from the livers of the poisoned geese."

Angela frowned. What had she missed? Rather than attend the banquet, she had treated herself to a pay-per-view movie. Had something happened downstairs?

In her zeal to move in for the kill, Verbiscar released Angela's arm.

"I know nothing about that," said Angela, stepping away.

Signaling her cameraman to keep the film rolling, Verbiscar tried to block Angela's retreat. "Agent Dimato —"

Frakus, of all people, came to her rescue, stepping in and blocking the reporter. "Linda, you must know Special Agent Dimato can't discuss an active case. Tell your viewers not to worry. They can rest assured. This was just an accident, and the Jamboree is on as planned. We'll be here until noon today."

Verbiscar smiled sweetly. "That's all from

the scene. Back to you in the studio, Dan."

Once the red light flipped off on the camera, Verbiscar scowled and teetered after Angela. "Was it Eric Linenger?"

Angela didn't answer.

"Off the record. He's a friend of mine. He helped me once."

Angela didn't stand to lose anything more by telling her. "Yes, it was."

Verbiscar's gloved hand fluttered up to her throat. "Is he going to make it?"

"I hope so."

Angela waited for the woman to collect herself, then added, "Now you answer a question for me. What's this about the Drummond guests being sick?"

Verbiscar's eyes widened. "You haven't heard?"

"Heard what?"

"You really don't know."

"Know what?"

Angela listened as Verbiscar recounted the highlights. The details were vague, but the picture was clear. Angela's thoughts flashed on the man collecting geese off the lake.

It had to be a coincidence.

Her stomach churned.

"What?" asked Verbiscar, studying Angela's face.

Angela shook her head and tried worming her way around the woman. Verbiscar planted herself in Angela's way. "You have to admit it seems fishy."

Her mind pictured the man again. *There's no way.*

The man culling geese from the ice on Saturday morning wouldn't have had time to make enough paté for two hundred people that night, she reasoned.

"Maybe it was the water," she suggested.

"You don't believe that anymore than I do." Verbiscar planted her hands on her hips. "Don't stand there and tell me that given this latest turn of events you don't plan on increasing the scope of your investigation?"

In spite of all her doubts, and the sick feeling in her stomach, Angela was forced to toe the party line. "I don't have the authority to make that decision, Ms. Verbiscar. My assignment, outside of watching for illegal catch, is to figure out what happened to the geese. Nothing more."

This time, Crandall came to her rescue. "I think she made herself clear."

"Crystal," said Verbiscar.

Angela averted her eyes.

"Then you're done here," said Crandall,

waving off the woman and cupping a hand on Angela's shoulder "Why don't you head out, Verbiscar?"

"Thanks."

"I still don't see why you can't send one of your own men up to the Raptor House?" sniveled Frakus.

"Because," said Crandall, pushing his nose up close to the director's face. "This is how it's going down. When Angela's done up at the Raptor House, she'll come back. Meanwhile, I want to see Mr. Tauer, in *your* office, now."

Angela considered pointing out that Nate had skated under the radar, but struck out for the parking lot instead. That was Crandall's problem.

Frakus stayed behind pulling down yellow tape, but Nate fell in step beside Angela. "It's not what you think," he said.

"How do you know what I think?"

Heck, she didn't know what she thought, other than that his fraternizing with Donald Tauer seemed like a conflict of interest. It was Nathan's job to inspect Tauer's crops, for god's sake.

Nate offered up a smile. She was pleased to find herself resistant to his charms.

"Peeps, you have to believe me. I'm sorry I couldn't help out. Trust me, there are things you don't know."

"Trust? That's a mighty big word." *For such a small man*. How depressing! Her life boiled down to a country-western lyric.

Nathan reached out and touched her sleeve. She felt a fissure open in her heart.

"I know we have a history," he said. "A difficult history. But can't we work our way past it? What happened between us happened a long time ago."

It was funny how people hang on to certain baggage. To her, it felt like yesterday.

"In case you're interested," he continued. "I'm single again."

The smooth talk rolling off his tongue raised her resolve. Angela smiled. Somehow knowing things hadn't worked out for him made *her* feel better.

"I still care about you, Peeps."

"So sad," she said, not caring if it sounded cold. "For the record, I'm not interested." She savored the rejection flickering across his face. "You know what bothers me most?" she asked. "It's the conflict of interest you've got here. Tell me, was your friendship with Donald Tauer the reason you couldn't help out with the geese?"

Nathan looked shocked. "Are you questioning my integrity?"

"Only if the shoe fits."

"I had a good reason for not helping. Besides, I was under no obligation to intervene for you."

"What was the reason?"

"Hey, Angel," hollered Frakus. "I expect you back here in an hour."

Angela resisted the urge to flip him the bird.

Nathan frowned. "He doesn't seem to like you much."

"Hmmmm." That was the understatement of the decade. "What reason?" she repeated.

"I'm not at liberty to say."

"Convenient."

Nathan stepped closer and dropped his voice. "Trust me, Angela, there's stuff going on you know nothing about. Let it rest, before somebody else gets hurt."

Angela stopped dead in her tracks.

His eyes locked on hers. "I don't want to see anything happen to you."

Her heart stumbled. The sincerity in his voice caught her off guard and, for a moment, she deluded herself into believing he cared. Suddenly, walking beside him was more than she could handle.

"Look, I've got to run."

Sprinting ahead, she left him panting at

the door to the Visitors Center. It felt good to leave him behind, like a karmic rite of passage, closure was at hand.

Once inside her truck, she allowed her emotions to dissolve into tears. In the past four weeks, she had been first on the scene in two separate incidents, both involving men she had worked with. First Ian. Now Eric. One dead. One clinging to life. What were the odds?

The situations bore similarities, but they'd occurred a month apart and in two different locations. The only commonalities were the proximity of water and the sick waterfowl. Was there a chance they were interrelated, or was she letting Linda Verbiscar get to her?

Eric had fallen through the ice hole of a locked fishing hut. Ian had strangled in the mist nets. Ian's death had been ruled a suicide. Eric's accident was under investigation.

A sudden chill caused her to rub her arms. Details of both nights played through her mind. She could feel the cold. Hear the call of the swan, the honking of geese. And in that instant, she knew they had missed something.

Chapter 11

Eric's accident and Ian's death were connected.

Angela found it impossible to shake the idea. She had never believed Ian's death was a suicide, or even an accident. From the start, she had thought it was connected with the person he had met with earlier on the afternoon of his death. Now she tried remembering what he had told her about the case he was working. She dug deep and surfaced with little.

There was the fact that he was out at Barr Lake investigating the report of a sick bird, and she seemed to remember some of his notes indicating he'd recorded a number of animal die-offs along the Front Range. Maybe he'd figured out the source of the poison, and someone had wanted the secret held.

The Raptor House loomed in front of her, and she felt the muscles in her chest tighten. Delivering bad news was one duty of being a law officer she had yet to perform. Her worst fears were realized when Dorothy collapsed upon hearing the news.

Angela helped the older woman to a car in the parking lot and assigned a volunteer to drive her home. After that, she answered a flurry of questions.

"Will he be okay?" someone asked.

Angela shook her head. "Truthfully, it's too soon to know."

"How did it happen?"

"The *accident* is under investigation." A fudge, but she didn't dare tell them the truth, that someone had pushed Eric through a hole in the ice. Not until the investigation was complete.

Most surprising were the number of questions focusing on details. Obviously some of the birdwatchers liked *C.S.I.* They pelted her with questions regarding the forensics of the scene.

Once satiated, the EPOCH volunteers resumed their work, and Angela seized the opportunity to duck into Eric's office and use the phone to call Kramner.

After briefing him on the situation, she tossed out her thoughts. "You have to admit, sir, there are common threads in the cases."

"You're reaching, Dimato."

Silence played on the line. Not knowing how to respond, she let it broaden.

"Let's say your idea has merit," he said.

"What is it you want?"

It was the first sign of concession, and Angela pounced on the opening. "I want permission to investigate the link between the poisonings."

Asking him to allow her to investigate anything more would be pushing the envelope, but she could do that in the process.

"We don't need a department scandal, Dimato. Nor can we afford to create ill will between U.S. Fish and Wildlife and the town of Elk Park." He sounded breathless, and she pictured him pacing. "I expect any findings to come straight through me."

It took a moment for his words to sink in. He was giving her the go ahead.

Angela sat up straighter. "Then I have your permission?"

"As long as you stick to the birds, Dimato."

"I pinky swear." She could tell he had no clue what she meant. "Scout's honor."

"And no big expenditures," he added. "There's a budget crunch on."

Fifty people sick! The number was staggering. Lark rubbed her eyes, hoping to blot out the figure scribbled on the desk blotter. According to the nurse at the Elk Park hospital, they had started referring

186

patients to hospitals in Denver. Given the facts and the symptoms, and pending official lab results, the victims were being treated for lead poisoning.

"We might as well lock the doors, Stephen," said Lark, glancing up at Velof. She was sitting at her desk. He was standing by the door. "The lawsuits will put us under in a week."

"Wait. There's more good news," he responded, marching to the window. "We've gone national." Pulling apart the slats in the blinds, he pointed to the KEPC-TV van in the parking lot. "Linda Verbiscar has been camped outside for an hour. The networks have picked up the story."

"Why isn't she down at the lake?" Lark, a volunteer firefighter, had called in when the siren sounded, so she knew someone had fallen through the ice. Enough volunteers had responded so her presence wasn't needed on scene, but didn't it warrant some television coverage?

"Maybe because we have multiple victims?"

"Good point," said Lark. "Besides, who knows? Our story might win her a Pulitzer."

Velof fixed her with a hawkish stare. "Might I suggest we have Bernie Crandall

187

remove her from the property?"

"And have her go live with the fact that we're squelching the public's right to know? I don't think so."

Velof's stiff demeanor crumbled. "Perhaps I should tender my resignation."

"What, you're not going down with the ship?"

Velof sat down, slouching in the chair.

"Pull yourself together, Stephen," said Lark, folding her hands on the desk blotter. "I need your help. Give me a couple of days to figure things out."

He lifted his head and regarded her through cool, blue eyes. "Do you really think you can straighten this out in two days?"

"Humor me. Look, I need you to do me a favor." She pushed back from the desk. "Keep Linda Verbiscar out front while I slip out the back. You don't have to lie or tell her anything. Just buy me a five-minute head start."

"You're leaving?" He frowned. "How come you can leave, but I can't?" Velof stood and marched back to the window, gesturing toward the media circus with both hands. "We're in the middle of a crisis, for god's sake."

"*C'est la vie*," she answered, knowing the

French would get his goat.

Velof scowled. "What do you expect me to do in your absence?"

"You'll figure something out. That's why I pay you the big bucks."

His lower lip quivered.

Was Velof afraid?

"This is over my head."

"You'll do fine," she said, pulling on her parka. She felt a bit guilty about acting so cavalier. "Look, just tell Verbiscar you have no comment about anything and ask her to leave the property. Then start calling the registrations for today and tomorrow. We may need to find alternative accommodations for some of the guests."

"Will you at least tell me where you're going?"

"The Raptor House."

His lips twisted into a snarl.

"I promise, I won't be long."

Folding his arms across his chest, he peered down his nose at her. "You should be here, not running off to look after the fowl that got us into this mess in the first place."

"The *fowl* are the key to the problem, Stephen. It wasn't the geese that got us in trouble. It was Pierre Ducharme."

Velof huffed. He clearly resented the reminder, but he had, after all, hired the chef.

In the end, he'd run interference, allowing Lark to slip out the back. Creeping behind a row of cars, she jumped into her truck and peeled out of the parking lot. Verbiscar's hand shot up. Lark waved.

As the reporter and her cameraman bolted for the news-station van, Lark turned left at the stop sign. She intended to throw them off her tail. Keeping one eye on the rearview mirror, she turned west onto Main Street and sped downtown.

Elk Park bustled with activity. People strolled along the wide, bricked sidewalks, scraped dry except for occasional stray patches of snow. The buildings were constructed of pink or sandstone stucco with tiled roofs, and brick or white-painted clapboard with asphalt shingles. Split lampposts were spaced evenly between slender, deciduous trees.

Lark waved at several people on the street, but only one or two waved back. The rest averted their faces, staring into shop windows, and avoiding eye contact.

Lark's face burned. Who did they think they were kidding? You learned who your friends were when the chips were down, especially in a small town. And, at present, she was a dangerous friend to have.

With no sign of Verbiscar, she blared the horn at Twilla Frakus, studying the fools-gold display at the rock shop, then doubled back on Bypass Road to the Raptor House. As far as Lark could tell, she'd left Verbiscar in the dust. To be on the safe side, she parked her truck out of sight behind Miriam's garage.

Inside, the rehab center bustled with activity. In the main room, EPOCH volunteers cleaned bedding, filled water dishes, and fed the geese. Muted sunlight crept through the windows, and dust particles swirled in the air in perfect rhythm with the honking of the geese. Winding her way through the room, she nodded to several people, who stopped what they were doing and stared. Surely they weren't upset with her, too.

"Has anyone seen Eric?"

The volunteers exchanged worried glances.

"Never mind, I'll check the office."

Lark barged through the building before anyone could stop her, half-annoyed by the reception — or lack thereof — and half-relieved not to have to discuss the food poisoning issue with anyone. Instead of Eric, she found Angela in the office, sitting in the desk chair making a list. Lark tried keeping her annoyance at bay.

"Have you seen Eric?" she asked.

Angela's head snapped up, and she paled, bringing all of her freckles to the surface. "Bernie Crandall didn't find you?"

"No. Why?" Angela's voice sounded strange and Lark began to worry. "Is something wrong?" Maybe Bernie was coming to arrest her. Wouldn't that be just her luck?

Angela stood. "Maybe you should sit down."

She stepped from behind the desk and reached for Lark's arm. Lark side-stepped her and frowned, a sick feeling rooting itself in the pit of her stomach. "Why?"

"I have some bad news."

Just like in the movies, when they tell someone somebody died, the tone of Angela's voice caused Lark's shoulders to seize. She grabbed for the back of a chair, and saw Eric's face bob in front of her eyes. Angela's hand, warm and strong, stroked her back.

"He was the man at the lake?"

Angela nodded, and her hand stilled. "He's alive, but —"

Lark's legs buckled, and she struggled to stand. "But what?"

"I'm not going to deny it. He's been hurt pretty bad," Angela said, shoving a chair under Lark's knees.

Lark sat down hard. "What happened?"

"There was an accident and he ended up in the water. Crandall was supposed to find you."

Lark groped for Angela's fingers. She squeezed them tightly, signaling her to go on.

"The firemen revived him and then took him to the hospital."

Hot tears welled up in Lark's eyes, and she allowed them to flow down her cheeks unchecked. Eric was her soulmate. They had just found each other. "How long ago?"

"An hour, maybe."

Lark doubled over and braced herself for the worst. "Is he going to be okay?"

When the woman didn't answer, Lark sat up. "Tell me, Angela. I have a right to know."

"It's too soon to tell."

Lark rocked back and forth in the chair, forcing herself to breathe. Finally, she stopped, and got to her feet. Her knees quaked, and she grabbed the arms of the chairs. "I have to go down there."

Nothing else mattered. Not the geese.

Not the Drummond. She needed to see Eric and hear the doctor say he would be alright.

She reached up and clutched Angela's arm. "Take me down there. Now!"

The hospital was a two-story white building situated on the west side of town, with beds for ten. In the reception area, cushioned chairs rimmed the outer walls, then formed two rows down the middle of the carpet. A long desk was carved out of the wall across from the entrance, and a collage of brightly tabbed medical files decorated the bookcase beyond.

The chairs were full of fishermen and, upon spying Lark, several booed.

Angela glared. Lark didn't seem to notice.

After depositing her friend into a chair, Angela banged on the bell at the desk. "Hello?"

"Hold your horses, I'm coming." A heavyset receptionist bustled into view. "Be patient. Can't you see there's a line in front of you?"

"We're here to see Eric, Betty," Lark whispered from the front row.

"Oh, you poor girl, come around this way." While Betty squeezed past the desk to let them into the inner sanctum,

Angela helped Lark to the door.

"Hey, what's the big deal?" said a man wearing flannel. "I've been waiting here for an hour. Why does she get to go in?"

"Hush up," said Betty, not unkindly. "This is a different matter. We'll get to you next, Clyde."

Angela slipped through behind Lark, and Betty closed the door in Clyde's face. "Big babies, all of them."

"Where is he?" asked Lark.

The floors beyond the doors were covered in white linoleum. The squares gleamed, giving the illusion they were slippery wet. Blue handrails, dividing white-washed walls, ran the length of the corridor on either side, and the air smelled of antiseptic.

"I'll have to check with the doctor to see if you can go in," said Betty, depositing them into two chairs in the hallway. "You wait here."

Lark plopped down, dropping her head between her knees and extending her hands to the floor.

After what seemed an eternity, a door across from them burst open, and a white-coated doctor bustled out into the hall. "I'm so sorry."

Lark's face drained of all color, and the

doctor back-pedaled. "No, no, not sorry like that. I didn't mean to scare you. I meant, I'm sorry about what's happened to Eric. He's fine. I mean, he's still alive. We're doing everything we can."

"Can I see him?"

"We need to locate his family," said the doctor.

"His mother lives in Norway." Lark's voice sounded flat, and Angela worried she was giving up hope.

"Does he have anyone in the States?" she asked.

Lark shook her head.

"That poses a problem," said the doctor.

"Can't Lark serve as the next of kin? She's the closest to him."

"By law, it might have to be his supervisor, Nora. She's the one who . . ."

Lark's expression caused him to trail off. Whoever Nora was, Angela could see the suggestion didn't sit well.

"I'll make any decisions that need to be made," said Lark. "Now, is he going to be okay?"

The doctor wrung his hands. "The water was cold."

"That's a good thing," Angela pointed out.

"She's right," agreed the doctor. "On top

of everything else, he took a blow to the head. The cold water kept his brain from swelling."

Angela perked up. "Did the blow come before or after he went through the ice?"

"It's hard to tell from my vantage point. But, you realize, he was clinically dead when they found him," said the doctor.

Lark reached for Angela's hand and squeezed until Angela's fingers hurt.

The doctor toyed with the end of his stethoscope. "The firemen revived him, but we want to warm him up slowly. The slower the better. We'll have a better idea of his injuries once he starts coming around."

"Have you seen other cases like this, Doctor?" asked Angela, hoping for reassurance.

"Personally? No. But I did some calling around. There was a similar case in Denver involving a man about Eric's age a few years ago. He remained in a coma for three weeks. He suffered a few mental and physical impairments from the accident, but he survived."

"Eric's going to be fine," said Lark. Her tone challenged either of them to argue.

The doctor dropped his bedside manner. "I'm not sure you understand the severity of his injuries."

Lark squeezed down on Angela's fingers again.

"Can she see him?" Angela asked.

"Of course." The doctor looked relieved not to have to say anything more, and turned back down the hall. "Follow me."

Eric's room was three doors down on the left. The doctor gestured for them to enter, instructed them to keep their visit short, then excused himself. Lark entered first, and Angela followed. Inside, white walls met a white floor, and white bedding covered Eric from head to toe. Tubes snaked from his arms up to an IV pole dangling fluid bags, and a row of machines overhead monitored his vital signs.

Lark rushed to the bed. Angela stood off to the side.

He looked better than he had the last time she'd seen him. His face still held a blue tinge, but there was a smidgen of color in his cheeks, and his chest gently rose and fell beneath the blankets.

Angela watched him breathe, in and out, matching her own breathing to the rhythm. Then, her breath caught in her throat. Getting in here to see him had been way too easy. Someone had tried to silence him earlier. What if the same person wanted to finish him off?

Chapter 12

Angela left Lark at the hospital standing guard, and went in search of Bernie Crandall. She found him at the Drummond questioning Velof.

"What's up, Angela?" he asked, clearly annoyed by her interruption.

She pulled him aside and asked him why there wasn't an officer watching Eric's room. "If anything happens . . ."

The sentence dangled, then Crandall keyed his radio, and barked an order to the officer who answered. "Done. Now, do you have anything else for me, or can I get back to Velof?"

That was her cue to leave. "Thanks."

Velof wasn't so anxious to be abandoned. "He's grilling me about the phone call from Frakus, Angela."

And your point is? What did he expect her to do about it?

"I told him what I told you. Frakus, or someone claiming to be Frakus, called and asked to speak to you. When I told the caller you were out, he asked me to relay a message. Which I did."

"Velof did track me down to tell me Frakus called."

Crandall glanced between them, then his gaze settled on Angela. "Do you know why someone might have pretended to be Frakus?"

"I can't imagine anyone wanting to be him."

"And I can't imagine anyone wanting to hurt Eric." Crandall scuffed the five o'clock shadow on his chin. "Any chance someone was after you?"

The question caught her off guard.

Velof's eyes opened wide. "Are you suggesting the phone call was a ruse?"

Crandall seemed to take to the notion and consulted his notes. "You said the call came in around five-thirty a.m., right?"

Velof nodded.

"Frakus says he was meeting Donald Tauer and Nathan Sobul at the time. Could you hear the caller clearly?"

"No." Velof shook his head. "It sounded like he was standing outside. The wind howled through the receiver."

"Anything else?"

"I thought I heard talking in the background, but it sounded from a distance."

"Like someone passing by?" asked

Angela. If the caller had used the Visitors Center's pay phone, it would have picked up voices from campers using the public bathrooms. There had been a few lights on and she remembered passing someone on the path. The grandpa of the boy who'd caught the undersized fish the first day of the tournament. Had he seen something?

Angela mentioned the camper to Crandall, who jotted the information down. "I'll ask him what he saw. In the meantime, don't either of you plan on going anywhere too quick."

"Thanks," said Angela. She felt good about Crandall's posting a guard to Eric's room, and relieved there were still avenues of investigation left unexplored. Velof just seemed relieved to get everyone out of his office.

She collected her things from her room, stood through a line at checkout, then headed to the lake. She had a commitment to oversee the fishing until noon — the official end of the Elk Park First Annual Ice Fishing Jamboree.

By afternoon, Angela was dragging. Packing her gear into her truck, she headed back to the hospital; and was relieved to find a policeman posted at the door, with Lark still sitting beside Eric's bed.

"How's he doing?"

Lark stroked his arm. "I feel so helpless."

"You're doing what you can." It wasn't much of a reassurance, but it was the best Angela could muster. "Are you hungry?"

"No." Lark's eyes lingered on Eric's face. "Why is there a guard at the door?"

Angela avoided eye contact, but there was no point in lying. Lark was going to find out sooner or later, and Angela figured she might as well be the one to tell her the truth. "Because there's a chance that someone tried to kill Eric."

Lark's eyes widened. "That's insane."

"Maybe, but the fishing hut was locked from the outside, and there were obvious signs of a struggle. I had to break down the door to get to him."

"Why would anyone want to hurt Eric?"

Crandall's question rang in her head. *Any chance someone was after you?*

"Maybe they didn't," said Angela. "But let's face it. What happened this morning wasn't an accident. I think it had something to do with the poisoned geese." She told Lark about Ian and the swan. "My guess is there's a correlation."

Worry lines creased Lark's brow. "Did Eric tell you, he and Ian talked a day or two before the accident?"

Angela's pulse quickened. "No."

"Ian called. He wanted to know if Eric had been seeing an unusual number of sick birds coming in."

"Had he?"

"No."

Feeling deflated, Angela sat down on the radiator. She realized she'd been holding her breath hoping that Ian had left Eric a clue to his case. "Did Eric say anything to you about going down on the ice?"

"No. After he left my house last night, he said he was going to stop by and see George Covyduck. That was around ten."

It took a moment for Lark's words to sink in, then the two of them registered at the same time.

"The lab results!" Both women shot to their feet.

"You better stay here, Lark."

"No. I'm going with you."

"It's not a good idea." Ian was dead. Eric was in a coma. What was the sense in making anyone else a target?

"I'm not doing Eric any good here."

The plea struck a chord with Angela, and she felt herself waver. She knew how it felt to be sidelined.

"I can appreciate how you feel, Lark. Really, I can. But this is an official investigation, and we already have two victims."

"How dangerous can it be going to Covy's office? Wait! Don't answer that." Lark circled the foot of the bed. "Look, I can't sit here any longer waiting for Eric to snap out of it. I have to do something."

Against her better judgement, Angela caved in. "Okay, fine. You can come. But only because I need help finding Covyduck's office."

Lark moved to hug her but Angela stepped back. "There's one more condition."

Now she was sounding like Kramner.

"Shoot," said Lark.

"If this gets the least bit dangerous . . ."

Lark nodded.

"You're out."

Covyduck's office was a small A-frame on the north side of Main Street near the library. Ceramic dog and cat bowls in various shapes and sizes filled the window displays of a brightly lit storefront. Inside, gourmet dog food, rhinestone leashes and collars, and a variety of play toys and treats filled multiple display racks.

"This is a different kind of veterinarian office."

"It's a small town," explained Lark. "The tourists are where the money is, but don't let the facade fool you. He's got a nice setup in back."

Lark was right. Past the front counter, double doors opened into a state-of-the-art clinic. Three examination rooms with stainless steel tables for pets were along the left wall of the hallway. The first door on the right opened into a surgical area, and the second into a bathroom. At the end of the hall, was Covyduck's office.

He sat at his desk. A medium-sized man with gray hair and black glasses, he wore a white lab coat with "George" stitched across the breast pocket.

"Lark." He stood up when he saw her. The lab coat fell open, revealing a plaid shirt. A pair of jeans bumped worn cowboy boots. He hugged Lark, and a number of surgical instruments jingled in his pockets. Then he grinned and shook Angela's hand. "Pleased to meet you."

The women exchanged glances. He hadn't heard.

Lark broke the news about Eric. Covyduck sat down and slumped into his chair. "I just saw him last night."

"Then he did come by," said Angela. With luck, maybe Covyduck could shed some light on what happened. He waved them both to chairs.

"Yeah. We had a few beers. He wanted to know about the lab results."

Angela scooted to the edge of her seat. "And?" At the risk of seeming insensitive, she was hungry for answers.

"And there's not much to get excited about." He dug through a pile of papers on his desk, and produced a letter typed on stationery from the Colorado Department of Natural Resources Central Animal Health Laboratory. "Basically, the report confirms what we already know. Based on the shape and condition of the organs, the cause of the poisoning is consistent with lead. I'm still waiting on the toxicology reports. The plant matter in the stomach is a combination of corn and wetland grasses, and there was shot present in the gizzard, most likely the source of the toxic poisoning."

"Did you say corn?" asked Angela.

"Yeah."

"What is it?" asked Lark.

"The closest cornfields around are fifty to one hundred miles east of here. That means the geese picked up the shot somewhere along the Front Range. Maybe we can figure out where."

"*East* covers a lot of territory," said Covyduck, skimming through the report. Pulling off his glasses, he pitched them on top of the desk and massaged the bridge of his nose.

Angela pressed. "What do we know about the shot?"

"Like I said, we're still waiting on the final shot report. From the prelim? The stuff's consistent with shot sizes number nine to number nine and a half on the American Standard Shot Scale. Some pellets were magnetic, some type of steel shot. Other pieces weren't. The nonmagnetic shot appears to be slightly smaller than the nominal diameter, which is consistent with what happens to lead skeet shot when it oxidizes." He tapped the report. "The only strange thing is, the pellets are breaking down faster than lead normally would."

Angela stared at the papers. "What are you saying?"

"It's like it's biodegradable."

"That doesn't make sense," said Lark. "Are you sure?"

Covyduck waggled the paper in his hand.

"Any idea why that is?" asked Angela.

Covyduck shook his head. "Unless someone is developing a new type of shot."

Lark frowned. "What would be the point?"

Covyduck shrugged. "A lot of hunters don't like alloy shot." He picked up his glasses and twirled them. "Steel has a lower density that negatively affects the shot string. In other words, it doesn't perform very well in the field."

Spoken like a true hunter.

"Okay, I get that," said Lark. "What I meant was, it's illegal to hunt with lead shot."

"Unless . . ." Angela reached for the report. "Could it be something else?"

Covyduck chewed on the stem of his glasses. "Anything's possible," he said. "But the damage to the organs, and the symptoms, are consistent with lead poisoning."

While he talked, Angela skimmed down the page. She hoped to find a clue and ended up disappointed. The contents spoke volumes on the condition of the bird and its vital organs, but imparted scant information relative to the shot.

"Where does that leave us?" asked Lark.

Covyduck shoved his glasses back onto his nose. "Waiting for the final lab results.

Meanwhile, Angela, is there any chance you can trace the shot?"

"I wish it were that simple. Do either of you have any idea how many birds die every year in the United States from lead poisoning?"

"A few hundred thousand," guessed Lark.

"More like two million." Angela handed back the report. "Almost none of the cases are solved."

Covyduck whistled.

Lark shifted in her chair. "So what would it take to unravel this one?"

"Luck." Angela could see that wasn't the answer Lark was looking for. "First, we would have to locate the source. The fact that the shot characteristics appear to be unique helps. It gives us a comparison."

Covyduck picked up the report and rustled it in the air. "Do either of you have any idea what a biodegradable shot that emulates lead in field trials would be worth?"

Both women shook their heads.

"Millions."

"Except, you're forgetting one thing," said Angela. "Lead or not, the stuff's still toxic."

Covyduck's words stuck with Angela on the trip back to the hospital. Millions of dollars provided a possible motive for the attacks on Eric and Ian, provided the attacks were related to the waterfowl poisonings, and the waterfowl poisonings related to the development of a new type of shot.

In any event, they would know soon enough.

Her mind flitted back to the night Ian died. What had happened to the swan? She didn't know. Her memories consisted of gruesome images — Ian swinging in the wind, his body on the ground, a black body bag being zippered shut — but she vaguely remembered that someone had taken samples from the bird. Would they have been stored somewhere, or discarded?

She made a mental note to check with the U.S. Fish and Wildlife lab on Tuesday. In the meantime, taking Ian's immortal advice, she would "keep working the problem."

"Whoever developed the shot has to be testing it somewhere," she said. "Maybe at a trap-shooting range?"

"Or a hunt club." Lark was twisted sideways in the passenger seat.

Most hunt clubs were open to members only, which would make the shot harder to trace. Club owners would be able to test the shot privately and get feedback at the same time.

"How many do you think there are along the Front Range?" Angela asked, trying not to show dismay.

"Too many," said Lark.

"So maybe we can narrow it down?"

"Any suggestions?"

Angela glanced sideways at Lark. "The vegetation from the goose's stomach indicated the bird fed in a wetland area, right?"

Lark nodded. "And somewhere near a cornfield."

"The area around Barr Lake fits that description."

"Right, along with twenty other lakes or ponds along the Front Range."

"True, but so far nobody has died at any of the others." The reference to Ian's death popped out, then Angela thought of Eric, clinging tenuously to life, and instantly felt bad. "Sorry, I —"

"No," said Lark. "You're right. It's a good place to start."

Angela parked the truck, then traipsed into the hospital behind Lark. Since Angela had conjured the image of death, the women had been silent. If only she could snatch back her words.

Lark headed straight to the back. Angela stopped at the front desk.

"May I help you?" asked the receptionist, buzzing Lark through.

"No business this afternoon, Betty? The last time I was in here, the place was packed."

"We cleared them all out. Had to send a few new cases to Denver, but not many. Just two homeless guys who must have been Dumpster-diving at the Drummond, and a six year old. Seems like the rest are getting better."

"What's the count up to?"

Betty's pen paused in midstroke, and the woman looked up. "Sixty-seven."

About half of the banquet attendees. Angela wondered how many lawsuits had already been filed. She was stunned by the number of cases. Were the biodegradable properties of the shot causing the toxin to hit the bloodstream faster?

"May I use your phone book?" she asked.

"Elk Park?"

"Greater Metro."

Betty clunked a thick volume on the counter. Angela thanked her, picked it up, and moved to a chair. Settling onto the cushioned seat, she flipped open the tome, and pored over the index. The effort proved a bust. There were no categories for shooting ranges, firing ranges, or gun clubs. She did find one listing under "Trap and Skeet Ranges," but the address placed it near downtown Denver, too far away from a water source.

Strike one.

Returning the book to the desk, she thanked Betty again, then waited to be buzzed through. Walking the hall toward Eric's room, she heard Ian's voice in her head. *Work the problem.*

It was time to come at it from a different direction. What had Eric figured out about the poisonings? He must have come up with something. What other reason would someone have for shoving him through the ice?

From the time she found him until he was transported, she couldn't remember anyone doing a thorough search of his clothes. Maybe there was a clue in one of his pockets, something his would-be assassin or the firefighters missed? It was worth taking a gander.

She nodded to the guard at the door and stepped through the doorway. The bright white glow of the morning was gone. Now, with the shades drawn and the lights dimmed, it took a moment for her eyes to adjust.

Lark sat beside the bed, her back to the door. Eric lay still, his face ashen against the pillow, his brown hair splayed out, his eyes closed. Angela imagined him sleeping, though his condition had never officially changed. He was stable but comatose.

"He looks better," she said, hoping she sounded encouraging.

"He's going to be fine," replied Lark, keeping her eyes focused on her boyfriend's face.

Angela refrained from comment and sidled over to the closet. A large puddle seeped out from the crack under the door. Was it coming from Eric's wet clothes?

Keeping one eye on Lark, Angela eased open the closet. Someone had hung his clothes up to dry and the cuffs of his pants dripped onto the floor. She checked the pockets of his khakis, his wrinkled shirt, and heavy coat, and came up empty-handed. Not even a wallet.

Then she thought of another place to try. Some of the new uniforms had hidden inside pockets, like the lapel pocket on a man's sports jacket. Her hand sought the slit. Her fingers struck paydirt.

"Will you take me home?"

Angela jumped at the sound of Lark's voice, and jerked her hand back.

"What are you doing?" Lark asked.

Caught red-handed, Angela opted for the truth. "I was looking for clues."

"Did you find any?"

"Maybe." Angela reached back in and pulled out the prize. It was a small plastic bag stuffed with two small plastic containers. Rectangular in shape, the containers measured three inches by one quarter inch by one half inch in size. A notation had been scrawled on the front of the bag in black felt marker. Eric had been collecting evidence.

"What is it?"

"The note says he found these in the debris left at the edge of the ice in the area where Frakus had plowed the dead geese." Angela held up the bag.

"They're fishing-sinker containers!"

"Maybe that's why he was down on the ice?" said Angela. "Maybe he was searching for clues."

The question is, who would have known he was there? And why would they care that he'd picked up two fishing-sinker containers?

Covyduck didn't mention anything about Eric's heading down to the lake.

Had he called and said something to one of the volunteers? Then again, it was possible someone had seen him arrive at the lake. Frakus. Tauer or Nate. Or any one of the fishermen camped out in the parking lot.

"I'll have them run for prints," said Angela. "With luck, we'll turn up something."

Lark stopped beside the bed on the way out, and by the time the two of them reached the truck, the day was spent. Stars dotted the eggplant-colored sky, and light twinkled from the streetlamps.

Angela stuffed the plastic bag into the glove box and started the truck, while Lark climbed into the passenger seat and laid her head back. Ten minutes later, they pulled up in front of the carriage house next to the Drummond.

"Here you go."

Lark sat up, taking a moment to get her bearings.

"Damn!" she said, once she realized where they were.

"What?" The stricken expression on Lark's face caused Angela's blood pressure to rise. "Did you forget something?"

"I forgot to cancel the EPOCH meeting." The panic in her voice seemed out of proportion to the problem.

"I wouldn't worry about it, Lark. I'm sure they'll understand when you don't show up."

"You're missing the point, Angela. The meeting's here." Lark waved her hand toward the house, and the lights in the living room winked back. "Come in with me?"

"No." Joining was not something Angela did. Not even the Brownies, in second grade, with all of her little friends. "Thanks, but no thanks. I'm not much of a joiner."

"You don't have to make it official. It's just . . . I could use the backup."

Lark's choice of words struck at Angela's core. The last person who'd asked her for backup had wound up dead.

Chapter 13

Lark took a firm grip on Angela's arm, screwed up her courage, and managed a weak smile for the EPOCH members assembled in the kitchen. She felt a little guilty pushing Angela to stay. Mostly she was grateful for the support.

"There you are," said Dorothy. The older woman was seated at the kitchen table. Two bright dots of rouge colored her cheeks. "We were beginning to worry about you."

"You look like you could use some tea, dear," said Cecilia, clattering a tea cup on the table. "Have you eaten anything?"

"Thanks, but I'm not hungry," said Lark, then on second thought, she turned to Angela.

"I'm fine."

"Oh my, you girls have to eat. Here, have some banana bread." Cecilia shoved a plate toward an empty place in the center of the table. Everyone had a plate in front of them. Andrew Henderson was the only one eating.

"Opal made it," he said, jerking his head toward his wife. Opal grinned, her skin tight on her bones. Harry sat on a stool at the breakfast bar, and Gertie reigned at the head of the table, her plump arms folded across her chest, a sour expression pinching her lips.

Probably mad I showed up, thought Lark.

Angela perched next to Harry. Lark took a place at the table.

"How's Eric?" asked Harry.

"He's going to be fine," Lark answered, forcing herself to believe it. She had to keep hoping.

As if proving the point, Angela piped up, "He's still in a coma. The doctor says it's too soon to know."

Maybe she shouldn't have invited her in, thought Lark, glaring at her. Angela refused to make eye contact.

"We found a clue as to why he was on the ice," said Lark.

This time it was Angela who glared.

"Tell them."

Angela told them about the fishing-sinker containers. "I'll give them to Crandall for fingerprinting, but I wouldn't get your hopes up. There are over two hundred fishermen out there this weekend."

Andrew shifted in his chair, and the wood groaned. "Any word on the banquet guests?"

Lark felt the blood drain from her face. She'd been at the hospital to see Eric and had forgotten to ask.

Angela carried the moment. "The nurse told me most of them were getting better."

"Whew!" said Dorothy. "That's a relief."

"What about the geese?" asked Lark. If the people were improving, maybe the birds were, too.

"We lost all but sixty-two," said Dorothy.

Harry looked surprised. "That's better than I expected. By the time symptoms of lead poisoning present themselves in waterfowl, it's usually too late. I figured we'd save ten percent, at best."

Lark's mind flashed to the banquet guests. Did the same percentages apply to humans? "It's possible it's not lead that's causing the problem."

Andrew paused mid-bite. "What are you talking about?"

Lark explained what they'd learned at Covyduck's office, about the biodegradable property of the shot. "It's possible it's some other substance that's making the birds sick."

A frenzied discussion followed.

"Are you saying it's some sort of natural product?" asked Andrew.

"We don't know yet," said Angela. "We're waiting on the lab analysis."

Lark was wishing she'd kept her mouth shut.

Finally Dorothy chimed in. "Whatever's causing it, the treatment appears to be working. Let's not upset the apple cart by going off half-cocked."

Mixed metaphors aside, Dot had a point. Except for the one mention on the report, all of the other evidence supported the lead poisoning theory. And certainly the fact that the lead poisoning treatment appeared to be working stood for something.

"Besides, regardless how many we save," said Andrew, "Harry's right. The secondary symptoms are the concern now. We would have been better off putting them down."

The words struck Lark dumb. He wasn't suggesting they quit now? She opened her mouth to challenge him, when Gertie stepped in.

"What a horrible thing to say."

"But true," he insisted. "For one thing, the amount of money we've spent is phenomenal."

"It's not about money," said Gertie,

puckering her lips even more.

Lark's eyes burned. Hot tears caused Andrew to swim. "I refuse to give up," she said, her thoughts flashing to Eric. "Not after the price we've paid."

Harry climbed off his stool, and placed a hand on her shoulder. "Are you okay?"

Lark tried to find her voice and failed.

"Oh my," said Cecilia. "Maybe we should have this meeting some other time?"

Angela stirred from her seat and took a flanking position on Lark's opposite side. "As long as the geese are alive, we need to keep trying."

It took a moment for her words to register.

"Why's that?" Andrew asked. "I don't see U.S. Fish and Wildlife footing the bill."

A murmur circled the table, indicating the EPOCH members agreed with him there.

Bolstered, he continued. "Besides, do we help the geese live in order to suffer a worse fate? What about the permanent damage — reproductive problems, increased predation rates."

Lark couldn't help but make the comparison between the geese and Eric. "Quitting is not an option. We're not giving up."

The strength of her words stunned even her. She blotted her eyes with her flannel shirt, and the smell of hospital antiseptic triggered another bout of tears.

Angela squeezed her shoulder. "Dorothy, are any of the surviving geese improving?"

"Quite a few." She cast a hard look at Andrew. "In fact, some are nearly as good as new."

"We got to them early," said Harry, refilling Lark's mug and redunking her tea bag. "That's the key."

Lark focused on Eric. Had Angela gotten to him in time? How long had he been in the water? She'd heard estimates of everywhere from twenty minutes to an hour. Still, there were cold-water drowning victims, dead longer, who had emerged to live normal lives.

The clock in the living room struck seven.

Again, it was Angela's voice that broke through. "Any idea how many of the symptomatic birds had shot present in their gizzards?"

Dorothy's answer was instant. "Two-thirds."

"The two-thirds that are dying," said Andrew, reaching for another piece of banana bread.

Opal swatted his hand.

"Shut up," said Gertie. "You made your point."

Lark wanted to hug her.

"What about leads on the source of the shot?" asked Gertie. "Do we have any?"

"No." Angela gestured toward Lark, then herself. "We figure it came from a designated hunting area, more than likely a hunt club or skeet ranch. I checked the Yellow Pages, but there are no listings. I'm hoping the secretary of state's office will have some sort of a registry."

Gertie looked skeptical. "Most hunting clubs are privately owned. Would they even have to register with the secretary of state?"

"If they're an actual club, they would," said Cecilia. "But you may find it's hard to locate them in the records." A retired CPA, she was likely to know.

"What about pinpointing direction?" suggested Dorothy. "Can we figure out which way they were flying?"

She might be on to something, thought Lark.

"Do any of you remember the night the geese came in?" asked Angela suddenly.

"Sure," said Lark. "We all do. That was the night of the big storm."

"That's what I thought." Angela walked back to the breakfast bar, and dragged her stool closer to the table. "When I was in college, I was asked to document a pair of trumpeter swans. From what we could gather, my lab partner and I determined that, after being blown off course by a storm, the cob was knocked down because of wing icing, and the pen followed."

"And . . . ?" said Dorothy, making an impatient motion with her hand.

"I see where you're going," said Harry, pounding on Lark's shoulder in excitement. "Lark, do you have a map?"

"Try the phone drawer." She pointed to a wide drawer under the counter, the most disorganized spot in her house. Inside, scissors, pens, pencils, rubber bands, and notepaper vied for space alongside twist ties, paper clips, and a few loose screws. "I doubt it's very detailed."

"Anything will do," replied Harry, digging in the mess. "Voilà!" He held up the prize, then spread it in the center of the kitchen table, and pointed to Elk Lake. "If we know the direction and the speed of the wind, we can use the information, factored with the distance geese fly in a day, and get a good idea of where the flock overnighted prior to landing here."

"Who among us knows how fast the wind was blowing that day?" Andrew asked.

Everyone shook their heads.

"We can find out on the Internet," suggested Gertie. "You can look up anything there."

Lark headed for her office, the second most disorganized spot in the house. The cramped, cluttered room stood off the kitchen hallway. Used primarily for storage, the desk stood buried in paper destined for the four-drawer filing cabinet in the corner. A bookcase crammed with tattered paperbacks, and topped with a picture of her mother, covered a hip-high area of the back wall. A small south-facing window allowed light to seep in from the overflow parking lot.

Flipping on the desk lamp, she booted up the computer and Googled the weather. The information popped right up. Scrolling down, she found Wednesday's record.

"It says the wind blew thirty to forty miles per hour out of the northeast," she hollered, hoping they could hear her in the kitchen.

"Great," answered Harry. "Now, how far do geese travel in a day?"

Lark switched her search but didn't

come up with an answer.

"Who knows?" she said, returning to the kitchen in defeat.

"I'll bet it's far," said Dorothy, pinching off a corner of a slice of banana bread and stuffing it into her mouth.

"Migrating Aleutian Canada geese fly over two thousand miles between take-off and touchdown," said Andrew.

Opal nodded her head. Angela wrinkled her nose.

"You know that off the top of your head?" she asked.

"I read an article about them in one of the birding magazines."

"What about lessers or Richardson's, then?"

"They weren't part of the article."

"Let's say one hundred miles," interrupted Harry, pulling a calculator out of his breast pocket. "It seems to me migrating geese fly between one hundred seventy to five hundred miles a day, but these geese would have reached their wintering grounds. They're stationary, for the most part. Any traveling they do is for exploration and to search for food. Let's factor using a hundred." He punched in some numbers, then stuffed the calculator back in his pocket. "Do you have a compass?"

Lark wobbled her hand. "North, south . . . ?"

He shook his head. "Math."

"Again, maybe in the office." She padded back down the hall. The center desk drawer coughed up a child-sized version. "Will this work?"

"It's perfect." Harry checked the gauge on the map, then adjusted the arc. Placing the pointed end of the tool on Elk Lake, he drew a wide circle. "Factoring in all the variables, I'd say it's safe to assume the geese were somewhere inside this circle."

Angela pointed to Barr Lake. "Look, it falls within the circle. I knew it." She told the others her theory about how Ian's death and Eric's accident were related.

"I hate to be the wet blanket," said Andrew, "but the swan could have flown in there from anywhere."

Lark studied the map. "That's true, Andrew, but it was there, and it suffered from symptoms similar to the geese." She reminded them about Covyduck's report. "Based on the vegetation, we know they fed on wetland grasses and corn. That knocks out the western region, and limits the eastern range by crops."

"And we end up with what?" asked Gertie.

"A swath of land in Adams, Weld, and Morgan counties," said Harry. He scratched the back of his neck, and sat down. "It's a lot of ground to cover."

"Maybe if we split up," suggested Cecilia.

There were miles of roads to cover, the task daunting. Still, Lark's need to do something overwhelmed logic. "I'm game."

Angela planted her hands on her thighs, and leaned out over the map, staring down. "What if we searched by air?"

"Can we do that?" asked Cecilia. She glanced around at the others.

"Why not?" said Angela.

"The U.S. Fish and Wildlife conducted a similar investigation in Wisconsin," said Harry, showing he'd done some research. "By flying over, the agents were able to pinpoint a shooting club in the general vicinity of Lake Geneva that fit the criteria they were looking for. As it turned out, the wetlands behind the skeet stations were contaminated, and the U.S. Fish and Wildlife Service was able to force a cleanup."

"I don't see why I couldn't justify doing the same thing here."

Andrew snorted. "With as much grief as you got over paying for one necropsy, what makes you think your boss will bend over and let you charter a plane?"

"As much as I hate to admit it, he has a point," said Gertie.

"We can't just give up," said Lark, realizing she was letting emotion drive her actions. "If U.S. Fish and Wildlife won't pay, I will."

All eyes turned on her.

"It can't cost that much to rent a plane for part of a day," she said. "Besides, maybe the answers will save the Drummond. Then I can write it off."

"Are you planning to go up with her?" asked Dorothy. The alarm in her voice reached the high decibels.

Lark shrugged. She hadn't really thought that far ahead. "Any reason I shouldn't?"

"One big one," said Harry. "You're scared to death of heights."

Just because she panicked the time Rachel Stanhope took her climbing. They had hung off the side of a cliff for god's sake. Besides, she'd flown in jets before.

"I'll be fine."

"Listen to Harry and Dot, dear," said Cecilia. "A small plane is different. My Jimmy —"

"I'll be fine!" The last thing she felt like hearing right now were stories about Cecilia's late husband, Jimmy. He'd been missing in action since the time of the Wright brothers.

Angela looked skeptical. "I'm not sure having passengers is a good idea."

Lark felt her heart bump in her chest. "Look, if I'm paying, I'm going."

Angela raised her eyebrows.

Lark softened her tone. "And anyway, it wouldn't hurt to have another pair of eyes scanning the ground."

"She's right about that," said Dorothy. "Besides, it's a lot less dangerous than driving a car."

Angela called Kramner first and left a message on both the office phone and his cell. When he didn't return her call, Harry arranged for a charter pilot to meet them at the airfield at the crack of dawn.

"It's too late for you to go home tonight, Angela. Why don't you stay here? You can sleep in the guest room."

Angela debated driving to Fort Collins, then opted to stay. After the others left and Lark had retreated to the bathtub, Angela arranged for Bernie Crandall to meet her at the house.

She let him into the kitchen when he arrived and handed him the baggie with the plastic containers. "I found these in Eric's pocket."

Crandall held the bag up to the light. "Fishing-sinker containers?"

"Do you think you could run them for prints?"

"What for? There must be hundreds of these out there." He gestured broadly toward the lake.

"But not that many mixed in with the debris Frakus plowed off the ice. Check out the notation. He picked them up in the pile of debris Frakus plowed off the ice *before* the tournament started."

Bernie tipped back his hat with a beefy hand and scratched his forehead. "So, let me get this straight. You think someone pushed Eric into the hole and locked him in Tauer's ice house because he found *these* on the ice?"

Angela shook her head. "If the person knew Eric had them, he would have taken them. No, I think someone scattered the fishing sinkers on the ice to cover up the real reason the geese were sick. I think that person was involved with Ian's death. And I think he figured Eric was onto him," she said, ticking the points off on her fingers.

"And the poisoned waterfowl is the link?"

"Correct." At least Crandall understood the connection.

He twisted the plastic bag in his hand. "I doubt we'll pull much off these containers."

"Maybe not, but it won't hurt to try."

"Think it's the same person who placed the phone call to Velof?" asked Crandall, slipping the containers into his coat pocket.

"It stands to reason."

"I'll be in touch."

After Bernie left, Angela headed to bed. She woke up surprised to find Kramner still hadn't returned her call. Should she should try and reach him again? Based on his "no big expenditures" lecture, she figured he would ground her. Better to follow Ian's advice. "Solve the case, make Kramner look good, then submit your expenses."

At five a.m., she knocked on Lark's bedroom door. No answer. She knocked a second time, then headed for the kitchen. There she found a note saying Lark had gone to the Drummond and would be right back.

Angela slipped on her insulated coat and headed out to warm up the pickup. If Lark wasn't back by the time the car blew warm air, she would drive over to the Drummond and get her. Leaning her head back, she wondered how Eric was doing, then a tap on the passenger-side window caused her to start.

Lark peeked her head over the sill and gestured for Angela to unlock the door. She wore a dark hat pulled down over her blonde hair, and she kept glancing from side to side.

"What the heck are you doing?" asked Angela.

Lark slid onto the passenger side, keeping low in the seat. "I had to ditch Linda Verbiscar."

"The reporter?" Angela glanced around. Why was Verbiscar following Lark? Because of the poisonings at the Drummond?

"Where is she now?" Angela dropped the truck into gear.

"As far as I know, she's parked in the hotel's valet parking."

Easing the truck out of the parking space, Angela crawled the truck toward the road. If she hugged the line of parked cars and moved slowly, maybe she could slip onto the road unseen. The last thing they needed was Linda Verbiscar following them around. The woman was aggressive and loud, and if she tracked them down, no doubt she would try and bully her way onto the plane.

"I think she knows about the flight," said Lark, stealing a glance out the rear window.

"What makes you think that?"

"She asked me a few questions."

Angela sought perspective. "Who would have told her?"

"One of the EPOCH members, maybe. I don't remember your telling anyone to keep the trip under wraps." Her tone was defensive, and the truth stung. Even Angela had told Bernie Crandall.

"Do you think Verbiscar put it out over the air?"

"Who knows?" Lark pulled off her hat and slouched lower in the seat. "Why?"

Even though Angela had left multiple messages for Kramner, she had never actually told him what she was doing.

"Your boss doesn't know, does he?" asked Lark, as though reading her mind.

"Let's just say I'm deep undercover."

"Is that why you're not wearing your uniform?"

Angela had brought one uniform and one change of clothes, and had ended up staying in Elk Park for the weekend. "I'm wearing the jeans and sweater because the uniform's dirty."

That, and the incognito factor. In the event they found something, and she asked the pilot to land the plane, it might make it easier to explain her presence on the ground.

When they reached the intersection to Highway 34, Angela could see the KEPC-TV mobile unit still sitting in front of the Drummond. She eased onto the highway and prayed Verbiscar wouldn't spot the truck.

"Is she following us?"

Lark peered past Angela, over the back seat. "No. They're still parked."

Angela drove, while Lark stayed slouched in the seat and placed a phone call on her cell. After a short conversation, she ended the call and announced, "According to Stephen, Verbiscar mentioned the flight in her six a.m. report."

"Great." Angela slammed the heel of her hand on the steering wheel. "Just great."

"She also leaked the information about the shot's unusual properties."

Angela stiffened. Who else but Lark and Covyduck knew about that?

The EPOCH members, but the more Angela thought about it, the more she doubted any of them would have spoken with Verbiscar.

"Do you think she talked to Covyduck?"

"It's possible," answered Lark, sitting up at last. "She started tailing me at the hospital."

Angela glanced at Lark. "How's Eric doing?"

"The same." Lark's body language and clipped monotone made it clear she didn't want to talk about it.

"Give it some time."

They rode in silence after that. Twenty minutes later, Angela wheeled the truck into the parking lot at the airport. A double-wide trailer served as the office and two rows of oversized Quonset huts housed some of the planes. Other small aircraft were lined up out near the fence, while two short runways formed a cross to the north.

A blue and white Cessna 180 sitting on the tarmac was being checked over by two men.

"Hello there," greeted the taller of the two when Angela climbed out of the truck. "Coot Hensley at your service." Doffing his baseball cap, he turned to his companion. "My damsels have arrived at last. It looks like we're good to go."

Damsels? Angela considered taking offense, then considered his age. He had to be in his sixties. Tall and lanky, he wore his grizzled hair buzzed short in military fashion. A five o'clock shadow dusted his face, and she wondered if he'd forgotten to shave. Then he flashed a toothy smile, and she decided it was just his style.

Angela grinned back, then reached into the truck, picked up the digital camera lying on the seat, and looped it around her neck. "Are you ready, Lark?"

Lark climbed out of the passenger seat, a stricken look on her face.

"You look a little green there, young lady."

Lark's grip on the truck rail turned her knuckles white. Her eyes stretched wide with fear. "Maybe we shouldn't be doing this?"

"You're the one who wanted to come along," Angela reminded her. "Don't bail on me now."

"What's the problem, girlie? Scared?"

Angela had to admit, the plane looked small, and Coot looked a little bit rogue.

"Don't be," he said. "I'm the best danged pilot this side of the Mississippi. It's a clear day, not a cloud in the sky. We should have smooth sailing all the way."

Lark looked less than convinced.

Coot pointed her to the backseat, and put Angela up beside him. "You'll have a good view from here, Angela. And you, missy, you're going to love the ride. There's just nothing like it. Put your headset on."

He picked up a pair of earphones attached to a mike and demonstrated the fit. Angela followed suit, nudging Lark to put her headset on, too.

"It makes communication a whole lot easier. Can you hear me?"

She shook her head, and he flipped a switch on the side of the headgear.

"Can you hear me now?" His words reverberated in her ears.

"Loud and clear." Angela glanced back at Lark. The woman had dug her hands into the cracks of the seat cushions and was holding on for dear life.

"Are there seatbelts?" asked Lark.

"Just like in a car," answered Coot.

While Lark dug for the belt, Coot turned the key, and the engine whirled to life. Angela glanced around the cockpit, surprised by how much it was like being in a car. The dashboard filled the front of the plane with wheels and dials like fuel gauges and speedometers.

"You can adjust your seat to give her more legroom, if you want. There's a lever under the seat."

Angela scooted forward, heard Lark's belt click tight, then fastened her own. Not that she thought it would do much good if the plane went down. Very few people fell out of the sky and walked away from the wreckage.

Coot lifted a thermos of coffee. "Anyone want some?"

"No. Thanks anyway," answered Angela.

Lark also declined.

"Well, I like my java in the morning." Pouring some into a disposable cup, he stowed the thermos under his seat, glanced over his shoulder at Lark, then winked at Angela. "Don't worry, kiddo. I've been doing this since before you were born."

Throttling up, he sped the plane forward.

Angela strained to see over the dashboard, to no avail. "I can't see."

"You will. The Cessna's a tailwheel aircraft. Wait until the plane gets up to speed."

In seconds, the tail lifted, and they were speeding down the runway.

"It's noisy," she said.

"Say what?"

She wasn't sure if he was teasing, or if he really couldn't hear. The roar of the engine vibrated the air around them, and Angela felt the plane build power.

"Everybody ready?" he asked.

Angela nodded and braced herself in the seat.

Lark didn't respond.

With a whoop, Coot pulled on the yoke, and the plane broke free of the ground. As they soared into the air, the earth fell away.

"This must be what a bird feels like," said Angela. "Wow!" The exhilaration of take-off triggered every nerve in her body. Her skin tingled. The colors of the ground brightened. The air tasted sweeter. "This is amazing."

Coot grinned.

As the plane banked, Angela glanced down. Below them, the KEPC-TV van wound its way along the road toward the airport. "Check it out, Lark."

Getting no response, Angela turned in her seat, and looked back. Lark's fingers still gripped the seat, and her eyes were pinched shut.

"It's okay," said Angela. "We're in the air. Take a look."

Angela coaxed until Lark loosened her grip on the seatback and inched her way to the window. After peering out for a moment, she appeared to relax. "It's really not a bad view, is it?"

"That's the main reason I picked flying this over my Piper Cherokee," said Coot. "In a Cessna, the wings are up above us. That way you don't get anything blocking your view."

Picking up the map, Angela oriented herself to the ground. "What do you say we start at Barr Lake, and work our way out?"

Twenty minutes later, they buzzed a cornfield to the north of the lake.

"See anything?" asked Coot.

Angela shook her head. "Can you take us up along I-76?"

"Wherever your little heart desires."

Below them, the earth looked sponge-painted, white on brown. Farm fields rolled toward the horizon. Canals and roads crisscrossed, chopping them into neat squares like powdered brownies on a baking sheet. In places, the irrigation systems formed perfect circles, creating a patchwork effect, and several lakes formed dark puddles on the land.

"What lakes are those?" asked Lark, pointing to a cluster just to the east of Barr Lake.

Maybe she was coming out of her stupor. Angela consulted the map. "The Mile High Lakes. They're named as a group. The larger one to the south is Horse Creek Reservoir, and beyond that is Prospect Reservoir."

Coot brought the plane around for another vantage. Angela pressed her nose to the window. Below them, just below the dam, a series of squat buildings hunkered on the northeastern side of the lake. "Lark, look at those."

"They're the hunting blinds at Barr Lake."

If that was the case, the buildings on the south side must belong to the Rocky Mountain Bird Observatory. But what about the cluster of buildings to the east? Peering down, she spotted a cluster of buildings buried deep in the trees.

"What about those?" asked Angela. Painted in camouflage colors and nestled into the cottonwoods and willows, the complex was hard to see.

"It looks like there are some skeet-shooting houses and some trap bunkers down there."

In addition, Angela could make out several observation blinds along a narrow wetland area. Farther east, a large building sprawled at the top of a knoll, while a private landing strip slashed the land to the north.

"Yessiree," said Coot. "If you want, I can set her down."

This place was exactly what they were looking for. Angela didn't see any cars or movement. "Let's go for it."

"Are you crazy?" asked Lark.

Angela and Coot exchanged glances.

She signaled Coot to proceed, then swiveled around in her seat to face Lark. "It doesn't matter. It doesn't look like anyone's there."

"But we don't have permission to land."

What Angela lacked in experience, she made up for in guts. From the stories Ian had told, this was the sort of thing undercover agents did all the time. "We'll just take a quick look around and pull a few samples."

"What if someone shows up?" Lark's voice rose in pitch.

"We'll say we want to join the club."

Coot nodded. "It looks like a great facility."

"The samples won't be admissible," argued Lark.

"Granted," said Angela. "But this way we'll know if we need to come back. Besides, what's the worse that can happen?"

The plane swooped lower. Lark's eyes widened with fear.

"We could get shot?"

Chapter 14

The plane rolled to a stop on the runway and Coot shut down the engine. Angela waited for his signal, then pushed open the door and disembarked. A white-crown sparrow trilled a greeting as her feet hit the ground, and she stretched, looking around.

They had come down three thousand feet in elevation from Elk Park. Instead of freezing, the air was balmy. Instead of pine trees, cottonwoods and sandbar willows buffered the view of Barr Lake to the west. Brown agricultural fields rolled away to the east. And, in the far distance, white-capped mountains etched across the bright blue sky.

Coot climbed out, then reached back to help Lark.

"I'll go look around," said Angela. "You two can hang here."

Coot gave a two-fingered salute, then lounged against the wing of the plane, slurping the dregs of his coffee.

Lark eyed him, then moved to follow Angela. "I'm going with you."

Was she was afraid of Coot? Slouched against the plane, he looked more like an old, stoned-out hippie than a retired air force pilot, but to Angela he seemed harmless enough.

"Suit yourself." She led the way along a path flanked by tall shrubs and strewn with high-grade stone. Crunching toward the clubhouse with Lark in tow, it occurred to Angela they weren't wearing any orange. Lark had on a dark coat, and Angela was bundled up in black down. "Let's hope we don't encounter any hunters."

Around them, branches snapped as the sap running through them warmed. Squirrels chattered incessantly from the trees. Small birds twittered. Distant flocks of geese and ducks quacked and squawked.

Keeeer. The call of a red-tailed hawk split the air. All around them, the day hushed. Lark moved closer.

Angela plowed forward, breaking free of the bushes, and the clubhouse sagged before them. It stood in the throes of renovation. Green paint slivered and peeled from the outer walls, like leaves drooping on a flower's stem, and a pile of abandoned screens rested along the side of the building. Scaffolding splotched with green paint climbed the back wall, blocking the only visible entrance. The parking lot was empty.

"Let's try the front door, just in case someone's here," said Angela, skirting the building and a pile of patio chairs on the brown grass. Leading the way, she climbed the stairs to a newly refinished, wrap-around deck. Before her, a bank of large windows spit back her reflection, broken in half by a set of wide double-doors. Over-head, a sign reading "Barr Lake Hunt Club, Founded 1887" banged in the eaves.

"This place is old."

"I thought you liked historical build-ings."

"I do. It's trespassing I'm not fond of."

Angela knocked on the door.

No one answered.

Cupping her hands around her eyes, she peered through one of the windows. A mounted deer's head glared back from above a massive stone fireplace. Navajo rugs were scattered in haphazard fashion on the wooden floor. Leather rocking chairs, couches, and floor lamps were clus-tered around the room in random order. "It's a pretty nice place, no doubt drenched in decades of cigar smoke."

Lark didn't look, she just wrinkled her nose in distaste.

Angela knocked again. "Hello? Anyone here?"

There were no signs of life.

She knocked a third time for good measure, then moved to the railing. Looking down toward the water, she could make out the skeet houses and trap bunkers tucked into the trees. In contrast to the clubhouse, each building sported a fresh coat of paint.

"Ready to head back?" asked Lark.

"Is anyone here?" asked Coot.

His voice caused both women to startle.

"Man, you scared me," said Angela, her hand patting her chest, keeping time with her pounding heart. "I thought you were back at the plane."

He held up his thermos and small bottle of freeze-dried crystals. "I needed a fix."

He rattled the door handle, and the door swung open. Sticking his head inside, he hollered, "Anyone here?"

A young man in his late teens or early twenties poked his head out from a doorway in the back. Tall and spindly, he had dark hair shaved within inches of his head. Acne marred his face in angry welts. "What can I do for you?"

"The name's Coot," answered the pilot, ducking his head through the doorway.

The man rolled his eyes. "So what do you want?"

Angela wanted to ask him why he hadn't answered her knock, but the blare of Led Zeppelin at his back answered her question. He must not have heard her. For that matter, how had he heard Coot?

"Great place you got here," said the pilot.

The young man puffed out his chest. "It belongs to my dad."

Angela stepped forward. "Any chance he's around?"

"Nope." The young man sized her up, from her feet to her breasts. "He ran into town," he said to her chest. "He's coming back, though."

"Mind if I make some coffee?" asked Coot, holding up the thermos.

"Sure, it's okay."

"Mind if I look around?" asked Angela.

The young man hesitated, then shrugged. "Sure. Want an escort?"

"Nope. I'm fine on my own."

Angela shot back out the door, leaving Coot talking with the kid. "Let's go," she said to Lark, scrambling down the stairs. "I can't believe our luck. The owner's son gave us permission to look around."

"He didn't ask why?"

"He wasn't the least bit interested, and he's over eighteen." Heck, if she had unbuttoned her shirt and showed cleavage, he might have collected the samples for her.

The hunt club outbuildings provided a great view of the wetlands. Each station was set so clay pigeons and shot fell toward the water. Shards of broken pottery littered the marshy grasses, along with numerous plastic shotgun wads. In addition to spent shot, toxins from massive amounts of broken clay presented a problem for waterfowl. At a glance, Angela decided they needed to test this area for polyaromatic hydrocarbons, too.

Producing a small vial from her coat pocket, she slogged to the edge of the marsh. Plunging her hand to her elbow in the frigid water, she scooped material from the bottom and watched the mud, clay particles, and shot settle into the vial. A murky layer of water settled on top, and she plugged the tube, slipping it back in her pocket.

"Hey!" Lark whispered, waving her arms frantically from the shadow of the skeet house. "Someone's here. Get out of there."

Angela complied. Lark was right about one thing. Permission from the son not withstanding, trespassers in Colorado risked being shot — even when guns weren't a prevalent part of the entertainment. No sense in making anyone's day.

Slogging up to the path, the two of them hiked back to the clubhouse. In the driveway, a well-dressed man unfolded himself from behind the wheel of a late-model BMW. Wearing short boots, wool slacks, a flannel shirt, and a down vest, he looked like he'd stepped off the pages of an L.L.Bean catalog. Gray tinged his sandy hair, and crow's feet crinkled the edges of his eyes. Angela recognized him immediately.

"Special Agent Dimato. To what do I owe the pleasure?" he asked, flashing a smile that gave new definition to the word charismatic.

Lark gaped.

"Mr. Radigan." It was the grandpa from Elk Lake. The one whose grandson had caught the undersized fish. "Nice place you have here."

"Thanks." He turned to Lark and extended a hand. "And you're Lark Drummond, correct? The woman who owns the Drummond Hotel?"

"That's me," said Lark.

Angela floundered for conversation. "I'm surprised to see you here."

252

"Out of context?" He smiled. "I own this club. One of my sharecroppers told me about the tournament. It sounded like a fun thing to do with my grandson." He looked up and down the driveway, then wrinkled his brow. "I have to admit, I'm a little curious about where you came from though. And why are you here?"

This was the part of the training with Ian she'd missed. Did she tell the truth or make up a lie?

Lark's face turned the color of mashed potatoes.

Angela opted for the truth. "We were conducting a search of this area and spotted your place from the air. I had my pilot land on your airstrip. I hope you don't mind."

"Not at all." The fact he remained un- ruffled, ruffled Angela's feathers.

"I noticed you have skeet houses and trap bunkers. Not all the clubs do."

"Shall we cut to the chase, Special Agent Dimato? My time's rather limited this morning."

Okay, she could give it to him short and sweet. "We've got one hundred and thirty-six poisoned geese in Elk Park. Some are sick, some are dead, and some are dying. All appear to be the victim of some type of lead poisoning, possibly from lead shot."

Radigan opened the rear door of his car and reached inside. Instinctively, Angela's hand moved back on her belt.

Her heart sank.

She wasn't wearing her gun. She'd left it inside her backpack, on the plane.

"How does that concern me?"

She kept her eyes on his hands. "Looking at weather conditions the night they arrived, and factoring in the storm and migration patterns —"

"You think the shot came from here."

Short and sweet.

"Yes." She watched for some reaction, but Radigan remained cool. "Lark and I took a walk down by the skeet stations. I notice there's quite a buildup of clay pigeons and spent shot cartridges in the water."

Radigan chuckled, and came out of the car holding a Wendy's take-out bag. "You won't find things much different at any of the hunt clubs around here, and the area's full of them." He shut the door. "Frankly, our operation is a helluva lot better than most."

"Are you talking about clubs along the Drainage Loop?" asked Lark, finding her voice for the first time. Angela noted her color looked better.

Radigan stared at Lark, as if assessing an adversary. "Are you a birder?"

She nodded.

"The Drainage Loop, as Lark calls it, follows the irrigation canals along the chain of reservoirs and duck ponds that run from the eagle watch at the Arsenal to Banner Lake. It's a great hunting area. We've taken some interesting species."

Lark scowled.

Angela refused to be baited by his choice of language, or his reference to hunting. But if the club sat along an irrigation system, it did mean any, or all, of the clubs upstream could be a contributing factor to the pollution. Samples would need to be taken up and down the drainage area.

"If it puts your mind at ease, we don't allow the use of lead shot on the premises. The club switched over to steel shot in the mid-eighties, *before* it was fashionable."

"What type of shot do your members use now?" asked Angela.

"Hevi-shot or Bismuth."

"No other type?"

Radigan leaned against his car and crossed his ankles. "Rest assured, Special Agent Dimato, none of what we use here is harmful to the birds."

His answer was evasive and hard to believe. "Except you're shooting them, aren't you?"

Radigan chuckled. "I meant not harmful when ingested. Speaking of which, I need to get my son's lunch inside." He started toward the clubhouse, then spoke over his shoulder. "I'm afraid you're looking in the wrong place, Special Agent."

Angela stared out at the birds gathered on the open water of Barr Lake. Why didn't she think so?

"Pretty, isn't it?" he asked.

She nodded, turning to find him stopped at the edge of the driveway.

"You know, at one time, all this land belonged to my great-grandfather." He swept his hand in a wide arch toward the lake. "Before the state built the reservoir in the 1880s, this was all short-grass prairie."

"Did your great-grandfather sell the land to the state?" asked Lark.

Radigan nodded. "It worked out well. The state got their reservoir, the birds flock to the water and fields, and we get to hunt them."

"Sweet," said Angela, making no attempt to mask her sarcasm.

He smoothed away a tire track with the toe of his boot. "You know, my company,

Radigan Enterprises, takes conservation and our relationship with the community very seriously, Special Agent Dimato. We do regular cleanups, sponsor youth events, operate during reasonable hours, and restrict the use of lead shot. You can't get much better than that."

Angela wondered how many times he'd given that speech. She toyed with the vial in her pocket. "Then, you won't mind if I collect a few samples?"

Radigan's eyes narrowed. He looked from Lark to Angela, then his gaze dropped to her boots. Angela stilled her hand.

"Funny, I was under the impression you already had."

Angela's fingers twitched against the sample. Should she confess or wait to see what happened?

He saved her the angst. "I don't mind at all. Now, if you'll excuse me?" He raised the Wendy's bag. "I'll see you back up at the clubhouse."

Braced for a different reaction, it took Angela a few seconds to realize they'd been given carte blanche to sample the area. "I say we get to work before he changes his mind."

"I was sure he was going to say no."

An unpleasant thought crossed Angela's mind. "What if he has nothing to hide?"

"Do you believe that?"

"No. I don't know."

Maybe they *were* wrong. Or maybe Radigan knew she'd come back with a warrant. Besides, even if he was developing a new type of shot, as long as no one hunted with it, it was perfectly legal to use it in the traps — provided it wasn't contaminating the wetlands. Was he convinced of that, or did he have some other trick up his sleeve?

Rather than stand around second-guessing his motives, Angela got busy taking samples. They collected from three separate areas. She scooped. Lark tagged and bagged. Once they had collected enough to justify ordering an assessment of the wetlands should the lab results test positive, Angela led the way back to the clubhouse to find Coot.

Cresting the hill, they discovered him lounging on the porch with Radigan, drinking coffee and smoking cigars.

"Ready?"

"Sure thing, Angela." Coot stood, swaying slightly on his feet. "Thanks, Chuck."

"My pleasure."

The men shook hands.

"Did you get what you need?" asked Radigan.

"Yes." His amiability unnerved her. She would have preferred Radigan to be a little more nervous. Most people under investigation were.

At the plane, she pushed Coot through the checklist and breathed an audible sigh of relief when the plane lifted off. Scanning the ground as the plane circled around, a sudden movement caught her eye. Radigan stared up from the deck of the clubhouse, his hand shielding his eyes from the sun.

Angela leaned back her head.

Then the plane dipped. Angela jerked upright. She blinked and tried orienting herself. She must have dozed off. In her dream it had been dark, and she was at the edge of a lake. In the light, she was in the cockpit next to Coot.

The plane swerved the other direction, setting off alarm bells in Angela's head. Lark sat paralyzed on the back seat.

"Keep it steady, Coot!" said Angela, wondering how long she'd been asleep.

Silence.

"Coot?" She felt a stab of fear, then a shot of adrenaline hit her veins.

Coot slumped in the seat, and his eyes fell to half-mast. He began to convulse.

"What's wrong with him?" asked Lark, her voice at the edge of hysteria.

"I don't know. Maybe he's having a seizure." Angela shook his shoulder. "Coot!"

No answer.

The plane dipped again, and Lark shrieked. Angela shook him harder, and his head lolled to the left.

"Coot, can you hear me?" Angela leaned closer to him, and sniffed. No alcohol, at least not that she could smell. Grabbing his cup, she took a drop on her tongue. It tasted like dark French Roast.

"Maybe he's having a stroke. What are we going to do?" Lark's voice sounded high-pitched and frantic.

"We're not going to panic." Angela handed his cup back to Lark. "Take this."

Lark reached forward, and the plane started down.

The woman froze, and Angela stuffed the cup back into a holder and grabbed the yoke on the passenger's side. "What the hell do I do?"

She tried pulling back on the yoke, like she'd seen people do in the movies.

The plane climbed. Then its engine speed dropped, and it started to slip sideways.

"We're going to crash," said Lark, panic edging her voice.

"No, we're not!" yelled Angela. "Get a grip, Lark. I could use your help."

Turning the yoke left leveled the plane, then the engine sputtered.

"Quit climbing. You're going to stall the plane!" The hysteria in Lark's voice snapped Angela to reason. She pushed forward on the yoke, and the nose of the plane dropped. The engine revved. Then, the nose of the aircraft cracked the horizon, and the plane started down.

"Back, back," yelled Lark.

Angela pulled back, and the nose crept up.

Aha!

"Forward down, back up," she said, proud of herself for figuring it out. "Somewhere in there we're level. Otherwise it sort of steers like a car." She pulled the yoke right, and the plane swerved right. Left, and it swerved left.

Angela glanced over her shoulder. Lark looked sick. "Can you call for help?"

"Let's hope so." Angela reached for the radio and fiddled with the knobs until she heard voices. Pressing the transmit button, she hollered, "Mayday, Mayday!" into the mike.

A deep, male voice boomed back. "What's your situation?"

"Our pilot's passed out. Requesting assistance," said Angela, lapsing into law enforcement lingo.

After a beat, the man's voice came back. "Are you a non-pilot?"

"That's affirmative."

"Do you have control of the plane?"

"Not really." Though, for the moment, they seemed to be okay.

"What's your location?"

Angela looked out the window. "Just east of Barr Lake."

At her movement, the plane veered.

Lark shrieked into the earphones.

Angela leveled the aircraft.

"What's going on up there? Is everyone alright?"

"We're fine. Fine," said Angela, soothing herself and Lark as much as possible. "We just need help. Now!"

"Okay. Stay calm. We're going to try and get you down. First, what type of plane are you in?"

"A small one." *Very small.* The front seat barely had room for Coot and herself. "A Cessna."

"Single engine," he said.

"I think I've got her on radar," said a

voice in the background.

"Are you flying on autopilot?"

"No." Angela described how she was controlling the plane.

"Do you see the pilot's clipboard?"

"Yes." She tried to curb her excitement. It was her first right answer. She stretched sideways, but, as short as she was, she couldn't reach without letting go of the yoke. "Can you reach it, Lark?"

Lark eased herself forward and reached over the seat.

"We've got it," said Angela.

"Good. Now find the airplane's checklist for descent and landing."

Angela watched Lark flip through the pages.

"It's a Cessna 180," she said.

"Great. Now I need you to look at your airspeed."

"Where?" Angela stared at the dials and knobs. None of them made sense to her.

"There's an airspeed indicator on the dash. It should have a green arc near the bottom." He waited a moment, then asked, "See it?"

"No." There were too many gauges. Shifting her gaze back and forth from the dials to the horizon, she found one that seemed to read knots. "Wait, I think this is it. I don't see the green arc, but it reads eighty-five knots."

"Good! Now just keep the needle between eighty and one hundred." The man paused. "Do you see the throttle? It should be a black knob."

"Is that the one on the dash that Coot used to add power?"

"Is Coot the pilot?"

"Was the pilot," she corrected. She wondered if the man on the radio knew him. If so, he didn't react.

"That's the knob. Find it, but don't do anything with it yet," said the man. "If you push it in, you add power. If you pull it out, you reduce power."

"Got it."

"Good. Let's practice."

Angela's chest tightened. *Practice?*

"Right now?"

"It's important you get a feel for the plane."

"I feel her just fine."

The man laughed, and Angela forced herself to relax, shaking out her shoulders like a boxer before a big fight.

"Seriously, try pulling up the nose of the plane."

"We did that before, and the engine sputtered."

"That's because you need to increase the power to the engine. After that, you're going to do the reverse and descend."

Angela felt paralyzed. "I can't."

"You can," he countered. "Listen to me, you can fly this plane. Do everything small. No quick movements. No large bursts of power." He paused. "Ready?"

Angela drew a deep breath. "I'm ready," she said, afraid he might quit on her if she told him no.

She pulled on the yoke, and the nose of the plane lifted, just like before. Only this time, when the airspeed dropped below eighty, she reached forward and pushed on the throttle.

"She's climbing," said the voice in the background.

Power surged through the aircraft. Excitement tingled along her spine. *I am doing it! I am really in control of the plane.*

"Now level her off, and let's try a descent."

"Ten-four."

When Angela started down, Coot moved in the seat beside her. Falling forward, he slumped across the yoke. The plane pitched down and to the left, throwing Angela forward.

Time slowed to a crawl.

Coot twitched.

Lark screamed, drew a breath, then screamed again.

Fear constricted Angela's throat. She opened her mouth to speak, but words didn't come. Blood pounded in her ears. The wind whistled. The earth rose in the window, as the plane hurtled toward the ground.

Chapter 15

Angela pressed herself back in the seat and tried yanking back on the yoke. Coot's weight countered her efforts.

"What's going on?" demanded the voice on the radio.

"They're dropping altitude!" exclaimed the person watching them on the radar.

"Talk to me. Are you okay?" demanded her instructor.

"Lark, pull him off the yoke," shouted Angela. "Get him into the backseat."

From the corner of her eye, Angela could see Lark grabbing fistfuls of Coot's shirt. The woman straddled the seat and was leveraging her weight, trying to pull him back. "He's too heavy."

"Why is he out of his seatbelt?" asked the man.

"Who knows?" they responded in unison.

Who cares? At this point, Angela just wanted him clear of the yoke. Her arms ached, and she was losing control of the plane.

Was there anywhere she could try and set down?

Beneath her, Barr Lake sparkled in the winter sun like a small puddle of blue on a white patchwork quilt. To the west lay Commerce City, an industrial wasteland of belching smokestacks, speeding cars, and scrawled graffiti. To the south was Denver International Airport, where there were too many bigger planes to contend with.

Her best bet lay to the east. There, the ground stretched flat toward Kansas. Acre after acre of agricultural fields, broken by an occasional tree or farmhouse, and dissected into squares by miles of one-lane country roads. If worse came to worst, maybe she could set the plane down on one of them. Or in one of the corn fields.

Static hissed across the radio.

First things first, said Ian's voice in her head.

Angela focused on the problem. To land, she needed the ability to level the plane.

Wrapping her arms around the yoke, she heaved back. The plane kept dropping.

"Do something!" screeched Lark.

"I'm trying."

Their airspeed was climbing. Reaching forward, Angela eased off on the throttle. The nose lifted slightly, but they continued to fall, plus now they were slipping sideways.

"Try scooting his seat back," she told Lark. It seemed like their only hope.

"I can't reach the bar."

"Okay, then I'm going to let go of the yoke," she told Lark.

"No!"

"It's the only way. Ready?"

Lark nodded.

Angela let go and bent down. The plane veered sharply to the right, then to the left. Her hand hit the bar under the seat and she pulled up, shoving her shoulder hard against the seat cushion.

Nothing.

She tried again, and the seat slid back. Coot lolled to the left.

Sitting upright, Angela reclaimed the yoke. She straightened them on the horizon, then pulled back. The plane started to climb. The engine coughed, and she throttled up.

"We did it!" screamed Lark.

"We're back in control," said Angela, checking her airspeed indicator.

There was a burst of applause on the radio.

"Good job," said the man. "Now I need you to find the altimeter."

That was it? No champagne?

She glanced out the window, realized how close they were to the ground, and the reality of the situation came crashing back.

"It measures in feet."

"Is it a round gauge?" she asked.

"That's it."

"It reads five thousand nine hundred. Wait! Five thousand nine hundred twenty."

"You're still climbing. That's good. Take it up to about sixty-two hundred, then bring down the nose, and level off. Try to keep the altimeter set there."

The reality of how close they had come to crashing into the ground hit home. If Denver was a mile high, they'd come within several hundred feet of the ground. "Thanks."

"Don't thank me yet."

Why? Didn't he think he could talk them down?

Panic bubbled up inside of her.

Maybe he was superstitious. Oh my god, had she jinxed them by saying thanks before they had landed the plane?

Suddenly it seemed important to know his name. "I'm Angela," she said. "Angela Dimato. What's your name?"

"Leo. Leo Kaminsky, Denver International Airport Air Traffic Control."

"Okay, Leo." She leveled the plane off at six thousand two hundred feet. "What do we do now?"

"How many of you are up there?"

"Two, plus the pilot," said Angela, giving him everyone's name.

Another voice broke in, this one a woman's. "Denver International, this is Carrie McCullough, a flight instructor out of Fort Morgan. I have a visual on the Cessna. Want me to lead her in?"

A flurry of conversation followed the offer, then Leo spoke. "Angela, do you see an airplane off your left wing?"

"A small, white one?" She had spotted it while they were talking. A dark-haired woman wearing a baseball cap hunkered behind the controls.

"That's correct. She's going to escort you in. I want you to shadow her movements. I'll be giving you the power, flaps, and pitch settings for an approach on runway seventeen."

"What about jets?" asked Lark, reigniting Angela's fear about landing at DIA.

"We've got them circling way above you. You don't need to worry."

That's easy for you to say.

While the white plane maneuvered in front of her, Angela focused on the directions Leo gave her for setting flaps and cutting power.

"Do you see the runway?" he asked.

She nodded, realized he couldn't see her, and said, "Yes."

"There's one more thing to remember."

What now?

"In a Cessna, you have to manually co-ordinate between the yoke and the pedals."

"I don't understand."

"Once you're on the ground, the yoke won't work. You'll have to steer the plane by working the rudder using the pedals on the floor. It may feel backwards."

"Anything else?" she asked.

"That's it. Good luck. You can make your approach now."

This time she nosed the plane toward the ground on purpose. Smooth and pale, the runway stretched toward the horizon in front of them, shimmering like a gray satin ribbon on a white package. To the west, the white cloth tepees of the terminal poked toward the sky.

The asphalt rose to greet them, and so did Angela's fear. Her fingers tightened on the yoke. She pulled up and veered away. "I can't do this."

"Yes, you can," insisted Lark, sounding

more desperate than convinced.

"No, I can't."

"Stay calm," ordered Leo.

Angela gulped in air, forcing her hands to relax. "Calm." *Yeah, right.* "I'm working on calm."

"You need to climb in altitude, Angela, and swing around for another try," said Carrie. "How's your fuel holding up?"

The gauge read low. "If I don't land soon, we'll go down under natural power."

Lark gave a little yip and pressed herself back in her seat.

"I'm moving above and behind," stated Carrie.

The white plane veered out of sight, and Angela's heart stopped, gripped by a momentary panic. Even with Lark clinging tight to the backseat, she felt alone and vulnerable. Her heart hammered in her chest. Her breath came in short bursts.

"You still with me?" asked Carrie, breaking the spell.

"Unfortunately."

"I'll walk you through it. You're doing fine."

They circled around until the runway came back into view.

"Now, set your flaps like Leo told you. Bring your nose down, then cut your power. Just pitch level."

"And pray," whispered Lark.

The ground came up fast, and the plane hit the tarmac with a force that jarred Coot awake. He grabbed for the yoke, but Lark pinned back his arms. Angela held tight.

The plane lifted and bounced. Her teeth slammed together. Pain shot through her tongue.

We are going to die.

"Pull the throttle all the way back, Angela," yelled Carrie. "And pull the red knob to kill the engine."

The plane bounced a second time, and Angela cut the power. Careening toward the edge of the runway, she depressed the right pedal. The plane straightened out, then veered in the opposite direction. She depressed the opposite pedal, over correcting, and the plane ran off the left side of the runway into a shallow ditch.

We're going to flip.

The plane dove forward, and Angela slammed her head against the yoke. Then the plane tore free of the grass and coasted to a stop on the taxiway.

The silence frightened her. Turning off the engine, Angela flung open the door. Spitting out a mouthful of blood, she gingerly checked her teeth. Her head throbbed but she seemed to be in one piece.

"Are you okay, Lark?"

Lark cupped her hands around her mouth and huffed a few breaths before throwing her arms around Angela. "You did it."

"We did it," said Angela, hugging her back.

Sirens blared, accompanying the cheers on the radio.

"Thank you, Leo, Carrie . . . everyone," said Angela, staring at the white plane swooping past the runway.

"Our pleasure," responded Leo. "Welcome to Denver International Airport."

Despite the fact they were okay, rescue personnel insisted on transporting Lark and Angela to the hospital. Except for a few minor lacerations, bumps, and bruises, both had emerged unscathed. The Denver County sheriff and investigators from the Federal Aviation Administration had asked a few questions, then they were allowed to go.

"How's Coot," Angela asked, pausing in the doorway on her way out.

"He'll live," the sheriff answered.

"What's wrong with him?"

The FAA investigator looked up. "We're working on that."

Angela bristled. Was he trying to stonewall her? "I'm a U.S. Fish and Wildlife Special Agent —"

"And a witness in this investigation," said the FAA man. "Close the door behind you."

Annoyed by his dismissive tone and the sheriff's smirk, Angela exited into the hallway. There was no point in arguing. But, borrowing a phrase from her Italian grandmother, there was more than one way to peel a grape.

A scan of the emergency room whiteboard showed Coot in cubicle seven. She flashed her credentials at the guard posted in front of the curtain. He allowed her to pass.

The lights were dimmed, throwing the tiny cubicle into twilight. The counter next to the sink was littered with cotton balls and blood-soaked gauze. Coot sprawled on the narrow gurney, a stream of wires connecting him to a bank of monitors on the back wall. Asleep on his back, his feet dangled over the end of the bed, and his short hospital gown crept toward indecent.

Angela averted her eyes and groped for his chart. It was where it belonged, tucked safely at the foot of the bed. She made a quick perusal of the chicken scratch on the chart.

His vitals looked good.

She flipped a page and found what she was looking for. A small notation in the doctor's handwriting read, "Patient is suffering from toxic poisoning."

"May I help you?"

The voice startled Angela, and she bobbled the chart. "Yes. No. I . . ."

The male nurse snatched the medical chart out of her hands. "What are you doing in here?"

"Special Agent Dimato," said Angela, introducing herself. "The guard let me in."

"No one but a nurse or the doctor is allowed to handle his chart."

"Fair enough. Would you mind reading it then, and telling me how he's doing?"

"It's hard to say. It sounds like he's lucky to be alive," said the nurse, jotting a note in the chart. Angela figured he was writing her up.

"I was one of the people in the plane with him."

"Yeah? Then you're lucky, too."

Being friendly wasn't working. Maybe it was time to try the official tack. "When will I be able to question him?"

The nurse slapped shut the chart and jabbed it in the direction of the makeshift interrogation room. "Lady, from where I stand, those two dudes are ahead of you in line."

Angela glanced over her shoulder. The sheriff and FAA investigator were standing in the hall. Angela ducked behind the curtain too late. The FAA investigator had spotted her.

He charged across the linoleum, and crowded into the cubicle. "What the hell — ?"

"I'm leaving," she said.

"Damn straight you are. You're lucky I don't put you behind bars." The FAA man turned to the guard at the door. "Take a good look at this one. She doesn't get in. If she shows her face again, arrest her."

Kramner was even less kind. Dorothy had picked up Angela and Lark at the hospital, and dropped Angela back at her pickup. She had called her mother from her cell phone, left a message saying she was alright just in case Verbiscar aired a story about the plane crash, then went straight from there to the duty station.

"I'm pulling you out of the field," said Kramner. "I want you in here come

Monday morning, where I can keep an eye on you."

She watched him pace, the fluorescent lights sparkling off the bald spot on the back of his head, creating the illusion of a disco ball on parade. His thick, black glasses perched on his nose, above nostrils flared with anger.

"What were you thinking?" he asked, stopping in front of her.

The lyrics from another country-western song popped into her head, and she banished them to the recesses of her mind. "I was doing my job, sir." A spark of fear filtered into her consciousness. "You aren't serious about the desk job."

"Dead serious."

"You can't pull me off this case." She had worked too hard. She had too much invested to see it handed off to someone else.

"I can, Dimato. I did. I suggest you take the rest of the week off, recover from your ordeal, then report in here on Monday morning."

"I don't want a day off." She wasn't giving up without a fight. "You gave me permission to investigate."

Kramner resumed pacing. "I never authorized a charter flight. And I certainly never authorized a crash."

"I figured it was better to try and land the plane, sir." She swallowed. "I heard Coot was poisoned."

Kramner swiped a hand through his hair. "The FAA faxed me a preliminary report. It seems your pilot ate something that didn't agree with him."

"Not by any chance goose paté?"

"No. Try a goose-meat sandwich."

Angela perked up. She was being facetious, but Kramner meant what he said.

"It seems your pilot helped himself to a snack while he waited for the coffee water to heat up."

"He suffered from food poisoning?"

"It appears that way. According to the sheriff, the kitchen boy at the club ended up at the hospital the same afternoon."

By "kitchen boy," Kramner had to mean Radigan's son. "Is he okay?"

"He's got a bellyache."

The important thing was it played to her theory that the bird poisonings and the two locations were interrelated. Angela skipped through the events of the previous three weeks. Ian's death, Eric's accident, the Drummond food poisoning, and the potentially fatal plane crash all had one thing in common — sick birds.

"Are they running tests on the meat?"

"We sent the samples to the lab this morning."

Her brain flashed on the swan at Barr Lake. "Sir, did they ever run tests on the swan we found the night Ian died?"

Kramner swiveled his head like an owl, staring at her while he paced. "I don't think so, why?"

"Because this is the third 'accident' related to waterfowl poisonings in as many weeks. It's too coincidental."

" '*Coincidence*, the remarkable happening of similar events by chance,' " he quoted.

"Unless they weren't by chance? What if all the events were intentional?"

That stopped him dead in his tracks. "You give me one good reason why someone would kill another human being over a flock of Canada geese."

"I'll give you a million." Angela produced the sample vials from her pocket and held them out. "Before he died, Ian was investigating a number of waterfowl poisonings in the Barr Lake area."

"That's old news."

"I think he figured out how the geese were being poisoned." She pushed the vials toward Kramner. He reached for the plastic containers and held the brackish liquid up to the light.

"Are you suggesting what I think you're suggesting?" he asked.

"If you mean, do I think Charles Radigan has something to do with this? Yes."

"He's a powerful man, Dimato."

"The partial report on the geese die-off in Elk Park shows the deaths may have something to do with the development of a biodegradable shot. Covyduck, the vet who handled the necropsy, says the new shot emulates lead, and that the formula could be worth millions, provided it's not toxic to the environment."

"And you think it is."

"I do."

"Which makes the formula worthless." He shook the vials, then set them on his desk.

"You have to admit, it makes for a secret worth keeping." She pointed to the samples. "Those came out of the wetlands at the Barr Lake Hunt Club. I'll bet money the shot inside matches the shot from the geese in Elk Park."

"Are you having tests run on the shot?"

"Yes." She felt a flicker of hope. "Chuck Radigan is hiding something, sir. I think Ian got too close. He talked with Eric before he died, then Eric reads Covyduck's report and ends up pushed through the ice."

"And Coot? Do you think that was intentional, too?"

"I don't know." It seemed hard to believe Radigan would risk harming his own son. "But if our plane had gone down, we wouldn't have those." She pointed to the vials. *And I wouldn't be around to keep forcing the issue.*

"So you're suggesting Radigan poisoned the pilot?"

"It's possible."

"What about his son?"

"That had to be an accident."

Kramner rocked back and forth on his heels. "Are these samples legal?"

"Yes, sir, they are. Radigan gave his permission. Ask Lark Drummond."

"It's still a reach, Dimato." He clasped his hands behind his back, and headed for the window. "Can you physically connect Chuck Radigan with Elk Park?"

"He competed in the fishing tournament with his grandson."

"Was he signed up before the geese ended up on the ice, or after?"

Her stomach tightened. "Before, sir."

"And what about the lead you found

283

scattered on the ice?"

She explained why the sinkers couldn't have caused the poisoning. "There wasn't time. We think someone scattered them to throw off the investigation."

"Who's 'we,' Dimato? I thought you and I were working this investigation."

Angela felt her face flush. "I've been talking with Lark and some of the EPOCH members."

Kramner pursed his lips. "Okay, what about the person you saw collecting geese off the ice? What was that all about?"

"I don't know. I haven't figured that out yet, sir."

Kramner made a few more laps, and Angela waited.

"It seems like you have a few loose ends to tie up," he said at last. "But, for argument's sake, let's say your theory's correct. Other than these three samples, do you have any proof?"

"There is some circumstantial evidence." She explained how they had come up with the migration pattern of the geese and located the Barr Lake Hunt Club, and reminded him about the necropsy samples Covyduck sent to the lab. "If the shot matches, and the vegetation and soils match, I think we could make a case."

"Maybe a thin one."

"Bernie Crandall is running fingerprints on two small vials believed to be containers for the fishing sinkers we found. Eric had them in his pocket. He'd picked them up from among the debris on the ice left from the night of the goose rescue operation. If we get a match there, we could have a strong case."

Kramner looked skeptical.

"It's thin," she admitted. "But I'm still building it."

He pivoted, then stopped. The second hand on the clock made half a sweep. "I'm sorry, Dimato. You're off the case."

His words numbed her. She figured once she presented the facts he'd reconsider.

"From my chair, all you've accomplished is to stir up a hornet's nest," he continued. "I received a phone call from Washington this morning. Linda Verbiscar went public with your aerial stunts and inferred on national television that the U.S. Fish and Wildlife Service is investigating Charles Radigan."

"We are," said Angela.

"Radigan's lawyer contacted the director. Do you have any idea who Charles Radigan is?"

"He's a local businessman."

"He's a powerful man. What do you know about his company?"

She felt the heat rise in her face. "Not much."

"You should have done your research, Dimato."

"I will. Just let me —"

"No." Kramner moved back behind his desk. "Face it, Dimato. You're lucky you still have a job. Your judgement in this matter is clouded."

Succinct and to the point. But the bottom line was, Kramner didn't like the press.

"Maybe, but my eyesight is twenty-twenty."

He didn't argue, but surprise caused his eyes to widen behind his thick lenses.

"With all due respect, sir, I think I've earned the right to follow through with this investigation."

"We're done here." She started to argue, but Kramner held up his hand. "You are not ready to be on your own, Dimato, and a birdwatchers' club full of amateur sleuths does not make a team. Your actions indicate you need direct supervision in the field, and, unfortunately, I'm a man short. And besides, we can't afford anymore *accidents.*"

She chose to ignore the insinuation. She couldn't force him to make the connections, anymore than she could ignore them. Her strategy now had to be in convincing him she was close to solving the case.

"If you'll just run the samples —"

The intercom buzzed, and Kramner punched a button on his phone. "I'll take it from here, Dimato."

His tone was dismissive. She moved toward the door.

"And if you find out I'm right?" she asked.

"All the more reason to have you riding a desk. You'll be safer there."

Chapter 16

The Elk Park Town Board met the third Wednesday of the month, and the town hall was crammed full of people out for blood. Chairs overflowed with parents and grandparents, their coats nestled on their laps, sour expressions pinching their faces. Kids, who should have been home with babysitters, wrestled in the aisles. And several teenagers, more interested in flirting than listening, lounged on the windowsills. The last time there had been a turnout like this was when Mayor McNamara had been recalled.

Bruised and battered from Tuesday's ordeal, Lark tucked herself securely into a corner at the back of the room. From there, she had a clear view of the proceedings but was close enough to the doors for a quick getaway. Across the room, Mayor Jane Lindor and eight board members sat fidgeting in stiff-backed chairs, sandwiched between a row of cafeteria tables and a bank of flags.

Lark could empathize. She'd sat on their

side of the tables before. She didn't envy them. Too often those in attendance wanted resolutions outside of the law.

"This looks official," said Angela, slipping into the tiny space between Lark and the door.

Lark experienced a momentary sense of panic over having her escape route cut off, then forced a smile. "Are you here for the show?"

"No," said Angela, patting her gun holster. "I'm here to escort you to safety should things turn ugly."

Lark started to laugh, then reconsidered. Her ribs ached, and there was too much truth in the comment. "Thanks."

Angela flashed white teeth. "Looks like all the players are here."

"And then some." There were more people in the room than attended church in Elk Park on Christmas Day.

Mayor Lindor banged a gavel on the table.

"Let's get started." The noise level dropped only slightly, and she pounded again. "I said, quiet! We're ready to start."

The crowd fell silent.

Someone coughed. Someone else sneezed. Then the mayor set down her gavel and picked up a sheet of paper.

"The first item on the agenda is the town treasurer's report."

There was a collective groan from the gallery.

"But . . ." Her gravelly voice carried over the rumble. "Since you're all here for the items at the bottom of this list, I'm going to dispense with normal procedure and move right to new business."

A wave of approval undulated through the room.

"The board has received a petition requesting the town secure a permit from the U.S. Fish and Wildlife Service for removal of the remainder of the Elk Park geese."

"I make a motion we do it," yelled Frakus.

"Second," hollered someone near the back.

The buzz in the room grew, and Mayor Lindor slammed down the gavel. "I have a motion on the floor. And a second. Is there any discussion?"

The room erupted. People shouted comments from all sides. Lark shrank back against the wall and tried to make herself look small.

"One at a time," yelled the mayor. "Brett?"

The room quieted again. Everyone

turned to look at Brett Bemster. A Tiger Woods–wannabe, he was decked out in corduroy slacks, a light-blue oxford shirt, and a navy-blue sweater vest. A yellow cashmere scarf was twisted around his neck, clashing with the olive tones in his skin. His face — tanned to the texture of shoe leather from too many days at the "Brown Baby" tanning salon — glistened with sweat. Blotting the shine off his brow, he played to the crowd.

"The geese are a health risk."

"They are dirty," said a woman near Lark, someone she had never seen before.

Mob mentality struck, and the crowd co-alesced.

"That's right," said Bemster. "They're pooping in the water."

"Not to mention what else," whispered Angela.

Lark choked and shook her head. No sense feeding the frenzy with sarcasm.

"That's not true," challenged Gertie, standing up in the second row.

"Shut up, Gertie," yelled a voice in the back.

"That's right," shouted someone else. "Sit down."

"Booooooo."

The crowd joined together, and the knot

in Lark's stomach tightened. Mob mentality frightened her. Even when she was leading the mob, like she had been the other night. When passions were aroused, a crowd took on its own energy. This group rallied in fear.

"You'll all have your turn," said Mayor Lindor, pleading for order. She glanced at the sheriff's men near the doors behind her.

Was she looking for help, or did she plan on bolting?

Brett flipped his hair and started again. "Canada geese are medically proven to cause disease. Studies show their crap contaminates the water supply, putting us all at risk."

"That's a lie." Gertie's round face was flushed. Despite the boos, she climbed up on her chair. "There have been numerous studies done, and there's not one drop of evidence that the fecal matter of geese causes illness. Not one."

"It's still gross," said the woman near Lark.

Frakus stepped forward into an aisle. "That's not true, Gertie. Why, in Seattle, we were issued annual U.S. Fish and Wildlife permits to round up and kill geese based on health risks. Now you tell me, why would they sanction extermination if there wasn't some proof? And now we have sick geese." He glanced around to see who was with him.

The majority of citizens in the room seemed to have jumped on board. Lark wished Angela would say something. She could explain to these folks that killing the flock wasn't a solution to the problem. Humans were the problem. The geese weren't diseased. They were sick because of human exposure.

"I can tell you this," said Frakus, taking a parting shot. "It cleaned up our parks."

"Aren't there alternatives to killing them?" asked a teenager near the windows.

Good for you, thought Lark.

"Trust me, nothing else works," said Bemster. "I've paid Lou Vitti thousands of dollars to keep the birds off the golf course, to no avail. The town's been shelling out for over a year. Since . . ."

Lark waited for him to indict himself by bringing up the bludgeoning incident. Instead, he switched gears.

"Suffice it to say, to keep on paying Vitti would be throwing good money after bad. The geese stay away while the dogs are around, then they come right back."

"That's because they've only gone as far

as the lake," said Frakus.

Andrew Henderson lumbered to his feet, taking an impressive stance. "We don't have many resident geese here. The sick geese are transients. They came in with the storm."

"We have enough geese to cause this town a problem," countered Frakus. "All the more reason I say we do something now. If we don't intervene, you can bet they'll multiply."

"There are other methods we can use to reduce the numbers," piped up Harry.

Lark hadn't noticed him sitting down front, but she felt a surge of relief he was here. He was the next best thing to Eric. Maybe the townsfolk would listen to him.

Gertie bobbed her head, while Petey Hinkle tried pulling her down off the chair.

"Give us some examples," requested Mayor Lindor.

"The most effective way is to replace their eggs with fakes to reduce reproduction," said Harry. "Essentially, you're tricking the birds into thinking they have a full brood until it's too late in the season for them to lay more eggs."

"Why not try that?" shouted a man near the doors.

Heads started nodding. Lark felt encouraged. Up until that moment, it had seemed like the EPOCH members were paddling against the tide.

"Because it's costly," said Frakus. "And it takes time. We have a problem now, and we'll have a bigger problem in the spring."

"We can train volunteers," said Gertie. "We don't have to pay anyone."

"It won't do any good," said Bemster. "The geese are worse than rabbits. Besides, Vitti's tried everything. He put out fake owls, scarecrows, Mylar balloons. He even sprayed the grass with methyl anthranilate."

Mayor Lindor frowned. "Which is . . . ?"

"Grape-soda flavoring," Bemster explained. "Supposedly the birds loathe the stuff. Trust me, it might have stopped 'em from eating, but not from dumping."

Lark leaned over, and whispered to Angela, "Have you ever witnessed a kill?"

The agent shuddered, clearly disturbed by the thought. "It's never been high on my list of things to experience."

"Mine either. I've read too many articles." The most graphic one had described how officials lured the geese into fenced areas, then herded them down a narrow shoot and into a pen where they were chased, grabbed, and gassed to death.

"And there's another plus," said Frakus, addressing the crowd like a prosecutor in closing arguments. "The town can donate the meat to charitable causes."

There was an audible, collective groan. Then Kip, the director of the local homeless shelter, shouted, "Don't do us any favors, Frakus."

"Are you hoping to kill off the needy, too?" asked someone else.

"Remember the Drummond!" shouted a man near the back.

The mantra was taken up, and a hundred faces turned to look at Lark. She forced herself to keep staring at Frakus.

"What happened at the Drummond is an isolated situation," he said. "Caused by using the livers of sick geese to make paté."

Lark pressed herself into the corner. Surely the townspeople knew she hadn't authorized use of the geese.

"It weren't just the livers," said Kip. "And it weren't isolated. We didn't serve no livers, but I had to close the shelter down because of those geese."

Lark drew herself out of the shadows. People at the shelter were sick?

Angela also pushed forward. "Did you collect the geese off the ice?"

From the manner in which Kip shrank

back, Lark wished she could see Angela's face.

"That's right," he said, bolstering his courage. "We were legal. Frakus called and donated the meat to the shelter." Kip shot him an accusatory glance. "Only, he forgot to tell us it was contaminated."

Lark's hand flew up to cover her mouth. In all fairness, Frakus might not have thought the meat was bad. But more to the point, if Kip was the person Angela had spotted picking geese up off the ice, where had Ducharme gotten the livers to make the paté?

The meeting degenerated into a shouting match, and Frakus came under full attack. Lark took momentary pleasure in his plight, then signaled to Angela she was leaving. The special agent bobbed her short dark curls and followed her into the parking lot.

"Wow!"

"Do you realize what just happened in there?" whispered Lark, afraid that speaking aloud might somehow jinx this latest development.

"Frakus got caught trying to kill off the homeless population?" asked Angela.

"Get serious. It means that Ducharme wasn't the one collecting geese off the ice."

Angela scrunched up one side of her face. "Not necessarily. For all we know, he could have collected the geese the same way."

The momentary crush of defeat caused Lark's lungs to deflate, and she sucked in a breath. In order to save the Drummond, she needed to prove she and her staff were not responsible for the poisonings. Maybe it was time to start grasping at straws.

"What if Frakus had given Ducharme permission as well?" she asked. "Then Frakus, or the town, would be responsible for the poisonings, right?"

Angela looked doubtful. "Maybe, if Frakus admitted giving permission. That's a big if."

They reached Lark's truck. She climbed in and rolled down the driver's-side window.

Angela rested her arms on the sill. "Plus you'd need Ducharme to testify. The fact he took off plays against you."

Lark slumped back against the seat. "That does look bad, doesn't it?"

She meant it as a rhetorical question, but Angela answered with a question of her own. "What if Ducharme bought the geese?"

"From Kip?"

"From anywhere. Wouldn't most places assume they could bill the Drummond?"

Lark's head snapped up off the headrest. They'd searched for a bill or receipt and touched base with their food distributors. She'd checked. Velof had checked. Heck, even Bernie Crandall had taken a whack at it.

But what if Ducharme had opened a new account with a new company? Maybe the paperwork hadn't arrived. Or maybe it had. Maybe it was sitting in her inbox.

Angela followed Lark to the Drummond.

The hotel, inviting in its holiday attire, projected a festive mood. Evergreen boughs draped the eaves, pinned with red bows and wrapped in bright twinkle lights. Music pumped through tiny Bose speakers drifted across the veranda, lulling the night.

By contrast, the lobby seemed somber.

"Things have been a little quiet around here," said Lark, nodding to the desk clerk and leading the way back to her office.

"Quiet" was an understatement. *Dead* seemed a better fit.

Unblemished by fingerprints, the opulent furnishings gleamed with an unnatural sheen, the red wool carpet showed vacuum marks, and music echoed off the sculpted ceiling. The only movement came from the sleepy desk clerk, and the eyes of the paintings, which seemed to track their movements, hungry for interaction.

Lark pushed open the office door and waved Angela to a seat.

"It's either here or it isn't," she said, pointing to the inbox on her desk. She picked up the stack of papers and handed half to Angela.

Water bill. Electric bill. Gas bill. All astronomical figures. But no bill for the birds.

"It's not in my stack," said Angela, setting it back on the desk.

"Damn," said Lark, tossing the last of the papers back on the pile. Tears made her eyes glisten. "I was so sure we'd find something."

Angela wasn't ready to throw in the towel yet. "Let's go at this from a different angle. How many places supply wild game to restaurants? There can't be that many."

"There's more than you think."

"All we need to do is find the right one."

Lark pulled out the Yellow Pages, and Angela dragged her chair around the desk.

"Try under food distributors," she said.

"First let's try under game." Lark flipped

pages. "It says to look under meat-processing or meat-wholesalers."

The meat page contained two columns of names. Angela counted thirty-eight meat-wholesalers, one meat-broker, and fourteen meat-processing facilities.

"We'll just have to call them all."

"In the morning," said Angela. "It's too late to call now."

There was nothing more they could do, so Angela and Lark headed down to the Warbler Café to meet the others. A town landmark, the coffee shop was housed in the corner of a strip mall on the east end of town. A painted mural depicting a variety of Colorado warblers marked the front door, while a wraparound deck stretched to the south overlooking the lake. Inside, tables crowded a hardwood floor. A long counter stretched along the back wall, covered with jars of beans and a variety of cappuccino and espresso machines. In the far corner, a copper roasting machine agitated beans, spewing the fresh scent of coffee into the air.

"Welcome," said Dorothy, throwing open the door. Taking Angela's coat, she shooed them toward a large round table in the center of the room, where Andrew and Opal Henderson were already ensconced.

The couple waved, and Angela conjured the image of Jack Sprat and his wife — only in this case, Jack was Jacqueline. Andrew was stuffing a piece of banana bread into his mouth, while Opal sipped her drink. No doubt a nonfat latte.

Gertie and Harry were making coffee.

"This is a great place you have here," said Angela.

"Why thank you, dear," said Dorothy, making a generous sweep with her arm. "You know we inherited it."

While Dorothy sliced more bread, Cecilia launched into the café's history. "It was opened by Esther Mills with seed money from the four of us — myself, Dot, Gertie, and Lark. A year and a half ago, Esther was stabbed to death in the parking lot."

"How awful!" Angela vaguely remembered reading something about that. She just hadn't connected the dots. "Did you ever catch the person who did it?"

"Oh my, yes. Thanks to Lark."

"It wasn't altruistic," said Lark. "Like now, I stood to lose everything."

Angela refrained from comment and accepted a fishbowl mug of coffee from Gertie. Warming her hands, she breathed in the coffee's aroma.

"How's Eric?" asked Andrew.

Lark glanced at Angela.

Did he think that's where they had been? Angela wondered. "As far as I know, he's the same."

Dorothy's eyes brimmed with tears, and she sniffed, using her napkin to blot her nose.

"Oh my, let's not go all weepy, Dot. We need to stay strong, for everyone's sake."

"He's going to be fine," said Lark.

Angela counted backwards, trying to remember how many days it had been since the accident. Two? It seemed like more. The longer Eric remained in a coma, the more likely he was to emerge with some long term damage.

She tried shaking the thought and fished for a better subject. "How's it going at the Raptor House?"

Checking on the geese had been a primary reason for her coming up to Elk Park. The town meeting was secondary. She had been headed out the door, when Verbiscar's face had flashed across the TV.

Now there was someone she'd like to see in a coma.

Dorothy set down her napkin. "It's a miracle, really. The geese have mostly recovered. You would hardly know they'd been sick."

Angela stared, convinced she'd heard wrong. Most times, no matter what you did, lead-poisoned geese died. Did that mean the toxin wasn't lead?

"No kidding," said Andrew. "That's weird. And there I was advocating we put them down."

"How are the banquet guests?" Angela asked.

"They're better, too," said Dorothy. "Of course, it didn't stop the health department from closing down the kitchen at the Drummond."

"We're waiting to see the results on lead-level tests," said Lark. "They're due in tomorrow."

"So where did you peel off to in such a rush?" asked Harry, joining them at the table.

Lark explained how it had occurred to her that Ducharme must have ordered the geese from a new distributor. "Angela and I did some checking and came up with fifty-three possibilities."

"Did any of them check out?" asked Harry.

"We'll have to call in the morning," said Lark.

"Did any of the names look familiar?" asked Gertie.

"Not to me."

"Me either," said Angela. She pulled out the page she'd torn from the Yellow Pages. "Do any of them look familiar to any of you?"

The EPOCH members passed the sheet around.

"I recognize this name," said Andrew. His finger pointed to "Organics Unlimited." Angela felt a tingle of excitement travel along her veins.

Opal wiggled in her chair. "I didn't know he dealt with meat, did you?"

"Who?" demanded Dorothy. "Don't keep us guessing."

Andrew pushed aside the paper. "Donald Tauer. Organics Unlimited is a subsidiary company of Agriventures, Inc."

Chapter 17

"Maybe we should pay them a visit?" asked Lark.

Angela swallowed, trying to dislodge the lump in her throat. It was time to come clean. "*We* can't do anything. Kramner pulled me off the case."

"What?" cried the EPOCH members in unison.

Angela looked down at the floor, her gaze tracking the uneven flooring, the shifts in color and light. When she looked up, she faced seven pairs of eyes.

"He doesn't think I have enough experience, or that I can be objective."

Gertie snorted. "If you ask me, I'd say you were getting too close and ruffling too many feathers."

"Either way, I'm out." She looked straight at Lark. "Take it to Kramner in the morning."

"Will he help?"

Angela shrugged. "It's what he needs. He rushed the tests on the samples. He should have the lead level reports back tomorrow. He knows his job."

"And if he won't follow through?"

For Lark it meant the difference between saving the Drummond and being forced to close down. Angela dropped her gaze and worked the toe of her boots against a crack in the flooring. "Then call me."

Angela slept in her own bed that night, and ended up sleeping in. The telephone rang in the morning and yanked her loose from a nightmare. She'd been running through the woods at Barr Lake, headed toward the mist nets, footsteps pounding behind her. Now, clawing her way up from the depths of sleep, her heart raced. She squinted at the alarm clock and reached for the phone.

"Angela?"

Lark. "What time is it?"

"Eight-thirty." Hysteria edged the woman's voice, prompting Angela to a sitting position.

"What happened?"

"I called Kramner. He said the samples came back negative for lead."

In a shift of panic, Angela's heart pounded. She clutched the comforter to her chest. "Okay. Let's think this through. Something is making the geese sick. What about PAH contamination from the clay pigeons?" Although that wouldn't account for the food poisoning in the Drummond guests.

"No."

"What about the alternative shot?"

"He claims there was nothing," answered Lark, her voice sounding calmer. "It appears to be natural. The samples were clean."

If that was true — and Angela had no reason to doubt Kramner's assessment — Radigan's willingness to let them take samples made sense. He had nothing to hide. They'd been looking in the wrong place.

"I guess this means Coot's food poisoning was really an accident," said Lark.

"Looks like." That would explain why Radigan's son ended up sick. So what had poisoned the geese?

Angela kicked her legs over the side of the bed and fished with her feet for her sheepskin slippers. "What about the lead levels on the banquet guests? Have those results come back."

"That's another thing. All but one came back normal."

"What was the exception?"

"It turns out one guy drinks orange juice from a pottery pitcher. His whole family tested high. He was actually lucky he attended the banquet."

Cold air from the slightly opened window wafted across Angela's shoulders, and she shifted the comforter to cover her back. If the wetland samples from Barr Lake Hunt Club tested normal and the banquet guests' blood samples tested normal, the lab work on the geese was likely negative for lead, too.

"Did you talk with Covyduck?"

"Before I called you. He's checking on the tests, as we speak. He promised to call me back." Lark sighed, and a tendril of fear curled from Angela's stomach to her throat.

They'd been working the wrong leads.

"Angela?"

"I'm still here."

I'm thinking.

"What other things could make the geese sick like that?" she wondered aloud. "What would make them toxic to someone who ate them?"

"You're asking me?"

"Come on, Lark, think! We have all the pieces. We just have to fit them together."

Angela climbed out of bed. Cradling the phone against her shoulder, she shut the window and sealed out the cold air. The day was bright. Sunlight played on the frost covering the birdfeeders in the back-yard, and a flock of LGBs — little gray birds, mostly house sparrows and pine siskins — mobbed the large feeder kicking seed to the squirrels on the ground as they squabbled. Flashes of red indicated a house finch or two frolicked among the bunch, and an American goldfinch pecked thistle from the tube feeder. Reaching for her robe, Angela cranked up the heat, then settled herself into a chair from where she could watch the birds.

"Dorothy told us last night that the geese and the banquet guests were all getting better."

"Right," said Lark.

"So that should have been our clue. Lead accumulates in the system. Whatever poisoned the birds seems to be working its way through."

"Like a virus?" said Lark.

Angela thought of Ebola and hemorrhagic fever, and nixed that idea. "No, more like —"

"Food poisoning," they said in unison.

Why hadn't she seen it before? thought Angela. It took less than a second for the epiphany to happen.

"It's the corn!"

Lark's silence at Angela's pronouncement was profound.

"Hold on a minute. I'm switching phones." Angela dropped the receiver and padded down the hall to her office.

A guest bedroom by virtue of the twin bed shoved into the corner, the prominent feature of the room was her grandfather's desk, a huge mahogany rolltop dominating most of one wall. A thin layer of bills coated the surface. An ergonomically correct chair — a throwback to dorm life — was stuffed underneath. On either side, stacks of books rose from the floor, like statues flanking a throne.

The rolltop's cubbies were crammed full of papers, and it took her a moment to locate a Colorado map. Spreading it open on the desk, she clicked on the speaker phone. "Lark, do you remember how Covyduck said they'd found a mixture of corn and wetland grasses in the geese's stomach?"

"Yes."

"At the time, I figured it would help us pinpoint the previous location of the geese, but what if it's the corn that's making them sick?" Angela traced her finger along the route of the Barr Lake Drainage Loop. There was farmland all around.

"Geese eat corn all the time."

"True," said Angela, "and people eat geese. Just go with me on this." She needed Lark's help to brainstorm. "Outside of the shot, the fishing sinkers, and wetland vegetation, corn was the only thing the geese had in common, right?"

"Right."

"And unlike lead, corn passes through, right?" Angela sat down, twisting her legs into the chair.

"Which explains why the banquet guests and the geese are getting better."

"You've got it!" Angela traced her finger along the eastern edge of Barr Lake. "What do you want to bet at least one of the fields near the Barr Lake Hunt Club is planted in corn?"

Lark hesitated. "That doesn't explain why it's making them sick."

"Maybe they sprayed the field with some new pesticide, or —" Angela broke off. There was another possibility, one she hadn't thought of until now.

"What?"

"Maybe the corn has been genetically engineered." Genetic engineering technology was still in its early experimental phases, and she knew next to nothing about it *except* that it was becoming more prevalent.

"But isn't GE farming regulated?"

"It's supposed to be. But I know of at least one case where a bunch of people died, and a few thousand more ended up disabled, all from taking some sort of GE dietary supplement." Angela paused. "That, and what I've read about Monsanto."

They were one of the largest producers of genetically engineered crops, and had been fined numerous times over the years for their planting practices — not leaving a large enough border around their GE fields, not monitoring for spread, and for planting test fields of GE crops without notifying APHIS, the Animal and Plant Health Inspection Service division of the USDA.

"Aren't they the ones that produce sterile seed?" asked Lark.

"Yes." The practice had spawned a big debate by forcing farmers to buy new seed every year. Since the onset, other companies had jumped on board, and now there were plants being engineered for insect resistance and pharmaceutical production. It was big business, and big money.

"Are you thinking what I'm thinking?" asked Lark.

"I am if you're thinking Agriventures is

somehow involved." Angela untwisted herself from the chair. "I think it's time to do some research."

"Is there anything I can do?"

"Yes. Have Covyduck send the sample back through the lab. Let's see if they can pinpoint a toxin in the corn."

Lark clicked off, and Angela spent the next hour on the phone. According to county records, the land adjacent to the Barr Lake Hunt Club was owned by Radigan Enterprises. Hadn't he mentioned something about sharecropping the land?

It didn't take long to find out who held the lease. According to a woman in the Adams County tax department, Agriventures, Inc. had declared profits for farming the land for the past two years.

Angela headed to the kitchen to make some tea and mulled over the facts. The only connection between Ian's death, Eric's accident, and the plane crash were the waterfowl poisonings. Try as she might, she had never been able to come up with anything else tying the three together. With this new information, and ruling out Coot's poisoning, the whole case pulled together. Donald Tauer was the common thread.

The more she thought about it, the more it all made sense. If Ian had figured out the source of the poisonings was the corn, he would have confronted Tauer. Was that the reason he was out at Barr Lake on the night he died? Was Tauer the person he had planned on meeting?

She knew for a fact that Tauer had been at Elk Lake on the morning of Eric's accident. Had Eric figured out the source of the poisonings and confronted Tauer prior to Tauer's meeting up with Frakus and Nate? Had Tauer placed the phone call to her claiming to be Frakus?

And why?

Thinking about Nate caused Angela's mouth to go dry. He was the commodities grader for the Agriventures' fields. Could he be involved in the scheme? Could he have accepted payments from Tauer for his stamp of approval on Agriventures' products?

Listening to the whistle on the tea kettle, Angela debated calling Kramner, then decided against it. No doubt she was in over her head, but he had ordered her off the case, and at this point she didn't have anything more than suspicions to go on. Besides, even with hard evidence, it would give him just cause to fire her for working the case against his direct orders.

While the tea steeped, she closed her eyes and relived the scene at the fishing hut the morning she'd found Eric. Donald Tauer had been more concerned about the contents of the fishing hut than about Eric's accident. Was there something inside the hut he was worried might be discovered, or was he really just worried about the firemen damaging things? Frakus had been upset about the ramifications that Eric's accident would have on the fishing tournament. And why had Nate been there?

She recalled his comment about things not being what they seemed. How so?

Angela sat up, squeezed the tea bag, and sipped at the bitter liquid. She guessed it was time to ask him a few questions.

Chapter 18

Nate's office was located in a building attached to the National Wildlife Research Center in Fort Collins, a facility engaged in developing methods to mitigate damage and reduce public risks posed by wildlife. It was through NWRC efforts that the Environmental Protection Agency was able to register methyl anthranilate as a geese repellant for use on turf and standing water. It was the NWRC that helped obtain FDA approval for the use of alphachloralose, an immobilizing agent that helps with the capture and relocation of nuisance birds. And it was the NWRC that worked to develop immuno-contraceptives, chemical repellants, and hazing and harassment techniques to discourage the presence of wildlife in certain areas. Needless to say, Angela had a problem with the NWRC.

Billed as the "leader in nonlethal wildlife damage solutions," the NWRC's international reputation for seeking "selective, effective, and socially acceptable" methods for conflict resolution between people and wildlife preceded it. But as far as Angela was concerned, the NWRC rested firmly in the people's camp. Nothing about harassing animals and birds seemed socially acceptable to her. And the money spent developing things like low-powered, nonlethal lasers for the dispersal of geese constituted cruelty to animals.

Dressed in civilian clothes — a pair of jeans, tennis shoes, and a pink sweater — Angela flashed her credentials to the guard seated at the NWRC reception desk. "Is Nate Sobul in?"

She hadn't called ahead, so she breathed a sigh of relief when the guard pointed her down the hall. Pushing through a set of double doors, she crossed into the USDA building, and poked her head into the third office on the right. Nate was seated at his desk.

"Hey, Nate."

The room was big and comfortable, and he had found a way to make it his own. Large oil paintings, splashed in the yellows and reds of the desert, graced the bone-colored walls. A black desk faced a ribbon of windows framing a long-distance view of the Continental Divide.

In keeping with the decor, Nate, himself, was out of uniform. Rather than brown and khaki, he was decked out in chinos and a black, long-sleeved polo shirt.

"Peeps."

Angela bristled at the nickname but forced a smile.

"What can I do for you?" he asked.

"Got a minute?"

Nate glanced at the papers on his desk. "Actually, I'm kind of busy."

She stepped into the room. "I'll only take a second, I promise."

Nate waffled, then cleared off a chair.

Angela sat down, then told him about the new twist in the case, omitting the part about having been sidelined. Perched on the edge of his desk, Nate's posture implied discomfort.

"Let me get this straight," he said, stretching out his neck. "You're asking me if Agriventures's cornfields are genetically engineered?"

"Correct."

"The answer's no." He stood and placed his desk between them. "They sell organic product. The fields processed clean."

"Look, Nate, we know it's not lead that made those birds sick. The only other common denominator is the corn. If you're covering up something, now is the time to come clean."

It was a bluff but she had made it sound good. Nate reached for his water.

"Do you remember the morning of Eric's accident?" she asked.

He nodded, keeping his gaze averted.

"You said the situation was something other than I thought."

His gaze shifted, and he pinned her with a stare. "Leave it alone, Angela."

"I can't." *Not if it means letting Ian's killer go free.*

"Would it put your mind at ease if I told you Agriventures is under investigation?"

"By whom?"

His body language told her he knew a lot more than he was saying. Had Kramner already replaced her on the case?

Nate set down the water bottle. "By me."

Angela sat in stunned silence. The heater fan whispered warm air into the room. Nate's chair squeaked. Finally, she found her voice. "I thought you were just a commodities grader."

That was a direct quote. It had been his excuse for not helping during Operation Goose Rescue.

Nate tipped back his head and laughed. "I guess I deserved that."

"You're serious?" she said. She tried to

keep the incredulity out of her voice and failed miserably.

"What, you don't think I'm up for the task?" Nate rolled back his chair and swung the door closed. "Look, what I'm going to tell you has to remain in this room. Since last year, I've been working undercover with the IES."

The Investigative and Enforcement Services division for the Biotechnology Regulatory Service division of APHIS. Nate was an agri-cop!

"I can tell by your expression, you're finding it hard to believe."

"A little," she admitted. "Okay, a lot."

Based on her knowledge of Nate, he lacked the perseverance and follow-through needed to make a good law enforcement officer. If he was telling the truth, there had to be an angle.

"It was my ticket into the BRS division. Trust me, Peeps, biotech is the wave of the future."

She knew it.

"You always were opportunistic."

If the barb landed, he ignored it. "Last year IES received a tip that Agriventures was selling a nonorganic product under their organic label. We checked it out. The product turned up clean."

"Using what criteria?"

"The basics. A farmer can't have used pesticides, chemicals, or fertilizer on the crops for at least three years. The soil samples and product samples showed Agriventures complied."

"What about genetically engineered plants? How do they factor in?"

Nate's dark eyes locked on Angela's. "It's hard to prove."

"How so?"

"You want the crash course?" Nate stood and walked over to the window. The sun danced off his hair, crowning his head in a reddish aura. "GE Farming 101. Farmers have been using genetics for years. They've bred plants together to come up with the best strain of peas, the best potato crop. But with today's technology . . ." Nate twisted the handle on the blinds, opening and closing the shutters. "Now, they can snip, insert, recombine, rearrange, edit, and program genetic material to create 'Frankenfoods,' bioengineered food crops that can be dangerous to consumers."

"Aren't there regulations?"

"There's legislation in Congress." He studied her for a second. "For instance, there's a bill on the floor that would require food companies to label all foods containing GE material, and one that would require the FDA to ensure compliance with special testing."

Angela wrestled with the information. "You mean they don't do that already?"

"Only if it is determined that the GE product is *not* equivalent to a conventional product."

That left room for definition. "Are there any more bills pending?"

Nate leaned against the window sill, and crossed his ankles. "There's one to protect the farmer by granting him indemnification from liability and placing the sole responsibility for any crop failure or negative impact on the biotech company that created the GE organism. And there's another that would place a moratorium on crops grown for pharmaceuticals. There's a real fear that crops containing the antibiotic marker gene might recombine with disease-causing bacteria and create antibiotic-resistant infections we won't be able to cure."

Angela got a bad feeling. "Like what?"

"Maybe a new strain of e-coli or salmonella."

Angela shifted in her chair. Despite the answers he gave her, all she could come up with were more questions. "Can you test products and determine if they're genetically engineered?"

"Yes. But it's expensive. And without just cause, not usually done. The truth is, if the product is tested, it's usually by the purchaser after it's in the market."

Scientists playing God.

"So where does the USDA stand on all this?" She hoped they were angling for more control.

"The BRS monitors the GE crops in field trials and evaluates the impact of any widespread environmental release."

"In layman's terms?"

"We want to know what effect the product has on weeds. And we want to know the effect on any other plants it comes in contact with. Most of all, we want to minimize contact."

"How do you do that?"

"All GE experimental crops must maintain a one-mile buffer zone to avoid cross-pollination and contamination of other crops."

Angela hooted. "What about birds and insects? Any animal moving between fields carries pollen on their feet. Contamination is inevitable."

Nate's face hardened. "Don't forget, you're preaching to the choir."

Time to switch tacks.

"So, basically, what you're saying is, it's not illegal for Agriventures — or anyone else for that matter — to grow GE plants."

"Not if they submit to monitoring."

Angela rubbed her temples and tried dispelling the faint throb in her head. "And if they don't?"

"Then we can fine them up to five hundred thousand dollars and/or force them to destroy the plants and clean up any contaminated areas. The FDA determines if there's a health risk and has its own fines. Hell, even the Environmental Protection Agency has a regulatory role." Nate pushed himself off the sill and moved back toward his chair. "If a GE plant manufactures its own pesticide, the EPA ensures the pesticide levels present in the plant are safe for humans and the environment. Same with the herbicide-resistant plants. If not, then they have their own set of fines."

"There isn't just one oversight agency?"

"No, which makes it even easier for these guys to slip through the cracks."

Angela considered his answers, then doubled back. "But if you suspect Agriventures of growing GE plants, why not test one of their samples?"

Nate picked a pencil up off his desk and

bounced the eraser on the desk blotter. "I have no reason to request another sample. Hunches don't count." He set down the pencil. "I'll let you know if I come up with anything more concrete."

"What about the samples we took from the geese?"

"There's no way to link them to an Agriventures' cornfield."

He was right. And the same would be true of the samples she and Lark had taken at the Barr Lake Hunt Club. What they needed was a sample taken directly from the cornfield. Was that what Ian had been after on the night he died?

"Did you talk to Ian about any of this?"

Nate didn't answer immediately. "I told him to leave it alone, just like I'm telling you."

Angela pushed up out of her chair, and headed towards the door. "Thanks for your time."

She knew what she had to do.

"I'm warning you, Angela. It's dangerous."

She thought of Eric and the phone call to Velof, and stopped midway to the door. Nate was Tauer's alibi. "What time did you meet John Frakus and Donald Tauer in Elk Lake?"

"Why?" His eyes narrowed. "If you're thinking Tauer pushed Eric Linenger into the water, think again."

"What time?"

He stared her down, then answered. "Five-forty. I was late, but he and Frakus were waiting."

She would check his answer against the accident report and the estimated amount of time Eric was in the water. It would be close. "Thanks."

She thought of another question as she hit the door. "Besides the fine, are there any other repercussions if Agriventures is caught growing GE corn?"

From what Nate had just told her, there didn't seem to be enough at stake to warrant Tauer's murdering anyone. With no laws in place monitoring GE crops, the penalties for noncompliance were practically nil. Exposure due to the deaths of a few migratory birds amounted to a slap on the wrist.

Nate cupped his hands behind his head and leaned back in his chair. "Sure, there are a number of possibilities. Criminal charges could be brought against the principals, though I doubt it. More than likely, boycotts against Agriventures, Inc. within the organic industry would dry up the markets. Tauer would be forced into bank-ruptcy."

"What you're saying is, anyone con-nected to the company stands to lose."

"Yeah, and on the flipside, any rival stands to gain." He leaned forward again. "I need to get back to work."

"Thanks for the information, Nate."

"It was good to see you, Peeps."

She wished she could say the same.

With her back to him, she didn't see him get out of his chair, but suddenly his hand gripped the door above her head, pre-venting her exit. He smiled down at her, but his eyes remained cold. "Now that you know IES is on top of it, I'm trusting you to back off."

He was telling her to drop the investiga-tion. Had he asked the same thing of Ian?

"It's out of my hands," she replied. There was more truth in the statement than he realized. She tugged on the door, but Nate held it in place, bending down until she could smell the pine scent of his aftershave and the residue of Ivory soap on his skin.

"Don't be stupid, Angela."

Was it the couched warning or his prox-imity that was making her tremble?

Angela tugged on the door again, only

this time he let it go. She stumbled, and he broke her fall, hard arms circling her waist. Her heart fluttered. A remnant of old love? It felt more like fear.

Clear of the building, Angela sprinted for her car, a slap-in-the-face reminder of her current position. Along with losing the case, investigating on her own time meant she lost the accoutrements of the job — the use of her truck, the uniform, the duty belt. The one exception was her gun, and that she kept locked in the glove compartment.

Sitting behind the wheel, she stared out at the farm fields stretching east to the Kansas state line. Most of them were planted seasonally in sugar beets or wheat. How many of them were genetically engineered? Or did anyone — even the USDA — know?

Despite her discomfort, the conversation with Nate had borne fruit. She had come away with a motive for Ian's murder, Eric's accident, and her own near brush with death. Whoever had perpetrated the crimes wanted to cover up the fact that Agriventures, Inc. had planted their fields in GE corn.

Of the possible suspects, Donald Tauer

led the pack. He had the most to lose, and he had been in Elk Lake over the weekend. Had he arrived on the ice early and discovered the geese? If so, it made sense he would scatter the lead sinkers on the ice, figuring any further investigation would be halted, and the geese would be treated for lead poisoning. It was his permit Frakus had used to instigate the carnage. Plus, he could easily have been Ian's mystery date, or caught Ian trying to sample his cornfield. Now that Coot had admitted to helping himself to the goose meat, all the pieces dropped into place.

Of course, Radigan had been at the lake, too. But Ian wasn't investigating the shot, or was he? She needed to check his notes. Frakus and Ducharme were ruled out when she connected the poisonings at Elk Park to Barr Lake. Which left Nate. What if her first instincts were correct? What if he and Tauer were friends, and the IES story was merely a coverup? Had Ian suspected Nate of rubber-stamping commodities?

The thought gave her a chill, and she cranked the heat up a notch. If that were the case, why would Nate give her so much information on the GE crop situation? Unless . . .

What if Nate had orchestrated Ian's death? Could he be trying to set her up, too? The case hinged on the corn in Agriventures' field. Before she tried proving anything, she needed proof that the corn had poisoned the geese. Nate knew her well enough to know she wouldn't drop the investigation, especially if the order came through him. Was he banking on her tenacity?

First things first, whispered Ian's voice.

Angela laid out a plan. First she'd check Ian's notes, and do her research. Then she'd gather the evidence. By then, she ought to have narrowed it down to one of the three suspects.

An hour later, she parked her car in front of the regional U.S. Fish and Wildlife offices in Denver. Avoiding Kramner, she picked her way through the maze of partitions and slipped into her cubicle near the back of the room. The space looked neglected, in the same sagging way a house did when no one lived there. An avalanche of memos spilled from her in-box onto the desk. A stack of manila folders begged to be filed. Two pictures were thumb-tacked into the wall — one a photograph of her parents in Italy; the other a computer printout of Samson, the elk, prior to his demise in Rocky Mountain National Park.

The desk chair canted slightly to the left, which she compensated for by curling her leg up under her bottom. Hunkering down, she booted up the computer and requested information on Agriventures, Inc.

Donald Tauer, CEO, owned fifty-one percent of the company. The other forty-nine percent was publicly traded. According to the prospectus, Agriventures, though new to the organic market, commanded a large slice of the nation's organic sales. Based on the quarterly report, millions of dollars had been invested over the past five years, implementing organic farming techniques across vast holdings. Assets outweighed the debts, and Agriventures appeared to be on the verge of paying dividends to its stockholders for the first time.

So why risk it all by planting GE corn?

She typed in Donald Tauer's name and it came up connected with a number of local and regional festivals like the Elk Park Ice Fishing Jamboree. A family man, an outdoorsman, his driving line was, "we focus on raising food that's safe for you and your families to eat."

By now, her foot was asleep, so she eased

it out from under her, tamping its dead weight on the floor.

Out of curiosity, she typed in "Radigan Enterprises," and pulled up some interesting stuff. Radigan's company had diversified in the seventies, gobbling up a hodgepodge of pharmaceutical companies, defense contractors, book publishing businesses, and banking cooperatives. The principal shareholder, Charles Embry Radigan, III, better known as Chuck, specialized in making money. The self-made billionaire — chairman of the Radigan Enterprises board of directors, active member of the National Rifle Association, and regional director of Ducks Unlimited — lived in a four-million-dollar mansion in Cherry Hills Farms. None of it reason enough to hang him.

"Glad to see you're working."

Angela looked up to find Kramner standing in the doorway to her cubicle. She clicked on the screen saver. "Research."

Without preamble, he said, "Bernie Crandall called this morning."

"And? Did he have the results of the fingerprint testing on the sinker containers?"

"They pulled a partial."

Angela sat up straighter in the chair,

causing it to shift and nearly dump her onto the floor. It took her a moment to balance. "Whose?"

"They think it belongs to a kid."

"As in little kid?"

Kramner bumped his glasses higher on his nose. "It's hard to say. They checked with Operation Kidprint and came up empty-handed, but it looks like the lead on the ice was a prank."

She wasn't buying that assessment.

Coincidence, the remarkable happening of similar events by chance. Hadn't that been Kramner's definition? There were far too many coincidences in this case for her to accept the randomness of the events.

"Thank you, sir."

After Kramner left, her cell phone rang. "Dimato."

"Angela, it's Lark. Covyduck just called."

More good news?

"You were right about the corn."

Chapter 19

Angela asked Lark to call an emergency meeting of the EPOCH members, then hung up the phone and hurried to Ian's office. Locating the notebook on waterfowl, she opened it to the first page. The more current notes — at least as far as she could tell from where they'd been positioned on Ian's desk — were near the front. Halfway down the first page, she found what she was looking for.

Waterfowl. Corn product. Meeting changed to six-thirty.

That was an hour before dispatch had notified her that Ian wanted backup. A little more than two hours before she'd found him dead. He must have realized he was walking into a trap at Barr Lake. More important, it proved she was on the right track, that it was the corn, not the shot alternative, that had caused the die-off.

Her next stop was dispatch. The dispatch center, located in the Denver City and County Building off Colfax Avenue, had taken Ian's emergency call.

Angela stopped in the doorway, and took in the scene. There were five stations, each occupied by a dispatcher. Each station housed several different monitors. From what she could see, one monitor displayed the address and personal information of the caller, one showed the location of the various emergency response teams, and another maintained a list of the calls being handled. When the phone rang, someone would answer and assess the emergency. Calls were triaged, and often a dispatcher handled two or more calls at a time.

One young man with a waist-length ponytail sat with his back to the door working a possible heart attack. He held a flip card with assessment questions open in one hand and was trying hard to calm down the caller.

"Please, ma'am, I need you to remain calm. Is your mother breathing?"

"Yes." The caller's voice sounded high-pitched and stressed.

"Is she sitting up?"

"Yes."

"That's good." The dispatcher kept his voice soothing and even. "Emergency personnel are on the scene. Can you go to the door?"

"I don't want to leave her."

"I need you to open the door."

Angela watched the tape spin. All calls were recorded, and recordings were archived by date. The other dispatchers were also on calls, so Angela waited. Finally, the dispatcher convinced the woman whose mother was having a heart attack to open the door.

"Hey there," he said, swiveling his chair around. "What can I do for you?"

Angela showed her credentials. "One of the dispatchers here relayed a message to me from my partner on the night he died."

The young man's face turned grim. "That would be me. My name's Taylor. I was sorry to hear the outcome. He didn't sound like he was in trouble."

"If I could just listen to the dispatch tape . . ."

The young man frowned. "Do you have authorization?"

"I'm a law enforcement officer. All I want to do is listen."

"Sure, why not? Hey, guys," he hollered to his coworkers. "I'm going on break." He led Angela to a back room and started down a row of bookshelves crammed with small metal canisters. "That was New Year's Eve, wasn't it?"

"That's right."

He found the tape and threaded it onto a reel-to-reel player. "You have any idea what time the call was made?"

She told him, and he cued up the tape.

Hearing Ian's voice brought a lump to her throat. The dispatcher had been right. Ian was hard to hear and the message sounded garbled. She could hear the swan in the background, and what sounded like someone else's voice.

"Do you hear that? There's another person there. Can you focus in on that voice?"

"You mean like isolate the track? Bring down the other stuff, and bring up the voice?"

"Yes."

"No."

"Can you turn it up, then?"

The young man complied, and Angela tried using her brain as a filter.

Run, man, run.

"I think he said, 'run,' " said Taylor.

"Play it again." Angela's blood turned cold at the sound of the voice. This time, it wasn't just the command, it was the voice she recognized. Donald Tauer's voice. It almost sounded like a warning.

"Hold on to this tape," she ordered. She jotted down its number and Taylor's name, then headed back to her car. She wondered why no one had ever mentioned the second voice on the tape. Surely Kramner had heard it. If not, she intended to play him a copy.

The day shift was over by the time she left dispatch, and Kramner was already gone. She tried catching him on his cell phone, but he didn't pick up. Even if he had, as hard as he was working to refute the case, she doubted he'd place much stock in the tape without additional evidence.

That's where the EPOCH members came in.

It took her an hour and a half to drive to Elk Park. By the time she arrived, the bird-club members were convened around the table in Lark's kitchen — Harry, Dorothy, Cecilia, Gertie, Andrew, Opal, and Lark.

"Good, let's get started," said Andrew, dipping his hand into a bag of corn tortilla chips. "What's so all-fired important that you pulled us away from supper?"

"I need your help." She told them about the toxicology reports on the geese and the guests at the Drummond. "I had Covyduck run the sample back through. It turns out the corn we found in the goose's gizzard has been genetically engineered."

Gertie's mouth dropped open. Andrew set his corn chip back in the bag.

"What's it being engineered for?" asked Harry.

"We don't know — pharmaceuticals, pesticide-resistance. All the lab can tell us at this point is that the genetic manipulation increased the levels of plant toxins, producing a poison that caused the geese to get sick."

A moment of silence followed her pronouncement, then the EPOCH members erupted with questions.

"Does that mean Ducharme's geese ate the same corn?" asked Gertie.

"Most likely," said Lark. "I did some calling around this morning, and discovered he'd contracted with Organics Unlimited for twenty-five geese."

"How bad is the poison?" asked Cecilia.

"Bad," said Dorothy. "It's killed fifty birds."

"You know what I mean, Dot. It's also worked its way clear of the system of the others. What I'd like to hear about is long-term effects."

Angela scanned the lab report. "It doesn't mention those here."

"Do we know who's responsible?" asked Opal.

The question hung in the air. All eyes turned to Angela.

"My money's on Agriventures," she said.

"Oh my," said Cecilia. "Are you saying that nice young man, Donald Tauer, is responsible for all of this?"

"I think it's possible he's responsible for everything — the geese die-off, the banquet guest poisoning, Ian's death, Eric's accident."

"He's not looking quite so nice anymore," said Dorothy.

"Do you have any proof?" asked Harry.

Angela looked around the table. "That's why I asked for this meeting. The U.S. Fish and Wildlife Service has samples from the wetlands at the Barr Lake Hunt Club. If there's corn vegetation present, I can have the lab run a genetics test to compare the results with the samples from the goose necropsy, and from the blood work of the patients. That should prove the corn is what caused the poisonings."

"What about the homeless guys?" asked Gertie.

"They ate the sick geese from the lake, so they fall in the same group. The problem is, the only real way to prove the corn is being grown by Agriventures is to collect samples from one of their fields."

Angela took a sip of hot tea and let the hot water bathe her throat.

"So collect them," said Andrew. "Isn't that your job?"

"I'm off the case, remember?" She pushed back her thick curls with both hands and pinned the hair in place behind her ears. "Besides, not even IES can go in."

"Acronym?" said Gertie.

"Investigative and Enforcement Services, they're attached to the USDA's Animal and Plant Health Inspection Service, APHIS."

Harry reached for the corn-chip bag. "Why not?"

"They don't have probable cause, and they're bound by due process."

"Meaning what?" asked Gertie.

"IES would have to file a request for samples, and be denied multiple times, before they can force Tauer into letting them collect specimens. If they handle it any other way, it becomes inadmissible in court."

Lark pointed toward the lab report. "Doesn't this constitute probable cause?"

"It might." Angela tipped her head back,

feeling the stretch in her neck. Then she rolled her shoulders and sat up straight in her chair. "I can ask Kramner to follow up, and he probably would . . ."

"You couldn't prove it by me," muttered Lark.

"Unfortunately, it would take some time, and the longer we wait, the bigger the risk of having evidence destroyed." She folded her hands together and rocked them against the table edge. "The bottom line is, there's nothing in this report, or any report, that proves the corn came from the field next door to the Barr Lake Hunt Club. All Tauer has to do is argue that geese migrate."

Lark wrinkled her nose. "That reasoning didn't fly when we wanted U.S. Fish and Wildlife to pay for the necropsy."

Gertie acted annoyed by the banter. "Do we have any other options?"

It was the opening Angela'd been waiting for. "We could collect the samples ourselves."

"Been there, done that," said Lark. "Have you forgotten the trouble we ran into the last time we went collecting?"

"No." It was even more dangerous now.

Harry stroked his chin. "What exactly does collecting samples entail? For all we know, it might be fun."

Once planted, the seed germinated. The EPOCH members talked it over among themselves.

"Hold on. One at a time." Lark rapped her knuckles on the table. "Do you have an idea, Angela?"

"As a matter of fact . . ."

They hatched a plan, and agreed to meet the next morning in the parking lot in front of the Visitors Center at Barr Lake.

Birders were common visitors at all times of the year, and it didn't surprise Angela to find a few others gathered in the parking lot at seven a.m. The weather, typical of Colorado, was perfect. The sun shone brightly in a cornflower-blue sky devoid of clouds. The temperature hovered near freezing, but promised to reach into the upper forties by noon.

Right on schedule, the Drummond van pulled into the parking lot, and the seven EPOCH members spilled out. Everyone was dressed warmly, with hats or headbands, mittens and boots, and sunscreen liberally applied. Angela followed suit. In addition, she carried her cell phone, two baggies, and her gun.

"Ready?" asked Lark.

Six people responded by raising binoculars draped around their necks. Angela joined them in their binocular toast.

"I'll keep the checklist," said Cecilia, bundled up to her neck in powder-blue Gore-tex.

"I've already got one started." Dorothy's outfit matched her sister's, only in pink, and she held a small, yellow notebook in her hand.

"It's not fair to have listed a bird, Dot. We haven't officially started."

"Oh, please," said Gertie. "Let's go already."

Lark struck out for the trail. Before even leaving the parking lot, she pointed to a black-billed magpie and an American crow fighting over a piece of bagel dropped by someone in one of the other groups. A quick stop at the Visitors Center to retrieve a checklist netted the group four house finches, seven house sparrows, and a European starling. LGBs played around a birdfeeder hanging on the south side of the trail. The starling darted in and out of an air vent on the side of the building.

Dorothy quickly checked off the birds they had seen.

"I don't think we should count the starling, Dot."

"For heaven's sake, why not, Cecilia?"

"It's not a native species."

"The same can be said for the house sparrow."

"Just count them both, already," said Gertie. "Jeesh!"

Lark waved her arm for the group to follow. "Let's go. We'll start along the trail to the banding station, then cut through the woods to the lake. After that, we'll head toward the dam, and the cornfield beyond."

Angela nodded approval. At least one person remembered what they were here for.

The group struck out, and within minutes, Andrew lagged behind.

"Just go on without me," he puffed. "I'm going to stop at the banding station anyway."

Opal hung back with her husband.

They'd only gone another ten yards, when Harry pointed to the sky. "Check it out."

Above them a red-tailed hawk made lazy circles, its creamy breast, red-speckled belly band, and rusty-red tail clearly visible.

The group stopped and lifted their binoculars. Angela fidgeted, anxious to press on. Then she succumbed and raised her binoculars. *When in Rome . . .*

The path to the bird-banding station was more of a road than a trail. Wide, graveled, and skiffed with snow, it curved only once along the canal before reaching the platform. To the northwest, giant cottonwood trees and willows blotted out the view of Long's Peak and the lake, but housed a number of birds.

"Look, there's a downy," said Gertie. "Three-quarters up in the snag."

She pointed to a tall, dead-looking tree, and Angela tracked it toward the top. Sure enough, a checkered black-and-white bird clung to the edge of a small tree. It was a male, evidenced by the red spot on the back of its head and nape. Its short bill looked more suited to eating seeds than drilling wood.

"Black-capped chickadee," said Lark, pointing right.

Two trees over, Angela found the bird. Gray with buff sides, its black throat and cap were unmistakable.

The bird watchers were on a roll. Before long they added the pine siskin, American goldfinch, and hairy woodpecker to the list. The hairy was elusive, hiding in the trees, and once Angela had her binoculars on him, he looked very much like the downy to her.

"He's bigger, dear," Dorothy patiently explained. "Plus, it has a much longer bill."

"Wait!" Harry's voice came in a stage whisper.

The EPOCH members stilled.

"There. Do you see him? Three trees back, halfway up, maybe two o'clock in the branches."

Angela squinted in the direction he pointed. She could only see grayish bark.

Then two big, yellow eyes blinked, and the shape of a great-horned owl emerged. It hugged the tree, in perfect form. Brown plumage with black barring rose to a white throat. Gold, feathery disks framed its face, and two feathery horns spiked from the top of its head.

Angela lifted her glasses and stared. The owl stared back, capturing her every move.

"That's rare," said Gertie, binoculars adhered to her face. "Great catch."

Angela found herself reluctant to pull away.

"Is that a life bird for you?" Cecilia asked.

"My first in the wild."

From the meadow behind them, a western meadowlark belted out a congratulatory song. The EPOCH members swiveled in unison, performing the dance of the birders.

It took only a moment for Angela to find the bird. It perched on a fence post, silhouetted by the sun.

The birders expanded the territory to include the meadow, and by the time they reached the banding station, they'd added the dark-eyed junco in gray-headed form, the white-crowned sparrow, and the horned lark to their list.

Cutting down through the woods past the mist nets, the EPOCH members didn't log any more birds. Angela hadn't been in this area since the night Ian died, and an uneasy chill crept along her neckline. The banding station looked different in the daylight. The riparian area stood at the edge of a cattail marsh, now dried up from years of drought. Narrow trails wound through an expansive understory of willows, and light dappled off ashen branches. The nets were furled, secured tightly around thin aluminum poles. None appeared large enough to bear the weight of a man. But, that night, the pole had been supported by a nearby tree.

Passing the rock he had stood on, Angela stopped. She climbed up on the rough surface and noticed the top was flat, easy to balance upon. She found it hard to believe an expert climber would have had trouble maintaining his footing, even in a storm. Pretending she was falling, Angela stretched for the pole. She was way too short to reach it. But even if she could have, there was no way the pole would have tipped in the direction of the tree. Someone had to have propped it there.

"Angela." Lark's voice jarred her from her thoughts. "Are you coming?"

She nodded, unable to speak.

"This is where it happened, isn't it?" asked Lark. "This is where Ian died."

It took every ounce of effort to push her voice past the lump in her throat. "Yes."

A few minutes later, they broke into the clearing at the east end of the lake. The brittle grasses crackled underfoot, and fish skeletons dotted the land, braised white with snow. Gertie set up a scope.

"Take a look."

Angela peered through the scope. She spotted a group of northern pintails. The males' solid brown heads with white stripes were clearly visible, along with the long, black feathers protruding from their tails. The females were a drab mottled brown.

To the right was a northern shoveler.

With its spatulated bill, it looked like a cartoon duck. Angela named it, then added a redhead, mallard, and common goldeneye. Reluctantly she relinquished the scope. "There you go."

She grew antsy as everyone took a turn. "Lark, we need to keep moving."

"Oh, look, there's a ring-necked duck," cried Dorothy. Uncommon on Barr Lake in the winter, everybody took time to look again.

"She's right," said Gertie. "You can see the brown neck ring."

Finally, Angela couldn't take any more. "I'm going on without you."

"Oh my," said Cecilia. "We should go with her. We can bird it on the way back."

With that solution in mind, the group packed up and headed further east.

"Stay on the trail," warned Angela. "And keep your eyes open."

When they'd gone as far as they could as a group, the bird watchers set up their scopes, and Angela struck out alone.

"If I'm not back here in half an hour, head for the banding station. If I'm not back there in an hour, call for help."

Picking her way through the cattail marshes and wetlands below the dam was more difficult than she'd imagined. More than once she ended up knee-deep in bog. It took her fifteen minutes just to reach the edge of the field.

The harvest had knocked down the corn plants, but half-chopped ears and scattered kernels lay in the ditch along the edge. The sun beat down, glinting off her jacket, and Angela realized she was a sitting duck out in the open.

With any luck, no one would realize she was there. But, if they did . . .

She quickly picked up several half-ears of corn and stuffed them into plastic baggies. Then she broke off pieces of the plants themselves and stuffed them into another bag.

A crack echoed, then a spit of wind parted her hair, followed by another crack.

A gunshot. Hunters?

Angela turned and spotted someone with an orange cap hunkered down in the field to the north.

"Hey," she shouted. "I'm not a bird."

A ring-necked pheasant flushed. Taking off in a whir of rich colors, its plump body sailed just above the vegetation. Another gunshot rang out.

This time the bullet thudded into the ground near her feet. The hunter wasn't shooting at the bird. He was shooting at her.

Angela started running along the edge of the field. Her only hope of cover was in the willows and cottonwoods bordering the Barr Lake Hunt Club property.

With several hundred yards to sprint, she considered serpentining, like Peter Falk in *The In-Laws*. Hitting a moving target was harder than hitting a still one; hitting a zigzagging target was harder still.

Another shot split the air, and Angela poured on the power. Moving right, she quickly switched back and moved left. Digging her cell phone out of her pocket, she dialed 9-1-1 for help.

Twenty feet more.

She got low to the ground and zigzagged toward the trees. Another shot fired. This one hit its mark.

Chapter 20

The bullet burned a hole into Angela's right shoulder and she dropped the phone. *Shit.*

Diving to the ground behind a tree, she bit her lower lip to keep from screaming in pain.

Don't give away your position.

She considered reaching for the phone, when another shot pummeled the ground beyond the trees. Were Lark and the others okay? She hoped they had heard the shots and gone for help.

A crackling in the field behind her urged her to move. While she sat there, the shooter was moving into range. She could draw her own weapon and return fire. Or she could conserve her ammunition and go for help.

Pushing herself up with her left arm, she clutched her right arm to her chest and headed for the Barr Lake Hunt Club. There was a phone there, and she needed to get out of the open.

With every step came pain, and her uncertainty grew. She had never completely ruled Radigan out as a suspect. Or Nate, for that matter. She would lay odds it was Donald Tauer firing the gun, but what if she was wrong?

Is this how Ian had felt? The hunter becoming the hunted.

She took the straightest route through the trees. Blood gushed from her shoulder, and poured over the hand clutching her elbow. It was warm and sticky, and she wondered if she needed to tie off the wound.

The sound of someone thrashing through the woods behind her propelled her on. The clubhouse loomed into view, and she bolted across the driveway for the front door.

Please let it be open.

Her prayer was granted. She rattled the handle, and the door swung wide. Quickly, she shut and bolted it from the inside. Traveling along the row of windows, she dropped one blind after another. If the shooter couldn't see inside, it might slow him down.

She bumped her arm on the last window frame, and her knees buckled from the pain. Footsteps on the deck prompted her back to her feet.

Angela reached for her gun, but the holster was designed to draw the weapon using her right hand. But, with her shoulder injured like it was, she only managed to nudge the weapon deeper. The door handles jiggled.

Abandoning the effort, Angela edged her way along the tables to the kitchen. Adrenaline pushed her to run, but logic told her to move slowly, quietly.

She eased open the swinging door.

No one was there.

Making sure the back door was locked, she dropped the back window blinds.

She heard the sound of breaking glass and the creak of the dining room door, then above her head a green light flashed over the doorway. So that was how Radigan's son knew Coot was there! The light was triggered by the door.

A shuffle of feet spurred her to action. She opened the back door, slammed it shut, then she darted into the next room. With luck, the shooter would think she had fled.

A clumsy retreat, and the front door banged. *Yes!*

Quickly she moved through the rooms until she found the office. She picked up the phone and discovered the line was dead.

Panic coursed through her. Her breathing quickened. She forced herself to stay calm.

Think. What would Ian do?

Setting down the receiver, her gaze dropped to a paper on the desk. It was a printout on the properties of the shot Radigan had under development. Picking it up, she studied the contents. One of the main components of the shot was a corn-based plastic.

Suddenly the pieces clicked into place, and a cold fear spread through her veins. Donald Tauer was guilty, but not of murder. He was guilty of growing the corn used in the shot Radigan developed. Radigan sharecropped the land. He received payment, or a percentage of the crop in payoff.

"Figure it out?" Charles Radigan stood in the doorway, a rifle cradled in his arms.

Angela startled. Pain wracked her body, and she felt her strength drain. "Why take the risk? The formula doesn't even work."

"It can, provided we find the right product. The corn has special properties. The plastic we made was tough enough to withstand the blast of a shotgun, yet it was biodegradable."

"And poisonous."

"We could have solved that, given enough time."

"Why not just get a license to grow it?"

"I was running out of time. Do you have any idea the hoops you have to jump through to grow and/or to use genetically engineered crops? My investors wanted to see results. Tauer never asked why I wanted my share planted with special seed. He didn't want to know."

"No," said Angela. "He needed the land you controlled in order to keep his business going."

Radigan smiled. "You're a smart girl."

"What about Nate Sobul?" She was afraid to find out, but figured the longer she could keep Radigan talking the better.

"The corn Tauer cleared for market was clean. I doubt there were even any traces of contamination. But your partner figured out the corn was causing die-offs."

"And he tipped off Nate." That made her feel happy. It meant Nate had been telling the truth.

"He must have reported his suspicions to the IES before I could silence him."

"Is that the new terminology for murder?" Angela watched Radigan's eyes. He didn't care much for the question.

"What do you think?" he asked, waving

the gun in the air. "Do you think I would stand by and let some gung ho environmentalist ruin me because a flock of geese died?"

No. Not any more than she would expect him to let her live now that she knew the answers. She dropped her left hand toward the edge of the desk. Radigan gestured with his gun for her to keep her hand on her elbow.

"Don't do that."

"I just needed to steady myself." Her shoulder throbbed. Luckily the bleeding had stopped, and the wound only bubbled now and then when she moved.

"The case was dead without your partner, and Nate's focus is on Tauer. As long as Tauer stays clean, there's nothing he can do."

"You don't think with me gone, the case will just disappear, do you?" asked Angela, sitting down in the chair. Let him shoot her.

Her gun bumped against her side. If she worked at it slowly, maybe she could maneuver her right hand to extract the gun, all the while keeping it covered by the left.

"It's my hope."

Even Kramner wouldn't buy that many coincidences.

"What about the geese at Elk Lake?" she asked, determined to keep him talking. She inched her hand a little closer to the gun.

"What about them? I figured they were off the Front Range, and it was obvious they were sick. I had my grandson help me scatter some sinkers around, hoping local animal control would assume they'd been poisoned from the lead. It almost worked, too."

That made sense, thought Angela. It was Radigan's grandson's partial fingerprint that Crandall had pulled off the lead-sinker container.

"Get up."

The preamble was over. Angela's fingers worked along the fabric of her shirt. "I need to rest."

"I said, get up." He prodded her arm with the barrel of his rifle, and her shoulder throbbed with pain. She struggled back onto her feet.

"Where are we going?"

"Back out to the field. You're going to be shot by a hunter. You're not wearing orange, and you're out here on your own. I'm afraid you'll look foolish, but it can't be helped."

Radigan stayed behind her, moving her through the house, out the front door, and to the driveway. The whole time, she gathered the fabric of her shirt into her hand. Finally, her hand captured the butt of her gun, and she slipped her finger around the trigger.

She took her chance at the treeline. Darting ahead of Radigan, she ducked behind the trunk of a cottonwood. He fired his gun, and the shot chipped at the bark.

"You can't get away."

This time, bracing her hand with her left arm, she fired back, hoping the action would gain her ground. Sprinting west through the cottonwoods and willows, she crashed through the understory, oblivious to the pain in her arm. Branches tore at her face and reopened the wound in her shoulder. Her blood spilled, and her energy drained away.

"Angel!"

She hated him using her nickname and considered stopping to shoot at him again. But common sense spurred her on. The birders were waiting at the banding station.

Radigan gained on her. She could hear him closing in, drawing closer and closer. Stopping at the edge of the trees, she stared out at Barr Lake. She had stuck to the treeline, but there was a section of dried lake bed to cross that measured thirty feet across. Thirty feet too many.

"Give it up, Angel. You'll never make it."

Maybe she shouldn't have played this one alone. That had been Ian's mistake. Not trusting his partner.

"Lark!" she screamed, hoping her voice would carry to the banding station. "Help! Someone!"

"They can't hear you."

No, but they could hear the gun.

Angela fired in his direction. She had eight shots left. There was no telling how long that would hold him off. She could only hope that the noise brought help.

Radigan fired back, the slug chipping the bark of the cottonwood at the height of her ear.

She waited until he fired again, then shot back.

After trading more shots, she was down to her last bullet when she heard Lark calling. With a sudden thrashing, Radigan took off through the trees.

Peeking behind her, Angela watched in stunned silence, as the EPOCH members walked hand in hand, crunching their way across the dried lake bed.

The reunion had been short-lived. Lark

called 9-1-1, and dispatch sent out emergency crews. Angela was taken to the nearest hospital, and the police issued an all-points-bulletin for Charles Radigan.

Two weeks later, her arm still in a sling, Kramner drove Angela up to Elk Park.

"What's going to happen to Radigan?" she asked, as they wound their way into the mountains.

"He's been charged with murder. Tauer cut a deal in exchange for a lesser plea." Kramner glanced at her sideways. "I have to admit, you had it pegged."

A small comfort.

"Does that mean I get to go back in the field?"

Kramner squared his jaw and nodded his head. "You still need some training, Dimato. But I think I've worked it out to hire someone to pick up where Ian left off with you. He can't come on board for a couple of months, so don't think it will happen tomorrow, but . . ."

Angela felt lighter. She needed a month or two to recover. The timing just might work out.

The truck crested the hill and coasted into Elk Park. The lake sparkled below them, nestled in the valley between Long's Peak and Lumpy Ridge. The weather had warmed. The ice had broken, heralding the onset of spring.

"What are we doing here, sir?"

"You'll have to wait and see."

He pulled the truck into the parking lot at the Visitors Center, and Frakus rushed out to meet them. "The others are already down by the lake."

Frakus glommed onto Kramner. Angela lagged behind, enjoying the day. The path was clear of snow, and birds twittered from the willows. In another month, the warblers would start returning.

Lark waited for her down by the lake. "How's the arm?"

"Better. Did I remember to thank you?"

Lark grinned, and the other EPOCH members rushed over to greet her. Bernie Crandall clapped her on her good shoulder.

"Hey there, Special Agent Dimato. How goes it?"

"Good, in spite of the extra holes."

Lark tugged on her sleeve, and the beefy cop stepped out of her way. "Eric, look who's here."

Eric Linenger stood at the water's edge. His muscular frame appeared wilted, but his blue eyes sparkled. "*Vell*, if it isn't my rescuer."

"You're walking!"

"And talking. Who would have believed?"

"I'm glad you're okay." She knew he'd improved, but now she knew he'd get better.

"Me, too."

"Me, three." Lark slipped her arm through Eric's. "Now comes the best part." She moved to the side, and Angela noticed the crates sitting beside the shoreline. She counted eighty-six.

"We decided to have a send-off party," explained Gertie. "John sent Petey and his crew up to bring down the crates. You get to do the first honors."

Angela blinked back tears and bent down to open a carrier. But before she could extract the honking goose, Pierre Ducharme swaggered toward them from the top of the boat ramp.

"I have returned to collect my paycheck," he announced in a thick French accent. "Stephen tells me you are on the ice."

Lark stepped forward. "I don't know what to say, Pierre. I owe you an apology."

"*Oui,* madame. I am waiting." Ducharme puffed up his chest, and Angela couldn't help but laugh. "You think this *eez* funny?"

Oui. She shook her head, and forced a straight face.

"I'm sorry, Pierre," said Lark, looking to Eric for guidance. Eric signaled her to go on. "I jumped to a conclusion, and I was wrong."

"You are forgiven, madame." A smile fractured his swarthy face. "I gladly accept back my job."

Angela choked. She doubted that's what Lark had in mind.

"But —"

"No buts, madame. I will go straight away and start preparing *zee* lunch."

Lark watched him swagger away, a pained expression on her face.

"Cheer up," said Crandall. "He's an excellent cook."

"No paté," Lark shouted. "Do you hear me, Ducharme? No geese, no ducks. Stick to chicken."

"*Oui,* madame. I am hearing you."

The geese had too, and they all set to honking. Angela turned back to the crate. Raising the lid, she reached inside and picked up the gander. As if sensing her injury, the bird stopped struggling the moment it entered her arms. She marveled at the creature, at its soft feathers, its gentle breathing. She basked in the moment. Then, opening her arms, Angela set the bird free.

CANADA GOOSE
Branta canadensis
Family: Anatidae

Appearance: A very large bird with gray-ish-brown plumage, a long black neck, and a black head with a white chin-strap. There are six species of Canada goose, each one varying slightly in size.

Range: Once known mainly as a wilderness bird, the Canada goose, or "honker" as it's sometimes called, is adapting to life on golf courses and in urban parks, expanding its year-round range. Northern flocks still migrate from Alaska, Canada, and the Arctic to northern Mexico.

Habitat: Canada goose can be found at reservoirs, lakes, ponds, marshes, wet meadows, golf courses, urban and suburban parks, and in open spaces.

Voice: Its voice varies from species to species, from a deep musical honking in the larger birds to a high cackling or gabbling in the smaller birds. Few can resist the haunting sound of Canada geese honking and calling as they fly in *V* formation overhead.

Behaviors: The Canada goose forms a long-term bond with its mate and produces young usually in its third year. Spring and early summer find the goose family swimming together on lakes and pond. The gander usually leads, while the young, fluffy, yellow-and-black babies trail behind.

Conservation: The goose feeds on shoots, roots, and seeds of grass and sedges; on bulbs, grain, berries, insects, crustaceans, and mollusks. Most grain consumption is post-harvest. Danger comes in the form of genetically engineered crops and hunting. More recently, the semi-domesticated goose found on golf courses and in urban and suburban parks faces increased predation by man.

Author's Notes

As one of Wisconsin's largest wildlife rehabilitation facilities, *Fellow Mortals, Inc.*, has
been serving the state-line communities in
and around Lake Geneva, WI since 1985.
Founded on the belief that a compassionate
act on behalf of another living creature is
one of the noblest deeds that can be per-
formed by a human, *Fellow Mortals* admits
approximately 1500 wild birds and mam-
mals every year, returning 60% of them back
to the wild — a percentage significantly
higher than the national average.

On January 17, 1992, *Fellow Mortals* received a call from a woman walking her
dog at the edge of Lake Geneva, who had
discovered a lead-poisoned Canada goose.
It was the first of hundreds of geese found
on the ice, and the worst lead-poisoning
case in Southeastern Wisconsin's history.
But through a cooperative effort with
Fellow Mortals, the department of Natural
Resources, other wildlife rehabilitators, an
army of volunteers, and the generosity of a
major pharmaceutical company, there were

survivors. And the U.S. Fish and Wildlife Service pinpointed the cause — the contamination of wetland area miles to the north. Their investigation fixed the blame on a skeet shooting ranch owned by a major U.S. corporation that was eventually forced to rehabilitate the wetlands. *Death Takes a Gander* is based on this case, though I've moved the location and taken great license with the story.

Rehabilitation of animals is a costly endeavor. The costs involved in the case of the lead-poisoned geese — thousands — nearly bankrupted *Fellow Mortals*. It was only through people's generosity and donations that they were able to recover. If you would like to donate to their organization, please visit their Web site at www.fellowmortals.org, or donate to a rehabilitation facility near you. Your gift to a wildlife rehabilitation facility is tax deductible, and your donation saves lives. Better yet, volunteer. In the words of Yvonne Wallace Blane, "[In the case of the lead-poisoned geese] the cost of lives saved cannot be told in dollar amounts alone, for they were also paid for by the people with disparate interests who invested their time and emotion in a seemingly hopeless cause for one reason — belief in the value of individual life."

The employees of Thorndike Press hope you have enjoyed this Large Print book. All our Thorndike and Wheeler Large Print titles are designed for easy reading, and all our books are made to last. Other Thorndike Press Large Print books are available at your library, through selected bookstores, or directly from us.

For information about titles, please call:

(800) 223-1244

or visit our Web site at:

www.gale.com/thorndike
www.gale.com/wheeler

To share your comments, please write:

Publisher
Thorndike Press
295 Kennedy Memorial Drive
Waterville, ME   04901